Fin Lune
and the
Clockwork
Phoenix

PHILIP JANVIER

Bluebox & January

Bluebox & January
St Stephen's Rectory
Belle Vale Road
Gateacre
Liverpool L25 2PQ

First published in the UK by Bluebox & January

ISBN-13: 978-0993517709 (Paperback)

ISBN-10: 0993517706

DEDICATION

To Jane with all my love…

CONTENTS

ACKNOWLEDGMENTS

This novel would not have been possible without the support of many people. Therefore, I would like to thank the following: Shirley Cowan who ploughs her way through all my manuscripts offering criticism, correction and encouragement. To my family, Jane, Josh, Matt and Beth who have endured without complaint endless discussions about Fin Butler and never ceased to be supportive. To God who has given me the desire to write and who recognises me as the work in progress that I am.

OMEN OF THE PHOENIX

I heard the child with smoke in its mouth,
I heard the chough on the top of its nest,
I heard the ravens in the thicket beyond,
And I heard the squeal of the bird in a snare.
I saw the bird frighten the crows away,
I saw the blind girl see in the dark,
I saw the trees walk like a man,
And I foresaw that the year would not
Go well with me.

Ancient Fragment

CHAPTER 1 – FIN BUTLER

The incessant beeping crawled into Fin's sleeping mind. He knew that he had to wake up but he was lost in a nightmare of flames and pain. He was burning alive, screaming but his voice was silent, trying to move but his legs were heavy. The fire alarm began to wail overwhelming the sound of the smoke detector, covered in a film of sweat, panic finally woke him. Smoke filled his room and he started to cough.

Falling out of bed Fin grabbed shoes off the floor and fumbled for the door. Grabbing the door handle he turned it and pulled. It would not budge and smoke began to seep under the bottom of the door.

Hammering his fist on the door, panic besieged him and he screamed, 'Get me out of here!'

Overwhelmed by the smoke he slid down the door and as his consciousness drifted away, he felt himself hit the floor.

'Are we keeping you awake Mr Butler?' the voice echoed sardonically around the courtroom.

Fin stirred in his chair next to his barrister, embarrassed, he sat up and looked at Mr Wheatear his representative from Eagle, Sphinx and Hawk, who closed his eyes and sighed quietly.

'Are these proceedings so boring that you can't keep awake?' continued the Judge.

Fin shook his head, there seemed no point trying to explain that he had not slept since the fire and when he did, the nightmares haunted him. He could smell the smoke and hear the screams. Everything reminded him of that night, the images of flames, the sound of sirens, the fire fighters, the police and the never-ending questions. Not to mention he was always cold, suffered constant headaches and had intermittent stomach ache.

'Then kindly pay attention!'

The Judge returned the focus of his attention to the barrister from the Crown Prosecution Service, 'Having outlined the seriousness of the charges against Mr Butler and why we are here, we will continue.'

Fin settled back into his chair, it was going to be a long, cold day. Looking around the court he searched for a friendly face, there was none. The gallery was unexpectedly empty apart from a dowdy member of the press playing on her smart phone. In the corner was an anonymous man, in a dark suit, fast asleep. He sighed and felt tiredness creep up on him again, even with his eyes open; he began to smell the smoke. Valiantly, he fought against sleep, loosing inevitably his head fell forward.

Fin having promised to tell the truth, the whole truth, and nothing but the truth, sat down and faced the court.

The prosecution barrister stared at Fin, 'Please state your full name?'

'Fenix Butler, but everyone calls me Fin.'

'Thank you Mr Butler. I don't think the court needed to know what everyone calls you. How old are you?'

'Thirteen, fourteen in April,' he replied.

Fin looked at the barrister and got the impression that he was watching a bird of prey hovering and waiting to pounce and was not surprised with his next comment.

'Thank you Mr Butler,' said the barrister, 'but after all your actions of late I hope you are not expecting a birthday card from anyone in this court!'

Grimacing at the sarcasm Fin was startled when the Judge spoke out.

'Mr Stock, please try to control your sarcastic comments,' he said, 'do I need to remind you that the defendant is a juvenile? You have chosen not to call Mr Butler by his first name but I will not tolerate any psychological games with him.' The Judge glared at the barrister, 'Is that understood?'

Sighing Fin stared at Mr Stock as he silently conceded the Judge's comments but as his eyes returned to stare at him, Fin realised nothing had changed. His solicitor had advised him to look good and wear smart clothes, adding that it will give him confidence and make a good impression. Fin was not so sure it had worked, his dark short spiky hair refused to lie down and his best clothes felt scruffy and out of place. Judging from Mr Stock's attitude it had not effected the court's approach to Fin and he accepted that today was not going to be a good day.

'Mr Butler, what is your date of birth?'

'I'm sorry, I don't remember,' he replied, 'it's in April.'

'What does your birth certificate say?'

'I have no idea, it was destroyed in a fire.'

A calculated look swept across Mr Stock's face, 'Which fire was this?'

A shiver ran down Fin's back and he could smell smoke again. The court fell silent; Fin could feel every eye upon him, even the reporter had stopped playing on her phone. Feeling the usual sense of cold anxiety creep over

3

him he grew distressed and struggled to reply.

Taking a deep breath he controlled his voice and said, 'The fire that killed my parents and my brother,' emboldened he continued, 'my mother and I survived the fire but she died later from burns and complications caused by inhaling smoke and carbon monoxide.'

A tear ran down Fin's face as he remembered his mother, sadly, all he could remember was her smile and the perfumed smell of her hair.

A chair grated and squeaked as Mr Wheatear stood up, 'Is this line of questioning really necessary? There is nothing relevant here concerning this case and the court has the police and fire service reports on record. There was no suggestion of my client being involved, as he was only aged three at the time.'

'Mr Stock, I will give you a little more leeway as I wish to understand where you are going,' stated the Judge, with a shrewd glance at Mr Stock, 'however, I warn you to tread carefully with Mr Butler's memories.'

Mr Stock nodded to the Judge, 'Mr Butler, what was the cause of this fire?'

Mr Wheatear groaned from his chair.

'Mr Stock?' said the Judge.

'I quite understand that this is a matter of record, however, I wish the court to comprehend Mr Butler's understanding of the event.'

'Proceed.'

Frustrated Fin's gaze drifted to Mr Wheatear, who nodded gently.

'My memories are patchy,' Fin replied, 'but I am told it was arson. We were all asleep upstairs and the fire started in the living room.'

Looking down at his notes Mr Stock continued, 'The fire service rescued you and your mother.'

'Yes, they did.'

'Leaving your father and twin brother still inside?'

'The house exploded unexpectedly, the debris was

spread for miles and their bodies were never found.'

'There is no doubt they were killed?'

The Judge intervened, 'Mr Stock, I think you have had your answer. The records are quite clear; the gas main exploded and took out half the street. As well the missing members of the Butler family, twenty-seven other people died, including three members of the fire service. The record also indicates that two immediate neighbours' bodies were never found either,' the Judge paused to rub his forehead, 'please move on.'

Taking a deep breath Fin looked around the court, anywhere other than into Mr Stock's eyes. Up in the gallery the anonymous man's eyes glistened as he stared back at him.

'Very well,' said Mr Stock, 'what happened to you next?'

Fin felt more confident moving away from this infantile memory, 'I was taken into the care of the Social Services and placed in a foster home.'

'Was that successful?'

'What do you mean by successful?' asked Fin.

'Did you find a home and a family that loved you?' explained Mr Stock.

'Yes, I did,' he acknowledged.

'You were fostered by Sarah and James Rooney,' said Mr Stock looking at his notes, 'were you happy there?'

'Yes I was,' acknowledged Fin.

Mr Stock seemed to swoop 'That's not what it states in your records.'

'I'm sorry I don't understand,' said Fin looking towards the Judge for help.

'Initially, the records indicate that you were quiet and sullen,' continued Mr Stock, 'clingy, demanding and constantly fearful about another fire.'

In silence Fin sat remembering those days, he had loved Sarah and James and they had loved him even when he became irritable and disruptive.'

'Always in trouble at school, swinging widely between temper tantrums and being silent and withdrawn,' added Mr Stock.

Mr Wheatear grated his chair as he stood up again. 'I believe that Mr Stock is cherry picking the evidence. The Rooney's rightly recorded Mr Butler's problems and working with the Psychiatrists and the Counselling Service they believed they were making progress, so much so that they began adoption proceedings.'

'What happened to the Rooneys?' asked Mr Stock, 'Mr Butler, what happened to your happy family?'

Hearing the Judge take a deep breath Mr Stock predicted the inevitable challenge and rephrased his question.

'Mr Butler, will you tell the court about your new foster family and what happened to them?'

Haltingly, Fin tried to describe his life with Sarah and James, how happy he was, despite the terrible nightmares, his fear of fire and anxiety about their safety. He described their annual holidays in the Scilly Isles, the fun and the ice cream, their patience as he struggled at school to be accepted.

The court listened in silence as he painted, with words, a picture of his new family and the growing sense of healing he received being a part of a loving family.

'So what brought this happy time to an end?' responded Mr Stock.

'A house fire,' he responded.

'Indeed a house fire,' Mr Stock paused and glared at Fin, 'and what was the cause of this fire?'

Fin took a deep breath knowing the day was about to get worse, 'Arson,' he replied.

'You were how old at this time?'

'Twelve.'

'In your own words,' continued Mr Stock, 'please tell the court what you remember?'

'I woke up to the sound of our smoke detector

beeping,' Fin's voice began to crack as he spoke, 'I ran into my foster parent's room and tried to wake them but they were unconscious.'

'Then you were unaffected by the smoke?'

'Of course I wasn't,' he snapped, 'it was terrible I couldn't see my hands in front of my face, it became difficult to breathe so I had to get out and get help. I ran back into my own room and climbed out of the window and dropped down into the garden.'

'What happened to your foster parents?'

'As I landed in the garden the fire engine arrived, I told them about my parents and they tried to rescue them,' tears started to form in Fin's eyes and his voice broke, 'they gave me oxygen but it was too late to save them.'

'What happened next?'

'I was taken away by ambulance and treated for smoke inhalation.'

'Did the police question you?'

Regaining his composure Fin replied, 'Yes Sir they questioned me about arson.'

Taking a deep breath Mr Stock half-smiled at Fin, 'Were there any similarities between this attack and the one you survived as a child?'

'I am told that, as before, the fire started in the living room and that there was evidence of an accelerant,' he replied.

'What type of accelerant?' asked Mr Stock.

Mr Wheatear jumped up from his seat, 'My client is not qualified to answer that question.'

'He would be if he was the arsonist,' replied Mr Stock, 'Mr Butler, did you copy your father and set your own house on fire?'

Fin shouted belligerently back at him, 'No, I didn't. He didn't!'

'Then how come you survived, unharmed?'

Cold and angry Fin was about to reply when Mr Wheatear silenced him with a dark look.

'My client is not here to be charged with the arson attack on his foster parent's home,' interrupted Mr Wheatear.

'And yet,' continued Mr Stock, 'the police investigated the fire and agreed that there were similarities in the unknown accelerant used.'

'But none with my client,' continued Mr Wheatear, 'unless you are implying that he left the three crow feathers.'

There was a commotion from the gallery as the press reporter dropped her phone and her voice burst out, 'The Firebird!'

The Judge addressed Mr Wheatear accusingly, 'You are well aware that the police have been keeping that particular piece of information confidential.'

The barrister embarrassed nodded his head in apology.

'You will not report that last detail about the feathers,' the Judge stated to the reporter in the gallery. 'I remind you that Mr Butler is a minor and that you may not use his name nor associate this case with the so-called "Firebird,"' pausing he waited to see if she was paying attention, 'If you do I will hold you in contempt of court!'

The reporter, looking crestfallen, nodded her head and sat down.

Taking a deep breath, the Judge considered the court and motioned with his hand, 'Continue Mr Stock.'

'Mr Butler, did you set fire to your foster parent's home?'

'No, I did not!' said a frustrated Fin.

Remaining seated this time Mr Wheatear looked at the Judge and said, 'Again, I wish to object to this line of questioning. The police have made no correlation between the event described and the charges my client is facing.'

'Mr Stock,' the Judge looked over his glasses at the prosecutor, 'kindly, move on, or at least explain your reasoning.'

'Certainly, it is my belief that there are links between

the arson attack on Mr Butler's foster parent's house and more recent events. That the "Firebird", is in fact, Mr Butler.'

The Judge glared at Mr Stock, 'Do the Police and the Crown Prosecution Service agree with you?'

Mr Stock shook his head silently.

'Then I suggest you move on. You have made your point and I am inclined to disregard it,' the Judge shook his head, 'please stop wasting the court's time.'

Fin's gaze moved from the Judge and he was not sure if he imagined it, but Mr Stock shared a look with his barrister and was smiling. Then Mr Stock looked Fin directly in the eye, he shivered and turned his gaze to his barrister. Mr Wheatear, looking dazed, shook his head and shuffled his papers.

Not sure if he had imagined it, Fin waited for the next question.

'Mr Butler, after your foster parent's death what happened to you next?' asked Mr Stock resuming his questions.

'Six months ago I was moved to St Matthew's Care Home,' he replied.

Watching Mr Stock play with his papers Fin could not escape the feeling that he was being toyed with as if this was a game of cat and mouse

Finally, Mr Stock looked at him, 'Mr Butler, how well did you adjust into your new home?'

'It was never my home,' he conceded, 'it was just a place I happened to live in.'

'Nevertheless, you made friends.'

'Yes.'

'Tell me about Jennifer Cato?'

Jenny was only person at St Matthew's who would talk to him, she had a dark olive complexion, bright blue eyes and the wildest hair he had ever seen. She was funny and she made him laugh.

'Jenny was my friend.'

'Was Mr Butler,' Mr Stock pounced, 'was your friend?'

'I have not heard from Jenny since the night of the fire,' he replied, 'whenever, I ask about her, the subject of the conversation is changed.' Fin's voice cracked, 'I can only assume something terrible happened to her.'

'Would it interest you to know that Miss Cato survived the fire?' said Mr Stock.

Hope sprang into Fin's face and his voice grew stronger, 'Yes it would!'

'Miss Cato, did in fact, survive the fire,' he continued, 'she will be giving evidence against you in this trial.'

Fin was about to speak but the Judge intervened, 'You will not be allowed to speak to her or communicate with her in any way. Do you understand this?'

Fin nodded, his face still showing signs of obvious relief, but now tinged with disappointment.

The Judge continued, 'For some reason, the fact of her survival has been kept from you. I have always disagreed with that decision and now we are in my court, it seems pointless to me you believing that she may have died.'

His eyes locked in combat with Mr Stock, the Judge did not notice Fin's nod of thanks. The Judge closed his eyes and the connection broke between them.

'Carry on Mr Stock.'

'So you were friends with Miss Cato?' Mr Stock said returning the focus of his attention back to Fin.

'Yes, I was.'

'Did you settle into well into your new home?'

Fin struggled to word his response; he had hated St Matthew's with its stupid and petty rules. He grieved the loss of the Rooneys and the growing independence he once had. The other young people avoided him because they believed he had killed his foster parents deliberately. Some of the residents decided to try to bully him, spit in his food and his steal his few prized possessions. On one occasion, he remembered, two of the biggest of them picking a fight with him. Fin smiled to himself, having nothing to lose he had lashed out with his fist, broke the nose of one and gave the other a black eye. They left him alone after that but the staff marked him down as a troublemaker.

'No Sir, I did not,' Fin knew he should keep silent but could not help himself, 'I hated the place and Jenny was my only friend there!'

Fin watched a smile creep over Mr Stock's face as he acknowledged the admission that Fin had just made.

'So you hated the place?'

Fin remained silent.

Mr Stock took the silence as a yes, and moved on.

'What happened at St Matthew's, Mr Butler?'

The stuff of Fin's nightmares spilled out into his waking mind and he struggled to describe that night. The smoke detectors beeping, the fire alarm screaming, panicking because his door would not open until Jenny rescued him by kicking it open from the corridor. Running through the smoke and fumes, the ceiling falling down and cutting them off from the exit and then clinging to Jenny with all hope gone.

Disorientated and waking up on a stretcher with an oxygen mask on his face, no sign of Jenny and no one listening to his demands for information. Finally, a tall dark police officer prizing his fingers open to release three feathers and watching them fall to the ground.

Mr Stock stood and stretched; Fin could not help but see the smug look on his face.

'So Mr Butler, what have you to say about how the fire started?'

'I have no idea how it started, I was locked in my room.'

'So you say, Mr Butler, so you say,' he retorted as he played with his papers, 'Would it surprise you to know that the same accelerant was used at St Matthew's as in your foster parent's home?'

Fin was not surprised at all, but knew that if he said so,

Mr Stock would use it against him so he simply shook his head.

'Sorry, Mr Butler, could you please say that aloud.'

Fin struggled to speak, but in the end, he realised that he had promised to tell the truth, 'No, I am not surprised.'

'No, you are not surprised are you? You are not surprised, because you started the fire!'

Shaking his head Fin replied, 'No I didn't, but there is a pattern forming and for some reason someone wants to blame me.'

'So you believe you are being framed?'

'Yes.'

'Then how do you explain the three feathers found in your hand?'

Fin's face drained and he felt sick, he had very little memory of the entire event and his memory was a blank. Finally, he spoke, 'I have no idea how the feathers got into my hands.'

Mr Stock smiled at Fin, 'You have no idea! It is obvious to me Mr Butler, you started the fire and you planned to drop the feathers as you escaped, but the fire overtook you and you were caught red handed.'

Lost for words Fin glanced over to Mr Wheatear thinking it was time his barrister intervened. Mr Wheatear was staring at a spot on the wall distractedly picking his nails.

The Judge sensed Fin's discomfort and looked at barrister, 'Mr Wheatear, are you still with us?'

Mr Wheatear shifted uncomfortably in his seat but remained silent.

Shaking his head, the Judge, addressed Mr Stock, 'Do you have any further questions?'

Mr Stock nodded and continued, 'I believe that I have proved that Mr Butler is the Firebird, however, I have a few related questions to ask.'

'Proceed,' said the Judge.

'Mr Butler, I have made my opinions clear about who

was to blame for the arson attack at your foster parent's house,' Mr Stock picked up a printed sheet of paper, 'I therefore, would like to check where you were when the Firebird struck previously.'

Waiting in silence, Fin had no idea where this was going.

'While you were living with the Rooney's there was a fire in your village do you remember it?'

Fin nodded, 'Yes it was at the Mackay Bakery.'

'Where were you when the fire occurred?'

'At home with my foster parents, we watched it on the local news.'

'Can anyone substantiate that?'

'Of course not,' replied Fin, 'because they were killed in the fire.'

'Yes they were, how convenient.'

The Judge cleared his throat and Mr Stock continued, 'Did you know that an accelerant and three feathers were found in the ruins of the bakery?'

Fin shook his head.

'Then I'll move on, six months after the fire at the Mackay Bakery, in the last week of July, there was fire in the Registry Office in St Mary's on the Scilly Isles." Mr Stock paused and then asked, 'Where were you?'

This question startled Fin more than he had expected. He had been staying in a hotel in St Mary's, in the Scilly Isles, with the Rooney's. Fin remembered the fire it had scared him so much, he had not slept for days and it had ruined his holiday.

'I was in St Mary's,' he croaked.

'And why were you in the Scilly Isles?'

'I asked my foster parents to take me there.'

'Why?'

'It was one of the last places I visited with my parents before they died,' he replied, 'and I was hoping it would help me to remember their faces. However, the fire ruined all that.'

'Did you to know that the arsonist used the same accelerant and left three feathers at the scene?'

'No I did not,' Fin replied.

'Mr Butler, it seems to me curious that whenever there is an arson attack, you are nearby. I believe that you are the Firebird and all this circumstantial evidence places you at the scenes of devastation,' turning to the Judge Mr Stock explained, 'I believe that Mr Butler is a danger to himself and to all around him. The circumstantial evidence alone points to Mr Butler, but even if we ignore that, he was caught red handed at St Matthew's.' Mr Stock sat down, 'I have no more questions.'

The Judge thanked Mr Stock and looked at Mr Wheatear, 'Your witness.'

Mr Stock stared at Fin's barrister, Mr Wheatear shook his head and his eyes turned dark yellow.

Grating his chair as he stood Mr Wheatear looked at Fin and then commented, 'No questions.'

Fin was dumbfounded, no questions, what about all the questions they had rehearsed together? Fin sat back in his chair and closed his eyes to his later surprise and for the first time in months he fell asleep, a dreamless sleep.

Twenty minutes later, deeply refreshed, hearing a familiar voice, he woke up.

'My name is Jennifer Cato.'

'Thank you, Miss Cato.' Then the Judge noticing Fin was awake greeted him with an unexpected smile, 'Welcome back Mr Butler, you are no doubt relieved to see your friend alive.'

Fin felt his heart leap and looked across at Jenny. Her normally wild hair had been fought back away from her face into a wiry ponytail. Three lines cut into Jenny's forehead, across her eyes and onto her cheek. Jenny turned to where Fin was sitting, horrified, he realised that Jenny was now blind.

The Judge nodded to Mr Stock, 'Your witness.'

'Miss Cato, please will you describe to the court your relationship with Mr Butler.'

Jenny turned towards Mr Stock and with a nervous voice answered the barrister, 'Fin and I are friends.'

'How did you meet?'

'We met at St Matthew's I had been there a while and hated the place. I didn't fit in and when Fin arrived, he didn't either. We sort of gravitated towards each other.'

Fin appreciated hearing her voice again but he could not help staring at her eyes. It was so frustrating he could not remember, what had happened to her?

'In your own words, Miss Cato,' continued Mr Stock as he fiddled with his papers, 'please will you tell us what happened on the night of the fire.'

Sitting up straight in her seat Jenny spoke with more confidence, 'It had been a normal day with nothing unusual about it and we were sent to our rooms at eight o'clock. I finished some homework, then sat and read until lights out at nine-thirty and then went to bed but I couldn't sleep. About ten-fifteen the fire alarm went off, I grabbed my clothes and shoes and ran to my door. It wouldn't open.'

'Was it normal to be locked in your rooms?'

'No, not at all, St Matthew's was full of petty rules and regulations but we could always leave our rooms if we needed the bathroom in the night.'

'What did you do?' asked Mr Stock growing interested.

'To be honest, after swearing at it, I put my boots on, and kicked it until it fell apart. I headed for the nearest exit, but I met a staff member running towards me and he redirected me down the boy's corridor to the rear exit. All the doors were open wide except Fin's and I could hear him shouting and banging on the door. I was so frightened, the smoke was terrible, I struggled with the door but it was jammed shut.

'So you kicked that door apart too,' observed Mr Stock and made a note on his papers. Noticing that Jenny had stopped speaking he motioned with his hand that she should continue.

'We ran towards the rear exit and nearly made it. Then the roof fell in and we were trapped.'

Interested, Mr Stock turned to Jenny, 'So you were trapped?'

Jenny nodded her head. Fear crossed her face as she tried to remember, 'It's all a bit hazy now. What I do remember is that the fumes became overwhelming, the ceiling then fell in, and we were trapped. I can't remember much else.'

'That's it?' Mr Stock's voice grew aggressive, 'I am sorry, Miss Cato, but your written statement, taken while you were in hospital, states you remember something else,' he paused for emphasis and then continued, 'Something really important!'

Jenny struggled to control herself, 'I don't know. I was confused.'

Fin was riveted by Jenny's account of the night as so far it matched his. To what was Mr Stock referring?

'Miss Cato, people died at St Matthew's and you were blinded. It is important that whoever caused this fire should be held accountable,' Mr Stock turned to face Fin and added, 'Even if that person is your best friend.'

Jenny started to cry quietly, 'I fell to the floor and lost consciousness. Briefly, I regained some sense, the flames were burning brightly and Fin was standing with his arms outstretched. He was holding the flames back and they were swirling all around us.'

Startled, Fin sat up in his seat, what was Jenny talking about? He had been unconscious the whole time.

Mr Stock pounced, 'So you and Mr Butler were surrounded by flames?'

'Jenny nodded, 'Yes.'

'Was there anything else unusual you noticed?'

'As the flames swirled around us, I could see Fin had feathers in his hands.'

'Then what happened?'

'I heard someone speaking so I turned around and I was struck in the face. The pain was terrible… My eyes hurt so much.' Jenny collapsed forward in her seat, 'That's it I don't remember anything else.'

Fin could hardly sit still; he was facing a barrage of internal questions. Why was Jenny lying? What would make her lie? I thought she was my friend. Surely, I would remember if she was telling the truth and I did start all those fires?

Mr Stock, cleared his throat noisily, and continued, 'So you clearly saw Mr Butler playing with fire and holding feathers in his hands?'

Jenny said nothing just hid her face in her hands.

Mr Stock's face grew dark and serious, 'Miss Cato, is it not the case, that you and Mr Butler hated St Matthew's so much that you conspired to burn it down?'

Jenny raised her head, her face now red and blotchy, 'No, of course not, why would we?'

The severe voice of the Judge echoed across the court, 'Mr Stock, do you have any evidence to support this line of questioning?'

'I think it's obvious that Mr Butler started this fire. However, it is highly unlikely that he acted alone. I believe that Miss Cato was his accomplice. They were found together after it all got out of control. Miss Cato's fantastical explanation is based on the truth. Mr Butler did start the fire and he did have the signature feathers of the Firebird in his hands.'

His voice now full of confidence Mr Stock continued, 'The police found the feathers in Mr Butler's hands. Miss Cato's injuries came about because she was where she should not have been. Why else would they have both still been in the building so long after the fire alarm went off.'

'Miss Cato,' asked Mr Stock as he changed his focus from the Judge to Jenny, 'Who was the member of staff you say turned you away from the fire exit?'

'I could not see his face in the smoke,' answered Jenny sitting up again, 'but I would recognise his voice again if I heard it.'

'You don't think it unusual that you didn't recognise the staff member concerned?'

'No the corridor was full of smoke and I was just trying to get out alive!'

'I think you are lying to protect yourself,' said Mr Stock turning to face the Judge, 'No more questions.'

Once more, the Judge spoke to Mr Wheatear, 'Your witness.'

Mr Stock turned and stared at Mr Wheatear. The look seemed to make Mr Wheatear unsteady on his feet.

'I have no questions for the witness,' croaked Mr Wheatear.

'What?' exclaimed Fin turning in his chair to glare at his barrister, 'No questions? You must have something!'

Mr Wheatear shaking his head, sat down.

Fin sat back forlornly and felt completely helpless. Meanwhile, an officer of the court led a crying Jenny away from her seat and back to an anteroom. Fin was so confused, why was this happening to him?

The Judge looking surprised, glared at Mr Wheatear, 'In which case we will adjourn for lunch.'

Fin sat in a featureless cell in the basement of the court. His lunch, of microwaved sausages and beans, remained untouched on the side. Mr Wheatear, having discussed the circumstantial nature of the evidence, had encouraged him to plead not guilty. Fin, frustrated at constantly having to justify his innocence, was relieved. Then his barrister having started well, seemed to be intimidated by Mr Stock. Fin felt cold and all alone.

Fin stared across the room and played with the disgusting hot drink he had been given sipping it slowly because he was thirsty. To his surprise, there was a tap on the door.

'Hello?'

'Can I come in,' asked one of the Court Care Officers.

'Sure,' Fin answered, 'why not?'

The officer was tall and had a friendly smile on her face, 'I'm here to talk about what is going to happen to you next.'

Fin began to feel a little cold, scared and the thought of prison terrified him.

The officer saw the fear in his face and tried to calm him down, 'It's not my place to predict what the court is going to recommend but I can assure you that you will not be going to prison. You may end up going to a young offender's institution, but even then, they are not that bad.'

Fin gave her a disbelieving look.

'Okay...' she sighed, 'They can be terrible.'

'That's what I thought.' Fin groaned and ran his hands through his hair. 'You said you're here to talk to me about what is going to happen next, what is going to happen to me?'

'Has no one told you the full range of possibilities?'

Fin shook his head.

'Your barrister and solicitor should have filled you in.'

'They probably did but, if I'm honest, I haven't been taking much notice.'

'Okay, briefly,' the officer tried to look relaxed because she could see the fear in Fin's eyes.

'Well, you could be found not guilty. In which case a new home will be found for you. However, if you are found guilty a long-term detention is likely. Arson carries a minimum sentence of five years, with a maximum of twenty years.'

Fin felt his was world ending, he was sure that he was going to be found guilty.

The officer smiled again and tried to reassure Fin that this was not the end of the world. Fin ignored her; nothing she was saying was going to make the slightest difference, as he knew in his heart he was going to be found guilty. He never noticed the officer leave the room.

CHAPTER 2 - RAVENSWOOD

Still cold and tired, Fin begrudgingly walked beside the anonymous man in the dark suit who had watched him from the gallery of the court. Pulling up the collar of his cagoule around his neck, Fin failed to avoid the evening rain seeping in. The only car he could see was old fashioned, black, covered in chrome and the registration plate contained a few silver letters and numbers on a black background.

'She's lovely,' said the man, noticing his interest, 'she's a 1963 Rover P4, it was designed in the 1940s and weighs one and half tons.'

Still dazed Fin said nothing and climbed into the leather back seat, just glad to be out the rain. Pulling the armrest down he settled back into the comfortable seat but seeing the man's smug look there was no way he was going to admit that to him.

'We are just waiting for Miss Gosling to join us, with our other passenger,' explained the man.

Not knowing whom Miss Gosling was Fin ignored him and let his mind drift back into the court wondering why nothing was ever easy.

The court resumed and Fin was led back to sit next to his barrister. Fin tried to talk to Mr Wheatear but he remained distant and distracted. After the fifth attempt, he gave up and sat back to wait for the court to start again.

The majority of the afternoon passed by in a blur as witnesses came and went. Social workers, doctors, teachers and care workers all expressing opinions on Fin's mental state. Fin tried to concentrate, but he was cold and tired and all he could think about was Jenny's description of him holding back the fire. Finally, the last witness of the day was called.

Detective Inspector David Llewellyn Jones was a tall, distinguished looking, man. He had short-cropped dark hair with a few whispers of grey in it and Fin guessed he was about forty but was not sure. His eyes were as dark as his skin and he spoke with a deep baritone voice with a slight Welsh accent. The Detective Inspector had interviewed Fin many times and Fin discovered that he was persistent, sharp and did not suffer fools gladly. Fin liked him and mistrusted him at the same time.

'Detective Inspector, please will you outline your involvement in this case?' said Mr Stock beginning the cross-examination.

'How far back would you like me to go?'

'Please give the court a relevant overview.'

'Certainly,' answered DI Jones, 'I have been tasked with investigating the arson attacks currently being attributed to the Firebird. My investigations lead me to believe that there are similarities in cases that go back twenty-five years. In each case, the same accelerant is used and three crow feathers are left.'

'Regarding these similarities, what can you tell us about the accelerant and feathers used?'

The Detective Inspector paused and picked up his case notes. 'There is nothing unusual about the feathers left at the scenes, they seem to be randomly gathered and they are just standard crow feathers. The accelerant is much more interesting. Chemical analysis indicates that it has the properties of a bio-fuel fashioned from a combination of naturally formed materials. However, here is our problem, we have been able to strip down the accelerant to its component elements, but we have never been able to reproduce it in the laboratory.'

'Is there a pattern to these historic crimes?'

'Few that we've been able to discover however, my superiors and I are working on the assumption that there are a number of common links.'

'Where does Mr Butler fit into your investigations?' asked Mr Stock.

Fin's heart sank within him and he imagined Jenny's sightless eyes, through the walls, looking at him.

'In all my investigations Fin is the first common element,' explained DI Jones.

'You deliberately have chosen to call Mr Butler by his preferred name, why is that?'

'I have spoken to Fin frequently, he is an intelligent young man and I do not wish to depersonalise him. If this was a youth court calling him Fin would be normal.'

'However, the seriousness of the crimes and the deaths involved has brought this matter here,' snapped Mr Stock.

'Nevertheless, guilty or not, he is thirteen years old and unless the Judge instructs me otherwise, I will call him Fin,' replied DI Jones.

'Thank you Detective Inspector I will make no such demands of you,' the Judge commented and then seeing a look of anger ripple across Mr Stock's face said, 'Mr Stock do you wish to object?'

Shaking his head in reply, Mr Stock indicated he did not and Fin felt warm for the first time that day.

'Detective Inspector in what way is Mr Butler the common link?' continued Mr Stock.

'I believe the court has been made aware of these commonalities,' replied DI Jones, 'the fires at Fin's parent's house, the Mackay Bakery, the Registry Office in

St Mary's in the Scilly Isles and of course the recent fire at St Matthew's.'

'Will you please share with the court what evidence you found that connects Mr Butler with these fires?' asked Mr Stock.

The Detective Inspector paused and then replied, 'Other than circumstantial connections there is no evidence whatsoever, that Fin was involved in any of these fires.'

Mr Stock turned and stared at the Detective Inspector as he did so he narrowed his eyes, 'Surely, you do not include St Matthew's in that generalisation? You were the officer that removed the feathers from Mr Butler's hands.'

A half-smile crept across the Detective Inspector's face as he replied, 'Are you well Mr Stock, because your eyes have glazed over and turned a shade of yellow?'

Obviously disturbed Mr Stock replied, 'I am fine thank you.'

Curious by the exchange Fin observed that Mr Stock's smile was forced and that he had a slightly disappointed look on his face.

'Yes, I removed the feathers from Fin's hands however, he was delirious and muttering all sorts of strange things.'

'Can you repeat them to the court?'

The Detective Inspector opened his notebook, 'No, no you can't! I don't know, I don't know. Leave us alone and go back to the flames where you belong.'

'And what do you think he meant by these ramblings Detective Inspector?' continued Mr Stock.

The Detective Inspector paused, and then said, 'I really have no idea.'

'Then why did you arrest him,' continued Mr Stock, 'surely your actions speak louder than your words?'

'I could not ignore the fact that Fin had the feathers in his hands. On that basis alone I wanted to know more.'

'So you arrested him on a whim?' snapped Mr Stock.

'Of course not,' retorted the Detective Inspector, 'but

in the circumstances I felt I had little option.'

'Thank you Detective Inspector I have no more questions.'

'Mr Wheatear do you have any questions for the Detective Inspector?' the Judge asked with an edge to his voice.

As Fin turned to look at his barrister, he saw the yellow-eyed look of the prosecution barrister as he glared at Mr Wheatear. Across the court, the Detective Inspector coughed loudly and Mr Stock's attention shifted to him. Mr Wheatear shook his head, as if to shake off a cloud, and stood up.

'Thank you, I do!' Mr Wheatear's voice was suddenly full of confidence. 'Detective Inspector, I just want to be clear about a few things. Was there any physical evidence, other than the feathers at St Matthew's, connecting my client with any of the fires?'

'No.'

'No, indeed,' brimming with self-belief he continued, 'Was there any trace of this mysterious bio-fuel found on my client or Miss Cato?'

'No, there was not.'

'Is it possible that my client could have found the feathers and just picked them up to bring out?'

'Yes, it is possible.'

'No further questions.' Mr Wheatear, with a smug look on his face, sat down.

Continuing to feel cold, Fin shifted in car his seat, tore his mind away from the court and looked away into the amber coloured darkness. From the direction of the main entrance to the court, a couple, with mismatched heights, struggled to shelter under a small transparent umbrella. The smaller one stumbled over the kerb and the taller one held her up. It was then that Fin saw Jenny's face and despite the cold, and his frustration, he smiled.

The taller figure, negotiated Jenny to the car, opened

the rear door and helped her slip into the back next to Fin. Closing the door she shook her umbrella out and climbed into the front passenger seat.

Suddenly Fin did not know what to say, Jenny was his friend but they had not spoken in months and she was blind now. Somehow, he could not escape thinking that it was his fault. Refusing to look at him Jenny said nothing and stared out the window. The driver started the car and they drove off into the night. As they travelled along the silence in the car became deafening. Overwhelmed by guilt Fin ignored the others closed his eyes and his mind again drifted back into the court.

Looking around the court, Fin found himself noticing it for the first time. The room was much smaller than he had expected it to be. The windows were frosted and the outside world was just a blurred image. The furniture was archaic; all apart from the Judge's desk that looked like it came from a charity shop. On the wall, there was a coat of arms containing two crossed swords and an eagle, coloured in faded red paint and peeling gold guilt. Like the court, it had obviously seen better days. The reporter was back playing on her phone and the mysterious man stared at him with dark hooded eyes. Fin felt uncomfortable and the drab room did nothing to lift his mood.

The Judge returned, the court settled down and Mr Stock with a great deal of waving of his hands gave his closing address. There was nothing new in anything he said, he just kept pointing out that Fin was a disturbed child, with a pathological need to start fires, a child who is a danger to himself and all around him. It was only when Mr Stock started talking about Miss Cato's involvement, that he sat up and took proper notice.

'In my opinion, Mr Butler is a dangerous young man who should spend the rest of his life in an institution for the disturbed. It is obvious, to me that Mr Butler had an accomplice at St Matthew's and I believe that Miss Cato was it. They plotted together to destroy a place they both hated. Miss Cato's fantastical testimony, from the locked doors, the mysterious stranger blocking her exit, to Mr Butler holding back the flames is pathetic. I urge the police to look further into this and try to ascertain Miss Cato's full involvement. That the fact that she lost her sight in this arson attack just shows how dangerous they are to themselves.'

Filled with righteous indignation, Fin leapt out of his seat. 'You idiot!' he shouted out before he realised it, 'How can you say such cruel things about Jenny? Don't be so ridiculous, posturing about like a giant vulture and blaming an injured girl who is totally defenceless!'

Instantly Fin regretted his outburst and sat down embarrassed. Detective Inspector Jones caught his eye, and while the Judge struck his hammer down, he smiled at him.

'I have finished my summing up,' explained Mr Stock, 'I do not think I need to say anything else!'

Mr Wheatear stood up as Mr Stock sat down with a flourish, 'While my client should have kept his anger in check, I agree with the sentiment of his words. Having heard all the evidence against Mr Butler I am convinced that the prosecution have produced nothing to prove his guilt. Unsubstantiated claims, circumstantial evidence and three feathers are not enough to prove my client guiltily. Then to fling such wild accusations at Miss Cato is disgusting and a complete misuse of his office.' Mr Wheatear paused and then said, 'I ask that this charade is ended and that Mr Butler be released from this court. It is high time he was allowed to get on with his life!'

Fin was astounded, where did his barrister suddenly find such courage? As Mr Wheatear sat down, Fin whispered a quiet thank you.

As the Judge shuffled his papers, the court went quiet. Expecting another adjournment the Judge surprised Fin by clearing his throat and speaking.

'Mr Butler has been charged with committing an act of

arson. Arson, as I understand it, is the deliberate act of starting a fire to cause damage to property. This is a serious offence, especially when, as well as damage to property, there has been injury and loss of life. In this case, Miss Cato was seriously injured and, sadly, one member of the staff died.'

Fin sat uncomfortably in his seat aware that the Judge was not going to wait and deliberate but was going to give his verdict immediately.

'The prosecution has tried to prove that Mr Butler is the "Firebird" and that Miss Cato was his accomplice. They have sought to show that Mr Butler is a psychotic and damaged young man. However, we have heard from the expert psychiatrists that after a fire many survivors may experience feelings, sights, and even smells that remind them of their ordeal. Fear of fire, concern for loved ones, insecurity, behavioural issues, sadness and depression are quite normal reactions.

To his surprise, Fin was paying attention.

'Many of these signs have been seen in Mr Butler's behaviour. The prosecution would have us believe that he emotionally damaged, when it seems to me, that Mr Butler has just been a victim of tragedy.'

Amazingly, Mr Wheatear reached out his hand and patted Fin's arm.

'I find myself believing that the prosecution's case to be too circumstantial and lacking in concrete evidence for my liking. As a result, I find Mr Butler, not guilty.'

Fin's heart jumped into his mouth and he gasped with astonishment

'However.'

The eyes of everyone in the court turned to the Judge.

'I believe that it is the duty of this court to protect Mr Butler, and indeed, Miss Cato, not from themselves, but from those around them who are seeking to implicate them in the antics of the "Firebird."' The Judge, paused for effect, and gave Mr Stock and the Detective Inspector a serious look, 'Therefore, I have consulted with Mr Chough, from the Ravenswood House Centre for Children at Risk, and he and I, believe that their educational institute and home would be the right place to situate them.'

A groan slipped from Fin's mouth, he and Jenny had hated St Matthew's so much he had been hoping for a real home, with foster parents, Ravenswood sounded terrible.

'I have spoken to the Youth and Children's Department,' continued the Judge, 'and they have agreed with this suggestion. Therefore, I am delighted to inform you, Mr Butler...' The Judge paused, 'Fin, that you and Jenny will be released to accompany Mr Chough, and a female member of his team, to your new home at Ravenswood.'

Nodding his head Fin accepted the inevitable.

'However, Fin...' the Judge's voice grew serious, 'I urge you, for your sake and those around you, to resist playing with fire!'

Fin felt his stomach rumble and he realised that he was hungry. The car pulled over for petrol and Miss Gosling, while Mr Chough purchased fuel, bought water and a sandwich for Fin and Jenny.

Once on their way again, Miss Gosling turned around and spoke to them both, 'The journey to Ravenswood House is going to take about two hours.' Her voice was clear and surprisingly full of joy, 'When we get there, the cook will have a meal ready for you both and temporary accommodation has been prepared. Tomorrow morning, we will show you to your accommodations, housemates and introduce to your house tutor who will be your designated teacher.'

Liking the sound of Miss Gosling's voice Fin smiled and then shivered. Miss Gosling noticed and pulled two travel blankets out from under her seat. Mr Chough adjusted the car's heater and hot air flowed through the car.

Jenny turned her head towards Fin as if to say something, but changed her mind. Wrapping herself up into her blanket she let the motion of the car rock her to sleep. Fin too found the warmth soporific and he fell into a deep dreamless sleep.

Waking up, Fin wondered where he was. It took a moment or two to realise that he was still in a car travelling to Ravenswood House. It took him even longer to realise that he and Jenny had cuddled together while they were asleep. Embarrassed, he tried to move, but when he did, Jenny clung to him instinctively. Thankful it was dark in the back of the car and that the two teachers were not paying attention to them, he gave up struggling, and went back to sleep.

The car slowed and entered a gravelled drive. Fin stirred and looked at Jenny, who was now awake but ignoring him. Looking out the window, he could see an old Tudor house that reminded him of Little Moreton Hall, a National Trust house, he had once visited. Ravenswood House was a large half-timbered manor house, with black oak beams that stretched across white walls. The three-storey building was highly angular and irregular; each floor overlapped the one below. Fin guessed it had been there for at least five-hundred years and by the way the house bowed and warped under its weight, made him feel it was likely to collapse if so much as a gust of wind were to hit it.

Thankfully, the rain had stopped and he and Jenny were led across a sandstone bridge into the entrance hall. Fin, as he crossed the bridge, was not at all surprised to see it that it once had a moat.

Mr Chough closed the large door behind them and asked them to wait in the entrance hall. Jenny reached behind her head, pulled out her hairgrips and shook her wild hair free.

'What's it like?'

'Mmm... What?' mumbled Fin, surprised that Jenny had spoken to him.

'What's the room like?' She turned on the spot, 'It feels vast and airy.'

'It has a large entrance hall with a giant sandstone fireplace, full of logs, against the far wall. The ceiling is high but plain, the walls are timber panelled.' Fin looked around,' There's a few uncomfortable wooden chairs with embroidered seats and an oak staircase.'

'What's the carpet like?'

Looking down at his feet Fin noticed their muddy footprints scattered across the thick, patterned carpet and he tried to describe it but found himself lost for words. Uncomfortably, he moved his feet, realising that this was the first time he had been alone with Jenny, 'I'm sorry.'

'What for?'

'Your eyes...'

Turning to face him, Jenny's hair swung around and brushed Fin's shoulder, 'I don't want to talk about it...'

Struggling to remain calm Fin tried to speak, 'But...'

Reaching out her hand Jenny placed a finger on Fin's lips and whispered, 'Shhh. I don't want to talk about it now.' Removing her hand she continued, 'This is not the place or the time and we don't know who is listening.' Jenny leaned closer to Fin's ear and whispered, 'It wasn't your fault.'

'So how do you like our little house?' cried Miss Gosling as she burst into the room, 'Come on, come on,' she laughed, 'there's a hot meal waiting for you in the little dinning room.'

Leading them down a dark corridor towards the back of the house, she let them into an oak panelled room that featured two crossed keys carved into the stone floor. A fire roared in the fireplace giving the room both warmth and light.

'Mr Chough will not be joining us,' Miss Gosling

laughed pointing at a large oak table laden with food, 'but that just means more for us!'

Crossing the room, they all sat at the large table and tucked in to a hot, thick, chicken and vegetable soup. Miss Gosling cut and served them fresh, crusty slices of bread. Very quickly, the three of them had consumed all the soup, made big inroads into a steak and kidney pie with boiled potatoes and finished off an apple crumble and custard. Fin sat back feeling he was going to burst if he ate another mouthful. Jenny's head slumped forward with tiredness.

'Come on, time for bed,' insisted Miss Gosling, and led Fin and Jenny down some even darker corridors, until they reached two rooms. 'These are your temporary rooms for the night.' She opened the door and directed Jenny into the room. Fin stood at the door as Miss Gosling helped Jenny find the bed, the en suite bathroom and the towels. 'We will come and wake you in the morning, but don't worry, its Saturday and you can have a lie in. You can lock the door from the inside, so enjoy the peace.' She them took Fin next door and invited him into a mirror image of Jenny's room, 'See you in the morning.'

With that, she closed the door and Fin heard her footsteps disappear up the corridor. Having washed his face and cleaned his teeth, Fin crawled into the bed and fell into a fitful sleep.

The candelabra swung with an unseen movement of air. The light flickered and wax ran down the sides of the old yellowed candles. Oppressive stone walls, decorated with hooks and chains, oozed moisture, and the room stank with mould and fear. Dark hooded figures, silently, entered the room and sat down at an old battered oak table. Shadows clung to the edges of the walls, frightened to come out.

At the head of the table, the Crow sat with his hood obscuring his face. 'So, Raven do you have the boy?' his voice emerged as a grated whisper.

'Yes, Lord'

'Good, good.' Dark piercing eyes gazed out of the hood's shadow, 'See that no harm comes to him,' he paused for emphasis, 'and the other.'

'But Lord,' the Raven croaked back at him, 'we have the opportunity to…'

'Silence,' the menace in the voice grew stronger, 'do not question my instructions,' the voice grew hard and cold, 'unless you want to take my place in the Flock with all that entails.'

The silence in the room grew stronger, 'Sorry, Lord,' the Raven's voice grew subservient, 'you know best as usual.'

'I do indeed, and you would be wise to remember that,' a strangled laugh slipped out, 'I could always use some more feathers.'

'What about the humans?' the Raven asked seeking to change the subject.

'Are you sure they are human?'

'I am certain. There is nothing special about them.'

'Certain, are you?'

'I would stake my life on it!'

'I accept those terms.'

'That's not what I meant,' fear entered the Raven's voice, 'they are just cattle.'

'Nevertheless, those are my terms,' replied the Crow, 'be careful Raven, be very careful, for I grow tired of you.'

'Yes, Lord,' acknowledged the Raven, 'what would you like me to do with the humans?'

'Leave them to squabble amongst themselves,' replied the Crow, 'for they are so very good at it.'

'They are starting to affect us again,' continued the Raven, 'maybe it is time to talk to the Royals about another cull.'

'Be careful what you ask for,' snapped the Crow, 'the Royals are not bothered who gets caught up in a cull!"

Smoke crept under the door of Fin's room and the smell crawled its way up his nose and into his sleeping mind. Fin struggled to wake up but he could not move. His arms were pinned down, his legs were trapped, and panic took over. Screaming in terror he woke up wrapped from head to toe in the duvet and fell out of the bed onto the floor.

'Are you alright?' Jenny yelled from the corridor.

Struggling free of his restrictive bedding, Fin stood up. 'Yeah, I'm okay, just a nightmare.' Falling back on to the bed, he closed his eyes. When, finally, he had stopped shaking, Fin took full advantage of the guestroom's private facilities and had a long, hot shower.

After a quiet breakfast with Miss Gosling, she took Fin and Jenny from the main house, to their new rooms, into the grounds. To Fin's amazement, and in stark contrast to Ravenswood House, the resident accommodation was purpose built and looked brand new. Set back in the grounds, with rows of trees behind them, were ten pine two-storey apartments, staggered, so that the view from the front of each building was that of manicured grounds and the rickety glory of Ravenswood House. Fin tried to describe it all to Jenny, but he was struggling to convey how great it looked.

Noticing Fin's struggle for words Miss Gosling explained, 'We had an anonymous donation from a rich benefactor. It was a condition of the gift that homes were provided for sixty young people who had nowhere else to go.' She pointed at the tinted windows, 'No expense was spared. The complex composes of ten flats, each with three shared bedrooms, a communal room, kitchen and separate, male and female, bathroom facilities. The bedrooms are upstairs, have large tinted windows, balconies, and are equipped with desks and chairs so that homework can be done away from the house. The communal room has a large stone fireplace, and comfy chairs.'

Taking Jenny's arm, Fin guided her into the communal space. The ground floor was open-planned; the kitchen was off to the right under the first floor and a fireplace stood in the centre of a room that went right up to the underside of the roof. Two staircases led up to the balcony bedrooms. Girl's laughter echoed down the stairs.

'We believe in the positive value of girls and boys living together. The left upstairs rooms are for the girls, and the right, boys.' Miss Gosling face became serious. 'There is an element of trust in this, but, let me make this clear, under no circumstances whatsoever, are you allowed on each others' balconies or in each others' rooms. The separate bathrooms are only accessible from the balconies, so there is no need for any of you get lost!'

Amazed by the luxury of the accommodation Fin simply stared around him.

'With your arrival we are nearly full although our numbers fluctuate occasionally as residents move on.' Miss Gosling indicated that they should sit down. 'You will meet everyone else in due course, but we want this to be your home, and those you share with, your family.'

There was silence in the room as they listened and even the laughter upstairs ceased.

'Each house, is named after a flower, this one, is Narcissus. The rest are Strelitzia, Iris, Aster, Helleborus, Vanda, Ranunculus, Orchid, Skimmia and Eucharis.' Starting to laugh at the look on their faces, Miss Gosling, continued, 'The mysterious benefactor liked his flowers! Don't worry you will remember them, eventually.'

Pulling out a pad from her bag, Miss Gosling checked her list. 'Okay, the accommodation, Fin you are in room one, sharing with Ash. In room two, we have Eiry and Sed. Jenny, now as we are a resident short I though it might nice for you, at least at first, to have a chance to get to know your way around your room without falling over anyone else's clutter. You are on your own in room three, I hope that's okay.'

Looking relieved, Jenny nodded her head and smiled.

'Each house had a designated teacher, or carer. I have a separate flat to the rear of this house so in practical terms, I am your house parent.'

'Miss Gosling, that's great!' Fin's enthusiasm burst out.

'Thank you Fin, your enthusiasm means a lot. However, if I am your house parent, then you can't keep calling me Miss Gosling when we are in this house, I am Elizabeth.'

Smiling at the warmth in Elizabeth's voice, Jenny said, 'That's good.'

'Finally, I try to be friendly, warm and available. I would like you to feel free to talk to me at anytime,' a dark look crossed Elizabeth's face, 'but not all the staff here are so approachable. Find your feet, settle in and be careful.'

This was too much for Fin, 'Why?'

Elizabeth sighed, 'Ravenswood House is a special place and it tries to be many things. It's a school, home, hospital, sanctuary, retreat, boot camp and prison.' Looking uncomfortable, she continued, 'No computer technology is allowed, no mobile phones, computer tablets, laptops or internet.'

'No phones?'

'None.'

'You must have computers in the library.'

'Books.'

'Game consoles?'

'Board games and cards.'

'Music?'

'Mr Chough, allows students to play an instrument, but no media players, radios or CDs.'

Silence fell on the room. Fin groaned, 'That sounds pretty harsh.'

'Make friends, be happy, do your work and try to avoid...' Elizabeth stopped, 'I've said enough for now please take your time to settle in and meet your room-mates. Lunch is in the main dining room, in the big house, at one. I will come and walk you over at about ten to.' With a parting smile, Elizabeth stood up and left them to find their own way to their rooms. In the doorway she stopped. 'Sorry, I nearly forgot, your belongings should arrive tomorrow morning and the caretaker will leave them in your rooms.' With that, she left, clicking the door shut behind her.

Fin led Jenny to the foot of the girl's stairs and then climbed up the boy's stairs to room one. He was just starting to like the place but something about Elizabeth's parting comments disturbed him, what did she mean?

Standing outside the door of his new room, Fin was not sure if he should knock or just walk in. He decided to both at the same time. 'Hello?'

The room was more spacious and comfortable than he expected. There were two beds in the room, well apart from each other, but each still having a panoramic view out the window. Lying on top of the bed furthest from the door was his new roommate. He was about the same height and weight as Fin, but his hair was blond and shaved short. Looking up from his book, he glanced at Fin and then ignored him. The desk chair next to the spare bed was empty, Fin sat down and took in the room and wondered why his roommate behaved as if Fin was invisible.

'Hi, I'm Fin.'

Ash looked over the top of his book.

'You must be Ash.'

Scowling he gave a long deep sigh, closed his book and sat up, 'Let's get this clear. I don't have any choice about you sharing with me, I didn't like the last person I shared with and I can't see me liking you.' Standing up, Ash threw his book on the bed, 'Don't let this place fool you with its good food and fancy accommodation. It's hell.' He walked to the door, 'I don't trust anyone, or anything and you're no exception. I have to live with you, so I will, but that's it. Don't expect my friendship in this pathetic prison family, don't talk to me and don't touch my stuff.' Opening the door, Ash walked out onto the gallery and left a bemused Fin sitting at his desk.

Hearing Jenny laugh Fin stood up and went downstairs to find Jenny talking to the girls. They were both about the same age as Fin and Jenny but the contrast in appearances was startling. One girl was short, black, with short-cropped hair and a wide smile and wearing a heavy fleece. The other was tall and thin, her complexion pale and she had long blond hair. The room was not warm, but she looked uncomfortably hot and was dressed in simply a vest and shorts.

Seeing Fin coming down the stairs, she turned and smiled at him, 'Hi, I'm Eiry, it's short for Eirawen, but that too much of a mouthful.' Reaching out her hand, Eiry shook Fin's hand, 'I saw Ash leave, so I guess you have met your room mate.'

'Yeah, it was... interesting.'

'He has his moments, but he's okay once you get to know him!' Turning and introducing the girl next to her, she said, 'This is Sed.'

Holding out her hand to be shaken, Sed continued the introduction, 'Sedna Purity ArnaaU.' She gave a little curtsy and burst out laughing, 'But call me Sed.'

Shaking Sed's hand, Fin smiled back and replied, 'I'm Fin, it's really Fenix, it seems we were all given interesting names.'

Sed was the same height as Fin; she had deep dark brown eyes and a full smile. Still smiling, Sed explained, 'My names all have meanings my mother believed that a beautiful name stays with you for your whole life. My middle name is Purity. Sadly,' Sed burst out laughing, 'I don't always live up to my name! My grandmother, who I used to live with, was from Kenya, full of Christian faith and life. That is, until she died, that's why I'm here.'

Finding one of the sofas, Jenny flopped down into it. Sed and Eiry showed Fin around the kitchen and they brought back drinks for everyone. Making themselves comfortable, they spent ages chatting, without really saying anything. Everyone has a story, Fin thought, but no one wants to share it. Without noticing it, time passed. They all started laughing, and began to relax in each other's company.

The front door opened and Elizabeth walked in and smiled when she noticed them all laughing, 'Time for lunch guys.'

Jumping up, Sed said helpfully, 'We're happy to take them over.'

'Great,' Elizabeth replied, 'then, I will see you all later.'

Standing up Sed and Eiry linked arms, one each side of Jenny and guided Fin over to the old house for lunch.

The weekend passed by in a blur of faces and names. Fin found himself, against expectations, beginning to settle in. Everywhere that was, except in his room, Ash as good as his word, had nothing to say to him. As promised his belongings arrived on the Sunday morning and it did not take Fin long to arrange his prized possessions. Even though he had been warned, Fin was still disappointed to find his old mobile phone and iPod had been confiscated. Aware that Ash was watching him Fin said nothing as he laid out his father's broken watch, two ancient Eagle Annuals, and a smoke-damaged collection of the Harry Potter books.

That night, Fin woke up screaming about the fire. Ash, disturbed by the cry, woke up, took one look at Fin, then rolled over and went back to sleep.

After breakfast, on Monday morning, while all the other students gathered for assembly, Fin and Jenny were taken into Mr Chough's office. After, inviting them to sit down, he began to speak.

'Good morning and welcome to Ravenswood. I hope you have begun to settle in okay?'

Hearing his voice aloud, Fin was surprised by the simple sound of it. He realised that he had not paid attention to it in the car. It was a confident voice. A voice that could inspire you and yet always get what it wanted.

'To all intense and purposes, Ravenswood, is a boarding school however, it is more than that. We are unusual, in that we are different from every other residential care home. The accommodation is superb, the food excellent and the education is set to an incredibly high standard.'

To his own amazement, Fin found himself listening to the monologue.

'However, some people find our methods strange, our discipline too strict. We demand the best and we get it, both from the students and the teachers. We specialise in getting the most from our students. Therefore, you will study Maths, English, Biological Sciences, and a rare form of a Classical Education. You will learn about history from unusual perspectives.'

As Mr Chough spoke, Fin could see pictures in his mind, of giant birds and brave warriors. Reaching out her hand to touch his arm, Jenny gripped Fin's elbow. The pictures faded, feeling Jenny let go of his arm, Fin relaxed, the moment passed, and he realised that Mr Chough was looking at him his introduction had ended.

'I will arrange for you to be given a timetable and your lessons will begin immediately.'

'Thank you,' Fin replied, slightly embarrassed for blanking out part of what Mr Chough had been saying.

'Sir,' growled Mr Chough, 'it's thank you, Sir.'

Going bright red, in response to the correction, Fin echoed his words, 'Thank you, Sir.'

Mr Chough dismissed them with the nod of his head.

CHAPTER 3 - THE NIGHTMARE ROOM

When lessons had ended for the day, Fin took a walk in the grounds. The light was beginning to fade and there was a chill in the September air. The truth was he felt a little bewildered and lonely. The day had passed him by in a rush of introductions and lessons. He had missed the start of term so he had a mound of catch up reading to do. Jenny had gone off with Elizabeth who was going to guide her through her assignments.

Ravenswood grounds were outstandingly beautiful and the leaves on the trees were just starting to turn brown. The grass was a lush green and the sunset cast a golden glow. Fin had never seen so much wildlife unbothered by his presence. Wild rabbits gambled in the shadows, standing on their back legs and twitching their ears in the wind. Birds were everywhere and Fin was even convinced that he saw a bat flickering in the air. The only annoyance was the racket the crows were making, no wonder; he thought they called it Ravenswood.

Making his way through the woods, Fin found his path blocked by an old red brick wall all pitted and scarred. The wall was quite a bit taller than he was and to deter any one climbing, the top was embedded with broken glass. Looking up, Fin realised, that one section was relatively clear. Gingerly he hoisted himself up using broken bricks as footholds. Looking out from this vantage point, Fin could see that what he thought was a line of trees was a lane. The birds were making such a noise that Fin could not hear if anything was using the road.

Back in the woods, Fin heard the sound of someone coming noisily towards him. Jumping down, he thought it was time to head back. Brushing his way through some branches, he crashed into Elizabeth.

'Miss Gosling…'

An agitated look crossed Elizabeth's face.

'Elizabeth, remember?' Elizabeth's anxious look was communicating something more than the surprise of being bumped into. 'I think you should head back to your room.'

'I thought you were guiding Jenny through her homework.'

'I was, but then I heard the birds.'

The birds had been noisy but Fin could not understand why it had rattled Elizabeth so much.

'I don't understand I was quite safe.'

Whispering intensely, Elizabeth pulled Fin close to her, 'No you were not!' she looked around making sure they were not overheard. 'Stay away from the walls, the birds are always watching, if they think you are trying to escape they will attack you.'

Out of nowhere, a crow landed on a branch near them.

'So you see,' Miss Gosling explained, 'we are very proud of the natural environmental biodiversity at Ravenswood. We have the most amazing variety of animals and birds here. All of the produce we grew in our own gardens is organic, we use no pesticides or chemicals and we are completely green. As part of our biology course we shall consider the merits of going truly organic.'

With a flap of its wings, the crow flew off.

'Was that crow listening to us?'

'That crow was a Raven, and yes it was.' Leading Fin back to Narcissus lodge Elizabeth continued, 'I think it believed me, the Ravens are not very intelligent, but they have amazing hearing and eyesight. I will have to write up an assignment plan to justify your walk in the woods,' Elizabeth smiled apologetically at Fin, 'and, I'm sorry I will need a five-hundred word report on your wildlife observations.' Elizabeth's face grew concerned, 'Mr Chough, will check up on us, by now the birds will have told him about our walk.'

They walked the last few paces to the lodge in silence. As she left, Elizabeth turned and faced Fin, 'I will need that report first thing in the morning you had best go and do it now.'

Spooked by Elizabeth's fear, Fin whispered, 'What's going on here?'

Overhead, a flock of birds flew over them. Elizabeth shuddered and walked off, with one last look up, Fin walked into the lodge.

An hour or so later, Fin had finished his report, completed his reading when his stomach rumbled. Downstairs he heard a burst of noise as the other returned from evening meal. Slowly it dawned on him; he had worked through the evening meal break.

The door burst open and Ash walked in, 'Are you mental?' he cried.

Taken a bit by surprise that Ash had started a conversation with him, Fin could only mumble, 'What?'

'I said, are you mental?' Ash glared at him, 'Elizabeth can only protect us so much.'

Still coming to terms with these new insights, Fin said nothing.

'If by your stupidity, you get Elizabeth hurt, I will kill you!'

Finally, Fin snapped, 'What the hell are you talking about? I have only been here a few days and have no idea what's going on. All I know is that I share a room with a self-absorbed prat. If there's something I should know, then tell me or shut up!'

Glaring across the room at each other, sparks seemed to fly. Then Ash, unexpectedly, laughed and walked out the door, turned at the last minute and growled, 'You'll learn soon enough.' With that, he banged the door shut.

Feeling hungry, Fin went downstairs to the kitchen and made a sandwich.

The following morning after breakfast, Fin handed his report into a relived looking Elizabeth and went on to his lessons.

On his first day, it had become apparent to Fin, that the average age range at Ravenswood was limited between eleven and sixteen. When he had asked about it, the answers he received were vague. It seemed the Governors of Ravenswood felt, as the centre was so new, it would be more appropriate to nurture a few younger cohorts through and evolve a sixth form. Still he thought fifteen in a year group made it difficult to hide in the lessons.

The first class of the day was history with Mr Byrd. Sed, Eiry and Jenny had saved Fin a seat near the back, which was just as well, for the moment he sat down the teacher walked arrived.

'I am sorry, I missed yesterday's lesson,' rambled Mr Byrd, 'but I was engaged in…' he paused absentmindedly, 'I was doing something unavoidable.' Staring round the room, he spotted Fin and Jenny, 'Oh, yes of course, we have freshers among us. Well you have missed weeks of work, I will give you extra reading and the rest will help you catch up.'

Jenny raised her hand.

'Cato, isn't it?'

Jenny nodded.

'I'm sure Butler will be delighted to share his reading with you,' Mr Byrd peered through his thick glasses at Fin, 'After all, you are in the same lodge and have to catch up the same work.'

Pleasantries over, Mr Byrd began to teach in the most

boring voice Fin had ever heard. As the lesson progressed, Fin could feel sleep creep up on him, that is, until he noticed something strange. The sunlight, streaming in the through the window, cast a dark shadow of Mr Byrd. The shadow however, seemed to have a life of its own. The angle of Mr Byrd's head and his long nose and glasses, cast the shadow of a bird's head. His teacher's gown, that fluttered as his arms gesticulated, cast the shadow of wings. Combined, they created the image of a large bird hopping from foot to foot.

Eiry, noticing Fin's attention on the shadow, whispered to him, 'Its weird isn't it! We call him, Birdie; he thinks it's because of his surname. It's not; it's because of his shadow.'

'Brooke!'

'Yes, Sir.'

'Do you wish to share your insights with the class?'

'No, Sir.'

'Then kindly cease whispering to Butler and pay attention.'

'Yes, Sir,' Eiry's face glowed red with embarrassment.

Behind them, Fin heard, Sed and Jenny giggle.

That evening back in the lounge of the lodge, everyone but Ash did their homework together. Ash had come in taken one look at them working together and had gone upstairs. Fin was not convinced Ash was muttering something under his breath, but the finger gesture he did not mistake.

'What is his problem?'

Sighing, Sed glanced up at the closing of the upstairs door, 'All of us here have our problems, otherwise we wouldn't be here. Ash's story is troubled, his mum died young and his dad died in bakery fire. He lived rough for a while till the police caught up with him.' She shook her head, 'No matter what he says, he liked his last room mate, Greg.' Seeing the look of doubt on Fin's face she added,

'Yeah, they were good mates and for the first time, he started trusting someone, then Greg vanished, overnight. We were told he had been moved to a new home, to be nearer a distant aunt he has. But it all happened too quickly.'

'People vanish here,' Eiry joined in, 'teachers, ancillary staff and students!'

'Why?'

'We don't know. It's just weird.' exclaimed Eiry.

'Ash is petrified it will be him next,' Sed continued, 'he has this theory that when teachers get too close to us, they are removed. That's why he is scared something is going to happen to Elizabeth.'

'He likes her?'

'Come on, you must have noticed how easy she is to get on with.'

Nodding his head Fin agreed, 'Yeah, she rescued me from the birds the other night.'

'Looks guys,' yawned Sed, 'I need to go to bed.' Picking up her books, she headed for the stairs. Stopping behind Fin, she indicated to Eiry to follow.

Eiry stood, 'I'm done in too see you I the morning.' Turning to Jenny who was untying her hair bands, 'Are you coming up now?'

'No, I think I will have a drink of hot chocolate first. Do you mind making it, Fin?'

'Not at all.'

Sed and Eiry vanished upstairs, switching off the main lights as they did so. A few minutes later Fin appeared with a couple of mugs of hot chocolate and some biscuits he had found.

'Have they gone?' Jenny shook her hair out, ran her fingers through her hair, then made herself comfortable with her drink.

'Just us, do you want me to read to you?'

'Why on earth would I want that?'

'Well, Birdie, said that I had to.'

Jenny smiled, 'You haven't a clue what's going on, have you?'

'You asked me to read to you…'

Dunking a biscuit into her drink Jenny went quiet for a moment. Fin watched, as she appeared to be thinking what to say next. Turning her sightless eyes towards him, she spoke quietly, 'When you were arrested, how did you feel?'

'Terrible.'

'You thought I was dead?'

'Yes, I thought it was my fault and the policeman said…'

'The policeman knows nothing,' she replied, 'what little he has pieced together is so far from the truth.'

'How do you know?'

'I know, because I am part of the story. I was there.' Jenny's face grew animated, 'I am going to tell you another story. It's important and a little wild.'

'I'd rather know what happened.'

'If you listen, I will tell you everything I remember.'

A growing sense of weariness was creeping over Fin, but his senses told something important was happening.

Putting her mug down on the table, Jenny reached out and touched Fin's hand, 'Trust me.'

Pain seared through Fin's eyes, in agony he grabbed the sides of his head but after a few deep breaths the pain receded.

'Are you okay?' asked a worried Jenny.

Nodding his head Fin wiped the tears of pain from his eyes.

'What was that?'

'I have no idea,' he said, 'but if it happens again I will ask to speak to a doctor.'

Concern etched on Jenny's face she added, 'We can talk another time.'

'No, I'm fine now, whatever it was has passed.' A weak smile crossed Fin's face, 'I was just getting interested.' Seeing the look on Jenny's face, he assured he was okay and that she should continue.

'I am going to tell you a story that my mother told me. A long, long time ago, before they kept written records, there was a war, but all record of that war has been destroyed.'

'The victors write the history. That was in some of the stuff that Birdie gave us to read,' said Fin. 'is Birdie trying to tell us something?'

'I don't think so, but, in this place you never know. Five parties lived together before this war. All of them were different but all of them complimented each other. No one knows where they came from, they were just there. As time passed by, they mixed and even intermarried. Some believed they were purer than others were but none of that mattered, because in the end they all looked the same. It is the basis for all the classic Greek, Roman, Scandinavian and countless other myths and legends.'

All of the tiredness that Fin had felt growing on him had departed.

'By the time of the war those five strands had become woven into each other and many had forgotten who or what their ancestry was. However, each strand had its own militant faction that radically clung to its past. As I understand it, there were the original humans, Homo sapiens. The guardians were the peacekeepers, immensely powerful mythical people with no wish to dominate. Then lastly, there was one other group.'

'I thought you said there were five groups?' queried Fin.

'That's because this last group split into three factions,' Jenny stopped, swung her head around, and listened. All was quiet, 'The third group won the war and rewrote the history. Sorry, I am jumping ahead. There is now no word that describes that original group, they were all birds, but they dived and it became more complicated. Firstly, there was the Royal Family, or the Royals, birds of prey, full of honour and truth, but ruthless, the absolute rulers of the three factions. Then there was the Flock, scavengers who liked power and glory but were evil beyond imagination. Finally, there were the Birds, they got on with everyone, humans, guardians, royals, everyone that is, but the flock. All they wanted was to live a peaceful life as a result the flock hounded them, bullied them and tortured them into submission, until finally; they became the flock's servants. I'm sorry it's hard to know what it was like before the factions, this is what we know now. The war nearly wiped out everyone. The humans who vastly outnumbered the rest, produced warriors who were not frightened of anyone and they often with the guardians' help, fought the royals and all the factions of birds. After years of bloody war, a truce was called. Terms of peace were agreed, but at the last moment, the flock betrayed everyone. Their faction won the war although they never truly beat the royals, but they subdued them. The flock exterminated the guardians until there were none left, save a few that are the basis for our myths and legends. The humans they saw as cattle, too many to wipe out, but easy to manipulate and bend to their will. The royals survive to this day; they grow stronger and are challenging the dominance of the flock.'

'It all sounds a bit farfetched.'

'Just give me a moment longer. One thing the flock did not account for, having wiped history clear, is that they were unable to follow the guardians' family trees. Guardians are resurfacing and living among the humans. Hiding, biding their time, growing stronger, all around us guardians are awaking. This terrifies the flock and disturbs the royals. The flock want to keep their power and the royals want to run the world their way.'

'Is that a bad thing?' asked Fin.

'It is if you are anything other than a royal. Their honour is absolute and unforgiving.'

'Why are you telling me all this?' asked Fin.

'Because, I am a descendent of the guardians and I

believe you are too. I am convinced that Ravenswood is a place where they gather possible guardians and try and turn them towards the flock.' Jenny shuddered, 'Any that don't turn, they exterminate. If the guardians are coming back, then the flock want to train them as guard dogs.'

'You realise, this is all nonsense?' exclaimed Fin, 'What about history, God, religion?'

'I don't have answers for all of it, but this much I'm sure of,' Jenny's face filled with confidence, 'history is full of the echoes of the war. It resounds in every culture and country. None of this disproves religion or the existence of God. It is our history not our origins, it is how things have happened and not why.'

Fin sat in silence and watched Jenny's face as she spoke her crazy hair was sticking out in all directions.

'You're looking at my hair.'

'How do you know?'

'I can see you.'

'But your eyes?'

'I'm not looking with my eyes.'

'Oh come on be serious!'

'I am being. Test me…' Jenny stood up, 'do it!'

Fin picked up a book, 'What am I doing?'

'You've picked up Birdie's reading book, "The History of the Minotaur."'

In his hand, Fin looked at the book, 'But you knew that was our homework, that's just a good guess.'

'Open it at any page.'

Flicking the book open Fin held it out for her to see.

'Page eighty-two,' Jenny smiled, 'You are wearing a dark blue fleece, charcoal jeans and your socks are not a pair.'

'Yes they are.' Looking down at his socks Fin laughed, 'No they are not. How?'

'I see with my hair I come from the family of Gorgon.'

'You can turn people to stone?' asked Fin while staring into her scarred face. 'Anyway you can't be, according to legend, the gorgon, has a hideous face. You are so beautiful and you don't have snakes for hair.'

'Fenix Butler, did you just call me beautiful?'

'No, yes, but...' he stumbled over his words.

'Shut up while you are ahead!' Jenny laughed and shook her hair, 'The myths have only passed on some partial truths and we have evolved. My hair can have independent movement and I can see with it. My eyes, if they worked could possibly stun people, but that is never going to happen now I am blind. My mother said that when I am older, my voice may gain some hypnotic power.'

'But I have seen you stumble over things.'

'If my hair is tied back it affects my vision, whatever they suspect about me, I don't want them to know for sure.' Sitting down Jenny indicated that Fin should do the same. 'What do you remember the night of the fire at St Matthew's?'

'Nothing much at all, I remember you kicking my door in, running with you to the fire exit and the ceiling falling in. That's it.' Fin struggled to remember, 'In court you said you saw me holding the flames back.'

'I did.'

'Why?'

'Because you did!' cried Jenny.

'What?'

'The ceiling collapsed and we were trapped. You tried to take us back the way we came, but there were flames at the other end of the corridor. You saw three feathers on the floor and you picked them up. We headed for a classroom to see if we could get out of a window but we couldn't. We saw someone running in the light of the flames and we tried to follow them. Then the air exploded and a ball of flame ran along the walls and ceiling towards us. Your eyes glazed over, you threw your arms out and held the fire back by creating a bubble of clean air around us. You saw someone come up behind me and tried to warn me. I turned around to look and something savaged my face and blinded me. You couldn't have helped me you were too busy holding the flames back.'

'I don't remember any of this.'

'You were looking into the face of whoever blinded me!'

'I don't remember.'

'No, I know you don't, but you might and until you do more people are going to get hurt. We have to stop them.'

As if a dam had burst, Jenny started crying. Footsteps flew down the stairs and she was suddenly embraced and comforted by an equally tearful Sed and Eiry.

'You were listening!' Jenny snuffled through her tears.

Sed wiped tears from her own eyes, 'Yeah, why do you think we went up so early?'

Eiry went to the kitchen and made them all hot chocolate and they sat down and talked. To Fin it seemed like it was only for a moment but when he looked at the clock it was three-thirty in the morning. This shook them all and they all went to their rooms. Fin closed the door quietly behind him, frightened that he might disturb Ash, but his snoring was annoyingly loud and persistent. Fin thought he would never sleep but he too, was snoring in seconds.

The following morning at breakfast Fin felt groggy with tiredness and it seemed that the girls were faring no better. History with Mr Bird was an ordeal. Fin's first lesson with Mr Mallard was interesting but it proved his undoing. Mr Mallard was not impressed that during the last five minutes of his lecture Fin fell asleep and gave him a double warning. This did not bother Fin too much, until Sed told him to be careful, three warnings in a day equalled a detention.

Frustrated, Fin tried to stay alert for the rest of the day and succeeded to stay awake through all his lessons. Realising, that he was in no condition to do his homework yet he headed back to Narcissus lodge. Turning the corner, he heard the noise of scuffling and saw Ash being held by two bigger lads and being hit by third. Rather than calling for help, Fin lost his temper and jumped into the fight. It was over in seconds, the three lads who found it easy picking on Ash decided that two was too much and ran off.

Still angry Ash shoved Fin away from him, 'If I'd needed help I would have asked for it!' and stormed off. As soon as Ash vanished around the corner and out of sight, Mr Mallard appeared from the other direction followed by two sulking older lads.

'So this is who you were fighting,' Mr Mallard assumed a strictly no nonsense look, 'Butler, who else was part of this brawl?'

Realising that one of the bigger lads had escaped as well as Ash, Fin decided he had had enough aggravation for one day, 'No one, Sir.'

'Smith and Fount, what have you to say?'

Scowling at Fin, they realised that they could not name Ash without their friend being named too, 'Nothing Sir.'

Mr Mallard looking intently at Smith and Fount, 'Are you sure because your friend Hastings is usually never far away from you and trouble?'

'It was just us Sir,' replied Fount, 'sorry Sir,' he whispered contritely.

'Two against one seems hardly fair,' continued Mr Mallard, 'What have you to add Butler?'

Remaining silent Fin did not dare speak in case Smith and Fount mentioned Ash had been there too.

Shaking his head in disgust Mr Mallard escorted the three of them to the main building and into Mr Chough's office. Once there Fin chose to be silent and sullen while Mr Chough proceeded to give them all a lecture on how lucky they were to be at Ravenswood. That fighting would not be tolerated under any circumstances and then he gave each of them a double warning. It was only when he returned to the lodge that Fin realised that had gained enough for a detention. When he got back to the lodge, he was horrified to see Elizabeth, with a face like thunder, standing outside it.

'Fin, it's only Wednesday and you already have a detention! What were you thinking?' Elizabeth was raging, 'What is the point of me taking risks for you if you then land yourself in more trouble?' Mellowing, 'Fin, detention here is not like anywhere else. Why do you think the behaviour here is so good?'

'Sorry Elizabeth.'

'The only way to survive detention is to be calm and rested,' Elizabeth turned to walk away, 'Tonight, I suggest you sleep as long as you can because tomorrow night you will serve detention alone in what the students call the nightmare room.'

Giving up any hope of doing his homework, Fin headed straight to his room, ignoring Ash he got ready for bed and dropped off into a fitful asleep.

Sitting in the student waiting room, Fin could not remember anything of the day. Teachers, lessons, his friends passed him by, all now a vague memory. He was frightened and was dreading detention.

The door opened and Mr Byrd entered, seeing Fin's face he smiled, 'You look terrified,' he said in a friendly voice, 'Let me guess? You've been told about the nightmare room.'

Unable to speak Fin just nodded.

'To put your mind at ease, we do not torture our students.' Indicating with a slight movement of his head, Mr Byrd led Fin out of the room and down a corridor. 'Detention at Ravenswood is a closely monitored study period, where we provide you with a set amount of work based on you PEP.'

A confused look crossed Fin's face.

'Sorry a PEP is a Personal Education Plan, which we have to have for you because you are in our care. So you will be given some work that will help you reach some of your educational needs.'

Walking at Mr Byrd's slow pace they went down a set of stairs Fin had not seen before. The walls were decorated in institutional magnolia paint, and on them hung pictures containing multicoloured inspirational texts. "If you do not understand my silence, you will not understand my words." "Life is a gift do not waste it." "Success only comes through failure." "To struggle is to live." Fin shook his head and shuddered.

At the bottom of the stairs, deep in the basements of the old house, they walked down a bright corridor until they reached a room at the end. Opening the door, Mr Byrd invited Fin into a small but neat room that contained a single bed with a brightly covered duvet and pillows on it. A desk, with a pile of books, pens and writing paper, off to the side of the room was a door that led into a small but clean bathroom and toilet.

'The students like to pretend that this room is a darkly lit prison. It is not, it is a quiet and peaceful place to work and reflect. On the desk, you will find some work set for you by your teachers, but most of it is reading for me. It will give you a chance to catch up on what you have missed. Please take notes you will need them to show that you have done the work, but you might like to read them to Miss Cato as she has also catching up to do.'

Pointing to a small cupboard and fridge, Mr Byrd continued, 'You will find things to eat and drink, so you won't go hungry. In case of emergency or if you want any help there is a bell-push by the door. In the morning someone will come and get you, check your work, and you can go to breakfast,' added Mr Byrd, 'Should you decide not to do the work set, you will return here tomorrow night to complete it.' Mr Byrd left the room and shut the door with a firm click.

Sitting down at the desk Fin looked at the work, he guessed it would take a few hours to do, but he thought it was a reasonable amount. A notion crossed Fin's mind, the click of the door closing when Birdie left sounded very loud, he could not help trying the door and it was unlocked.

Three hours later, Fin fell asleep at the desk. Closing the books, he got ready for bed and put the light off. His last thoughts as he fell asleep were that was not too bad.

Waking up suddenly, Fin realised that he had heard something. Straining to hear anything above the silence, he listened, but there was nothing. Fin felt himself begin to fall asleep, when he felt and heard a rumble. It only lasted a moment or two, but once he had heard it, he realised it had been there, in the background, all the time. It was not loud, Fin could feel it more than hear it, but once he had noticed it, he could not stop hearing it. Finally, Fin dropped off into a troubled sleep.

Smoke crept under Fin's door and he turned restlessly in his sleep. Snuggled down under his duvet, his waking mind fought with his subconscious. The wailing of the siren pulled him out of his deep sleep. Jumping out of bed, he grabbed his clothes and shoes off the floor, moved to the door, and pulled. It would not move. Fin told himself not to start panicking, calmly; he pulled his clothes and shoes on. Taking a deep breath, he turned the handle and pulled the door. It was locked; this was not his imagination playing games with him. Challenging himself to think, Fin looked around the room, what could he use to get out? The bell-press, Fin pressed it as hard as he could but nothing happened. Panic began to creep up on him again and he hammered on the door with his fists and screamed, 'Get me out of here!'

Suddenly the door burst open, hit him on the shoulder and pushed him across the room. Standing in the doorway was Jenny, her wild hair swirling as if taking in everything, was sticking out in every direction. Fear was in her bright blue eyes as she yelled, 'Fin, Fin, where are you?'

Fin climbed up off the floor rubbing his shoulder. Noticing, something unusual in the dust, he picked up a pile of feathers. Jenny grabbed his hand and together they ran down the corridor. The emergency lights had come on and the green exit signs glowed in the dark. Together they ran for the exit, but before they could get to it, there was an explosion and the ceiling fell down blocking off their route. Turning they ran back seeking another exit, but there was none. Another explosion sent a ball of flames dancing down the wall and ceiling towards them. Fin threw himself between Jenny and the flames. Somehow, he created bubble of clean air around them. Feathers in hand, he protected Jenny only to see a figure move out of the darkness and strike her in the face. Jenny screamed and blood poured from a wound on her face. Fin saw the face of her attacker, it was familiar, he had seen it before...

Screaming Fin woke up.

Covered in sweat, Fin went to the bathroom and washed his face. The memory of the face echoing behind his eyelids was hauntingly familiar but it was fading and he could not remember it. Still shaking he returned to his bed and waited for the morning.

CHAPTER 4 - THE LIBRARY

Everyone laughed as Birdie flapped his arms in class, to illustrate a mythical bird, Imdugud, in a painting by Sir Walter Edmund Cranmer. Even Fin found himself laughing, he had not realised that Birdie, not only knew his own nickname, but also was able to show self-disparagement.

'The Imdugud Rising is a stunning piece of work. Cranmer, greatly influenced by the Pre-Raphaelites Brotherhood, rejected their fascination with painting everyone the same. I do not suppose it is surprising they all used the same models, for example, William Morris' wife, Jane. Sitting on the fringes of their fame, influenced by Evelyn De Morgan, he produced paintings of great power.' Birdie was in his stride, and knew it, 'His choice of paint, texture and brushwork was outstanding. Yet it was the subject and scale of his work that drew him both praise and ridicule.' Opening a large book, Birdie drew their attention to a painting, "The Field of the Slain," 1916, by Evelyn De Morgan, pictures an angel of death gathering up skulls. Evelyn, as a pacifist, plagued by the bloodshed of the First World War, sought to capture its horror. Cranmer did not see an angel but a bird of prey, devouring the world. This set the tone for his mythical works, of which, The Imdugud Rising, is typical.' In a grand gesture, Birdie continued, 'Earlier I mentioned the scale of his work, this painting was vast, and now fills a whole wall at the Sedgesworth Gallery.'

Sitting round a large, circular table, Jenny, Fin, Sed, Eiry and a reluctant Ash looked at each other. Birdie, was about to give them their task for the week.

'I want you to explore the Ravenswood Library and find a Pre-Raphaelite painting that you like. As a group, you will produce a copy of that painting; give a joint presentation on what fascinates you about it, and write an individual essay on the subject of the painting and what it means to you.'

A collective groan filled the room. Capturing everyone's thoughts, Sed said aloud, 'How will we find the time to do this with all our other work?'

Overhearing this, Birdie responded, 'I was coming to that. Every year, we spend a week on a subject; all other lessons have been put on hold until this project is finished.' Looking serious for a moment, Birdie continued, 'The timing of this works well for Ravenswood and for all the teachers, as in a few weeks we have a governmental school inspection due. In preparation for this inspection, there will be a special meeting of our private sponsors, local authority representatives and the Governors. It is important for us all that everything looks at its best. That means you will be working relatively unsupervised in groups.' Birdie stopped to look around the class, 'Do not misuse this freedom, as there will be a detention for anyone who fails to play a full role in the exercise.'

Feeling a cold shiver run down his back, Fin knew nothing would make him go into that room again.

'Finally, you will be spending a lot of time in the library, Dr Swan is dreading it.' Looking directly at each table in turn, Birdie shook his head, 'Last year he gave three whole groups detentions, for eating, drinking and smoking in the library. None of you will be that stupid, will you?'

The room remained silent; everyone was excited at the thought of an independent week. 'Doctor Richard Swan', Birdie continued, 'loves his books. However, I warn you, he is a frustrated man. The no computers rule means that in the three years, we have been running this facility; Dr Swan has yet to catalogue all the books in it. Our library is vast and extensive, filled with thousands or even hundreds of thousands of books, many of them old and very rare. No one knows everything in it.' Noticing signs of boredom creep across the class, he concluded, 'Help Dr Swan catalogue his books, show interest when he talks about his friends in royalty and he will help you in any way he can. Treat the library with disrespect and you will suffer his wrath.' Taking a deep breath, Birdie finished the lesson, 'Today is Friday, and you have two weekends and five schools days to complete your assignments. We begin the presentations at nine o'clock precisely a week on Monday.'

The class filed out past Birdie and out into the autumn sunshine. Stopping in his tracks, Fin groaned his notebook was missing from his bag. Turning, he headed back into the building, down an empty corridor and past the staff room. Hearing raised voices he stopped to listen.

'This inspection is the last thing we need.'

'Well, if you had been careful with the older students they would not have complained!'

The first voice, Fin recognised as Mr Chough the second as Birdie.

'Are you questioning my judgement, Mr Byrd?'

'Somebody has to. That boy, Greg Matthews is still missing.'

A murmur of shock echoed around the room and Fin realised the staffroom was full. Curious, he moved closer to the door.

'Mr Bird, it is a tragedy that Matthews is still missing. Yes, the police have been here, but you know, we all know, that he went missing after he had left here. There is no connection, whatsoever between his disappearance and

Ravenswood.'

'Sometimes, Mr Chough you forget how rigorous it is for the young people here. That detention room…'

'Sometimes you forget, Mr Byrd that all of our methods have been approved by the Governors and our sponsors. It is necessary that all of our students reach their full potential. Only then, will they fit into the place reserved for them by our society.' Mr Chough's voice grew teeth, 'However, I will raise your concerns this afternoon with the extraordinary meeting of the Governors.'

'Do so!' bumbled Birdie, 'It's time we showed more care for the students.'

The staffroom remained silent, Fin decided it was time to disappear and ran to the classroom to collect his notebook. On his return, the staff room door was wide open and the room was empty.

The oak door creaked open and the hooded figures, silently entered into the dimly lit room and sat down. Apart from the sound of water dripping, the room was silent.

'It is time we pruned the staff again,' croaked Raven breaking the silence, 'Birdie is an embarrassment, he protects the stock, he cannot teach and he challenges my authority in front of the staff.'

The room filled with a sense of unease, the hooded figures kept their faces hidden in case they were drawn in to conversation.

'Is that all you called us together for, to complain about the staff?'

'It is important, the inspection is coming and we can't afford any slip-ups.'

'No, you cannot!'

'Birdie is a liability, he teaches them about us and what he doesn't know, he guesses.' blurted out Raven, 'He's a nightmare. How can I be expected to check and evaluate the stock, with some old fool protecting them?'

'Must we go over old ground again, Raven?' Dark eyes glared out of the shadows of his hood, 'Mr Byrd is under my protection, he once did me a great service and although he does not know it, still does. You will leave him to me, when the time is right I will deal with him.'

'Yes, Lord,' in a reluctant voice, Raven conceded, 'Gosling is becoming too attached to the stock. If left unchecked she may develop into a problem.'

'I am aware of Elizabeth Gosling; she is Mr Byrd's favourite niece, so she is to be given some latitude.'

The voice grew dark and cold, 'Favourite niece or not, I will have her wings should she grow too inconvenient.'

Saying nothing, Raven felt his anger and frustration mount.

'Raven, you do not speak but your eyes betray you.' The Crow stretched out his hand and Raven convulsed, rose into the air crying in agony. 'I warned you, I grow tired of your insolence.' Crow dropped his hand and Raven crashed onto the table. 'Yet, you may have some use to me, so I will tolerate you a little longer.' Suddenly standing up the Crow turned towards the rest, 'Your lack of loyalty to Raven has been noted!'

'Lord, if I may speak?'

The Crow nodded his head and said, 'I am listening, Jackdaw.'

'Magpie is not here, and no one has seen or heard from him in days. I fear he may be lost!'

Sitting down wearily, the Crow replied, 'I fear he has been taken by the Royals.' Noticing the mummers of apprehension that ran around the room, he said, 'Magpie will not betray us, he knows I have his family and that they will all die a painful death if he says anything. If he keeps quiet, his family will prosper. It is unfortunate but he served his purpose well. None of you are indispensible and you know the risks and rewards for failure.'

As Fin's workgroup approached the library entrance,

the presence of Dr Swan blocked the entrance. Staring down at the students, he dared anyone to try to get past him and go in. 'Can I help you?'

Full of charm and confidence, Sed approached him, 'Excuse me, Sir, we would like to like to access to the library to research,' stopping for a moment, Sed looked at her notes, 'the works of Sir Walter Cranmer and the Pre-Raphaelite Brotherhood.'

Losing none of his strict countenance, Dr Swan stepped aside to let the five of them into the library. Walking passed Dr Swan, Fin had the most amazing feeling of déjà vu; he had met Dr Swan before, but where? The library seemed incredibly dark after the brightness of the autumn day outside. It took all of them a moment to get their bearings, all except Jenny, who had her hair down and was running up and down the stacks in wild enthusiasm. Fin had not realised it before, but Jenny's hair could see in the dark. Hearing Dr Swan enter the library, Fin not wanting a detention, quickly caught up with the excited Jenny and grabbed her hand. Instantly she stopped, realising what she had almost done to the group, only to find Fin clutching his face in agony. Falling to the floor Fin lay there while shivers of pain wracked his body. Eiry rushed over and put her hands on Fin's shoulder, he was freezing cold. Standing at the end of the stack, Sed indicated it was safe to talk; Dr Swan had gone out to speak to another workgroup approaching the library.

'Fin,' asked Eiry, while placing her hot hands on his forehead, 'what's the matter?'

Sitting up, Fin shook his head, 'I've no idea, but it's gone now.' Struggling to sit up the others helped him to a chair at a table. 'I tried to stop Jenny running and it felt like someone had stabbed razorblades into my eyes. It was excruciating but it's completely gone now, apart from the memory.'

Passing a book to Fin, Sed joined them, 'Flick through that and see if there's anything of interest.'

Doing as he was told, Fin sat there and flicked through the pages of the book. Every few minutes or so, one of them, including Ash, would walk passed him to check he was okay.

Engrossed in the book, Fin did not notice Dr Swan until he sat at the table with him.

'Butler, isn't it?'

'Yes, Sir.'

'How do you like Ravenswood?'

Wondering why he was interested, Fin, answered generally, 'I'm settling in.'

'Good, good.'

'Sir, may I be honest?'

'Yes, of course, always.'

'You obviously want to ask me a question; otherwise, you would not have sat down to make general conversation. I don't want to be rude, but why don't you just ask me whatever it is that's bothering you?'

Squirming in his chair Dr Swan sighed, 'I wanted to ask about your past.'

Sitting still Fin just waited.

'Many years ago, I was on holiday in St Mary's in the Scilly Isles with my two nephews, I made friends with a lady called, Adalinda, I cannot remember her surname. Adalinda had twin sons; I can only remember the name of one of them, Fenix. It was such an unusual name that it has stuck in my memory.'

'My mother's name was Adalinda,' whispered Fin, shocked that this stranger had met his mother, 'What was she like?'

A sad look crossed Dr Swan's face, 'She was frightened and there was nothing I could do to help. She said that there were two men following her and that they wanted to take the twins from her. Her husband was helping the police with an enquiry about fire he had witnessed at a hotel there.'

Out of the corner of his eye, Fin saw the others behind

a stack, listening intently just out of Dr Swan's sight.

'Your mother was lovely and it disturbed me to know how frightened she was. It was our last day, my teenage nephews had to return to college, so we got our ferry back to the mainland and I never saw her again.' Dr Swan shifted in his chair, 'I don't know who or what frightened her but I hated feeling so helpless. There is nothing I can do to help her now but if you ever need my help, just ask.'

As he watched Dr Swan leave the table and go outside the library, Fin was convinced that he had seen a tear in his eye.

'What a load of balls!' commented Ash as they all sat down at the table.

'It may be the truth, I'm sure I've met him before.'

'His voice does sound familiar,' added a puzzled Janny.

Suddenly realising that he was showing an interest in Fin's life, Ash stood up, 'I need a juice, I'll see you back here in half an hour.'

Hours later, all of them covered in dust from the books, stood by the library ladder Jenny had found to reach the highest shelf. Balancing precariously, she had spotted in the darkest corner, with her hair a thick book marked, 'The Wonderful World of Walter Cranmer.' Dropping it down into Ash's hands Jenny swung back onto the ladder only for it to slide away, leaving Jenny hanging from a bookshelf. Sed rescued the ladder and climbed up to help Jenny. Laughing, with no harm done Jenny climbed gingerly down the ladder. Sed, however, stayed where she was, behind the shelf which had contained the book, a secret panel had opened. Reaching inside, Sed found an ancient, leather bound book. Squinting in the light, she read, 'Ravenswood House.' Quickly, she joined the others and they opened it carefully. Inside the handwritten book were pages of barely legible writing but slipped inside there was a loose set of parchment plans.

'That's the priest hole!' an excited Sed pointed out, 'look, there are tunnels and passages all over the place.'

'Do you think they are still there?' asked Eiry.

'Well the priest hole is, so maybe the rest are too.'

A noise from the doorway indicated that Dr Swan had heard their excitement and had seen the book. Facing away from the book, Jenny using her hair to see behind her back slipped the old plans into her bag.

'What have you there?'

'When we took this book from the shelf up there,' pointed Sed, 'a secret panel opened and this book was inside. I am sure there were other books there too.'

Picking up the book and reading its title, Dr Swan nearly swooned with excitement, 'You wonderful children, I have been looking for this book for years,' holding the book to himself with a rapture like smile on his face he realised that there might be more books up there. 'Show me the panel.'

Leading him to the ladder Sed pointed up. Dr Swan ran up the ladder and moments later came down with a handful of books.

'This is fantastic,' looking round at the youngsters' smiling faces a thought crossed his mind, 'You doing Mr Byrd's Pre-Raphaelite project aren't you?' They all nodded, 'Everything you need is in section two, stack six and shelf four.' A sly look crept across his face, 'you will find them hidden behind a selection of 1970's Haynes car manuals!' Seeing the shocked look on their faces he added, 'This is the third year running that Mr Byrd has set this project for his class. Last year it took me weeks to sort out the library again. Now collect the books, sign them out, and take them to your lodge and work there. If you do the work immediately, you should have time bring them back on Tuesday and have next weekend free from work.'

The group left a happy Dr Swan with his books and they returned to the lodge.

Tumbling into the lodge, Ash locked the door behind them. Gathering around a large table, they laid out all the books. From her bag, Jenny produced the plans, they all gathered around excitingly when there was a knock at the door. Ash swore so loudly that all the girls gave him a look. Jenny hid the plans again, tied her hair back and sat down. Sed ran to the door and let Elizabeth in.

'Why was the door was locked?'

'We decided that we would tackle Birdie's…'

'Mr Byrd!'

'…project while we were fresh, we locked the door so we wouldn't be disturbed.'

Smiling at their enthusiasm Elizabeth nodded, 'Good, good, if you get it started now you may have some free time next weekend. Have you considered how Jenny is going to contribute?'

A slightly flushed looking Jenny replied, 'They are reading everything out aloud to me and describing the pictures. I hope to be able help them write the assignments and I will speak during the presentation.'

Admiring Jenny's creativity, Fin continued, 'We're all excited to be working together on this!'

Not quite believing what she was hearing, Elizabeth looked at Ash. Realising that he was looking far too happy about this arrangement and that it would cast suspicion on them, Ash scowled. Seeing the scowl on Ash's face Elizabeth relaxed.

'Excellent, then I will not worry about you working. I will be functioning from my room for the next few days, if you need me, pop round.' Stopping at the door, Elizabeth turned with a smile on her face, 'Don't forget to lock the door behind me.'

Unravelling the elastics from her hair, Jenny looked at each of them. 'I think it would be better if we wait until later to look at the plans. I will go and hide them in my room.'

Although frustrated at having to wait the others agreed.

'We have no choice but to get this projected started,' said Ash, 'I suggest we forget about the plans until we have all finished. It'll give me an incentive to actually do some work.'

The days passed by in a flurry of activity. Ash turned out to have an artistic eye and his copy of "The Siren." by John William Waterhouse drew praise from them all. Jenny and Eiry prepared a presentation on the subject that featured a poem written by Sed and Fin.

Slightly embarrassed by the attention, Sed read the poem aloud, '"The Siren," by Sed ArnaaU and Fin Butler,' pausing, she took a deep breath and began to read:

The sailor shipwrecked
Both in body and mind
Heart captured by a beautiful voice
No mermaid was she
He failed to see her wings
Half bird, half woman, lyre in hands
Golden hair, soft lips, all lies
Long before the water took him
He drowned in her deep blue eyes
Laughing she led him
To where the sirens play
With sailors that fail to sleep

'We need to work on it a bit more, but we think that captures the essence of the painting.'

Looking at everything, they had prepared Eiry said, 'No leave it as it is. Let's have a break and after dinner tonight get the old plans out.'

Ash and Sed went to gather everything up.

'No leave it, if anyone checks we can still say we are working,' said Eiry.

As evening fell, the rain began to pour down and the wind drove against the windows. To Fin's delight they lit the fire and only Eiry thought it was too hot. With the door locked and the weather inclement, there was little chance of them being disturbed. Just in case they had all their works books out, ready to use should anyone try to brave the weather and visit them. Clearing a fraction of the table, Jenny laid the parchment out for them all to see.

The document was full of tiny diagrams and almost indecipherable writing. It was broken into three parts, the original house with its walls and compartments, a bird's eye view of the house and grounds and cross section of the house and hill.

Leaning across the table, Ash pointed at the priest hole just outside Mr Chough's office, 'I've heard about that, some of the staff told me that they had explored once but it was blocked by a cave in.'

'This plan is so much older than the present house,' observed Fin, 'the Victorians extended the kitchens over this part. Ash, could you copy the parts of the map that are still here?'

Taking a thick, soft pencil and tracing paper, Ash gently traced the plans out. Remembering that she had a Ravenswood prospectus with a plan in it, Sed ran upstairs and collected it. The two plans were nowhere near the same scale so Eiry and Sed did there best to redraw it to the scale of the old map. It was a little bit of a struggle but an old ruler made all the difference. It took them all, over and hour to redraw and line up both sets of plans. When they had finished, Ash laid his traced drawing over the top of the modern illustration. Everything they knew about lined up perfectly, stairs, doorways and offices, even the priest hole.

Tapping the overlaid drawing, Ash said, 'This is amazing, so many of these passages must still be there.'

'They may have caved in like the one connected to the priest hole,' Eiry said, thinking aloud, 'these look like dungeons under the house.'

They all leaned over at the plan. It did look indeed, as if there were dungeons under the house. It was all very confusing there were multiple routes to the underground rooms Eiry had indicated.

'Some even come in from outside,' Eiry had a mischievous look on her face, 'I would love to explore them.'

'That entrance is in Mr Chough's office,' indicated Ash, 'I'm all for exploring but I don't fancy being caught by him!'

'Do you think he knows about it?'

'Eiry, I wouldn't want to bet that he doesn't.'

The excitement of earlier seemed to drain from the room. Jenny not wanting to let the moment pass refused to be beaten. 'I agree, he must know about those rooms, they are too obvious. This map however, is so much more extensive than those rooms. Why don't see if we find can find one of the more obscure ones.' Jenny's excitement reignited everyone's passion for exploring and adventure.

Looking thoughtful, Fin looked at the plan, 'I suggest that we make a map of the tunnels we think may still be there. These plans map the routes of the secret passages, if they are still there then they are going to well hidden.'

Draping her wild hair over the plans, Jenny concentrated, 'That symbol there, I'm sure I have seen it before, carved into the wooden panelling.'

Holding the plans under a light, Ash struggled to make out the image Jenny had spotted, 'The rose in a circle?'

'Yes and no.'

'Helpful!'

'Yes it is the symbol I'm looking at, but no, it's not just a rose in a circle. When we arrived here, we were waiting in the main entrance hall. Fin described it to me, while I was standing with my back to a carved section of wall. My hair explored that shape. It's a double circle, with another circle in the middle, two layers of petals and what felt like a cross hidden behind the petals.'

'Oh Jenny, I could hug you!' said Fin bouncing up and down on the spot, 'one of the books you gave me when I had that excruciating pain in the library, was much older than the rest. It was book on Tudor codes and ciphers. What was it called?'

'Does it matter?' asked Ash, signs of his usual disposition creeping back into his voice.

Refusing to be riled, Fin responded, '"The Hidden and Lost in Tudor Architecture." Anyway, there was man called Sir Francis Walsingham, he was a bit of a git and the spymaster to Queen Elizabeth I. He approved of the torture of countless priests, in fact, anyone he suspected of working against the Queen, suffered and died at his hands. To hide priests away from him and his spies, rich householders built priest holes, like the one here; some even built escape tunnels and passages. It's the reason many of these buildings are so irregular. Anyway, there was a section on symbols and signs, just like that one there. If I am right, you hold the inner petals, push the circular button in the middle and twist the cross. That releases a mechanism that opens the door, once you click the door back into place the carving returns to its original position.'

Frowning, Ash asked, 'If it's that obvious, why hasn't someone else already found it?'

'The historian, the writer quotes was discredited in the eighteen hundreds for falsifying his records.'

'He made it up?'

'That's what everyone thought.'

'Then why should we believe him?'

'Because you are looking at one of his illustrations, and we have nothing to lose by testing his theory!'

'Not wanting to pour cold water on a good idea, but if we want to go exploring secret passages and tunnels, we are going to need torches,' groaned a disappointed Sed, 'I haven't got one and I doubt if any of you have either.'

Unable to contain her excitement, Jenny bounced up, 'That's not a problem to me, with my hair I can see in the dark. I think this passage here goes from Ravenswood to the well in the next-door farm. If I take Fin with me, we could sneak out to the local village and buy some torches and batteries for us all to go exploring.'

In the absence of a better suggestion, they all agreed that they would try to see if they could gain access to passage tomorrow, Friday. Ash helped them all trace copies of the plans so they each had their own map. Taking the original back, Jenny went and hid it in her room. Outside the wind howled and the rain violently beat against the windows. Tired, they all went to their beds excited about what the next day would bring.

CHAPTER 5 - THE SCHOOL TRIP

The spiral staircase went down steeply. The initial euphoria of finding and mastering the fiddly carving had worn off, now Fin was in the dark, totally reliant on Jenny being able to sense where they were going.

Yesterday was such a disappointment. They had all got up early and met in the lodge kitchen ready to get moving. The plan was simple, Eiry and Sed were going to meander over to the old house and if anyone questioned them they were going to say that they wanted to see the painting collection. Meanwhile, Ash was going to wait outside to watch the main entrance, if any teachers became interested or suspicious he was to distract them. If the coast was clear, then Fin and Jenny's aim was to get to the wall carving and enter the passage.

Excited they headed for the door when there was an almighty crash. The wind and the heavy rain brought one of the old silver-birch trees down, completely blocking the entrance. The commotion outside was horrendous and it was not long before someone knocked on the door. The nearest to the door was Ash, when he opened it there was a completely bedraggled Elizabeth, her hair blowing about in every direction and full of leaves and twigs.

'I'm sorry guys, but you are going to have to stay in

today, or at least until the tree surgeons have sorted this mess out.' Shrugging her shoulders, Elizabeth's expression was one of, that's life get on with it, 'We will send you hot food over later. It shouldn't inconvenience you too much as you probably still have loads of work to do on Mr Byrd's project.'

Now trapped inside, they had little to do, except argue with each other. As usual, it started with Ash but eventually, they were all at it. In tears, Jenny ran to her room. A scuffle developed between Sed and Ash, and only ended when Sed punched Ash in the arm. After an expletive or two, in which Ash declared Sed, more or less, illegitimate, an old-fashioned two-fingered gesture followed him upstairs. That left downstairs, an ailing Eiry who was running a high temperature, and Fin, who was freezing cold and had the shivers. Both feeling unwell was a recipe for disaster and the game of chess they were playing quickly turned into a missile throwing competition in which one queen ended up in the log fire.

It was late afternoon before the tree surgeons finished, the logs carted away, the branches mulched, and the debris cleared. The kitchen staff excelled themselves and brought over a wonderful, hot evening meal. Elizabeth who had heard the arguments and expletives through the walls, felt sorry for them and joined them. Realising that they needed a boost, she brought with her a giant bar of chocolate and a selection of games, by the time she left, the atmosphere had changed from sullen to bright.

The following morning, after a quick breakfast, they put their plan into action. The weather, now clear but cold, all signs of the wind and rain gone. Everything went perfectly, they struggled to get the mechanism to turn, but when it did, the door slid to one side. The entrance, covered in a mat of cobwebs was easily accessible. Pushing through the sticky screen, Fin and Jenny found themselves at the top of a stone spiral staircase. Slipping the door back into position, they opened it from the inside to make sure it worked before the others left. The simple locking system activated the door easily from inside, so they said their goodbyes, shut the door and headed down.

The slow crunch of their feet echoed down the stairs. Stopping, Jenny stretched her senses out in every direction, 'We've come down about a hundred feet, although it feels like more. There is a corridor going off here and the main staircase continues. This corridor gives me the creeps.'

Squeezing passed Jenny, Fin look down the corridor, light filtered in from a room to the side, 'Just stay here a moment, I can see light ahead.' Walking as quietly as he could, Fin moved towards the light only to discover spy holes in the wall. Fin gazed into a desolate room; water oozed from the walls, instruments of torture hung from the walls and in the middle of the room was an old battered oak table. The room, lit by candlelight, was the most unfriendly room Fin had ever seen in his life. Finding the cold oppressive, he rejoined Jenny and they continued to descend.

As they descended, the darkness seemed to close in on them, the air grew stuffy and Fin struggled to breath. Sensing his distress, Jenny reached out her hand and gripped his arm, 'It's starting to freshen up.'

Taking a deep breath Fin realised that Jenny was right. The steps ended and they both breathed a sigh of relief.

'It's hard not being able too see anything at all,' whispered Fin, 'without you I would have had to go back. There's no way we can all explore these tunnels without torches.'

Once away from the constant descent the walk became much easier and they made better time. The passage way changed as they travelled along, to Fin as he trailed his fingers along the walls, what started out as brick turned to quarried stone. They whispered to each as the moved along, for some reason they did not want to make any noise. Stopping suddenly, Fin crashed into Jenny.

'What's up?'

'There's a door blocking our way.'

Scrambling around the door they both struggled to move it, it would not budge. Jenny's fingers found the mechanism, she twisted and pulled and door swung open. Light streamed into the tunnel, it was so bright that Fin had to shield his eyes; the change in lighting had no effect on Jenny's at all.

'Be careful, there's a drop,' said Fin slipping past Jenny, 'we have found the well.'

Passing Jenny, Fin leaned out into the well. Looking up he saw thick iron spikes driven into the wall. Reaching out Fin took a firm grip on one and tried to haul it out of the wall. It would not budge.

'There are spikes going all the way up the side to the top. I'm going to try and climb up, it doesn't look far.'

'Do I need to say it?'

'I will be careful.'

Swinging himself out, Fin nimbly climbed up the nails, the top was only a short distance above them. On reaching the top, Fin poked his head out between the bars that prevented anybody falling in. The farm buildings, all derelict and desolate showed no sign of life. That removed one problem, he thought but how do I get through the bars? Planting his feet firmly on the spikes, Fin pushed up with all his strength, nothing moved. Frustrated, he examined the bars more carefully. The bars had been designed to stop people falling down the well not keep them in. On one side, he saw giant hinges welded to the frame of the bars. Good, he thought that means they should swing up if he could free whatever was holding them shut. On the other side to the hinges, a simple bolt, out of arms reach from the top, slid into a hole in the well wall. The bolt, rusty and stiff, slid out of the rock and Fin, pushed the frame open.

Climbing down to Jenny, Fin noticed just how deep the well actually was and decided to be little more careful. After a quick conversation, they climbed up and out of the well.

Lowering the cover back over the well, Fin said, 'Without a special tool to reach down I can't lock it. So getting out is easy, getting back in if it is fastened would be impossible.'

A quick investigation around the farmyard proved it had been deserted for years. It took them a little brush the dirt and cobwebs off before they headed for the village. There were few birds around, and thankfully no crows or ravens so they set off.

About forty minutes later, they reached the outskirts of the village. Fin stopped Jenny from tying her hair back. 'Pull the hair down over your eyes to hide your scars. No-one will know you're blind.'

The village of Huntley and Wart, was like so many Fin had been to before. There was a small supermarket, a butcher's, a bakers, a news agent and post office, a Chandler, a chemist and five charity shops. Their first stop was the Chandler, but buying five torches there was too expensive for their limited resources. The charity shops seemed a better option.

Passing the newsagent, Fin stopped in his tracks, 'Jenny, hang on!' Picking up a local newspaper, he read it aloud, 'Gruesome murder baffles police. Police are still struggling to comprehend the violent death of Graham Arthur Stock, a Crown Prosecution barrister, whose tortured body was found on Greyhound Fell. "I have never seen anything like it," said Detective Inspector Jones, the head of the special unit investigating his death, "the poor man had been tortured to death and his eyes pecked out by birds."

'It can't be the same man.'

'It is there's a photograph of him.'

'Does it say anything else?'

'Not really, no,' Fin, noticing the look he was being given by the shop assistant put the paper back on the rack, 'we better keep moving, the less time we spend out in public the better.'

Trawling through the charity shops, they found five torches for sale within their limited budget. It was as they were testing the last one that they over heard two old women talking.

'Those two look like they escaped from a convict ship.'

'I've not seen them around here before.'

'Well you know we get all sorts of weird ones around here since the refurbishment of the old house.'

'That house gives me the creeps, all those evil looking birds; I would swear they are sometimes listening to us.'

'Go away with you.'

'Think I might ring them and see if they have lost any of them kids, I'm sure I've seen a phone number for them. There all delinquents I hear.'

Picking up a few packs of spare batteries, Fin and Jenny left the store and rushed back to the farm. The return journey was so much easier for Fin now he had a torch and they got back to Ravenswood very quickly. Using a well-placed spy hole, they checked their exit was clear and rushed back with their illicit purchases. After returning to their rooms for a quick shower and change of clothes, Fin and Jenny, joined the others and shared their adventures.

Opportunities for further exploration dwindled as the daily routine returned to normal. The combined presentation for Birdie went well and they each received a commendation for their efforts.

'Have you seen it, have you seen it?' Sed burst into the lounge, scattering her books down on to the table, 'Birdie has organised had a school trip out!' Throwing a poster down for them all to see she read out aloud, 'Those students who have been studying Cranmer and his mythical paintings are invited to join Mr Byrd and Miss Gosling in a trip to Sedgesworth Gallery and Museum. Only students with an up to date assignment list and no sanctions are eligible.'

The thought of a trip out filled Fin with excitement, since his and Jenny's visit to the village he had started to feel trapped and claustrophobic. The group's merits meant that their places were guaranteed on the trip; however, Fin did not believe that it was really going to happen until the door shut on the old coach and they set off.

Sed and Eiry were whispering intently, so Fin lent forward in his seat, 'What's going on?'

Eiry, gathered all of them around, 'I might as tell you all at once,' she began, stopping she looked around to see where Birdie was sitting, he was at the front in deep conversation with Elizabeth, 'I have just heard Birdie and Mr Chough arguing.'

'So you are going ahead with the trip against my wishes!'

A stubborn Birdie faced up to the principle, 'This trip has been on the books for months.'

'And I have always thought it folly and a waste of time and money.'

'Nevertheless, the governor's gave me all the approval I need. This trip is important to the education of the children.'

'They are not children, they are students.'

'The students need to see this work if they are ever to find their place in our world.'

An angry retort came from Mr Chough, 'Futile, and an argument that at best is pitiful, they are subjects, no more and no less. When the time comes they will take their place or move on.'

'Some of them know nothing.'

'What is that to me?'

'Are you so proud that you do not see the potential that they have? They are our future too.'

'Again a futile argument, we hold the future in our hands.'

'Well, I disagree and the governor's agree with me so

the trip is going ahead.'

A fierce and calculating look crossed Mr Chough's face, 'Mr Byrd I grow tired of your pathetic and antiquated view of the world. The students are just cattle and soon the Governors will see things my way.'

'Well when that happens I will face the consequences but until then I will not be bullied by a principle that is wet behind the ears,' shouted Birdie and stormed off up the corridor.

As one, they all glanced down the bus to Birdie, who seeming to sense their attention briefly stop talking and looked back at them.

'Where did Birdie get the balls from?' asked Ash in his usual forthright way. 'Are you sure?'

Eiry nodded, 'What did he mean, we are all cattle?'

Shrugging her shoulders, Jenny's body language conveyed all their thoughts. Outside the weather turned nasty and a hailstorm battered the coach, overhead a murder of crows, oblivious to the storm followed the coach.

The rickety old coach pulled into the parking bay outside the gallery. Fierce stone angels glared down at them from their fixed positions. The storm rattled around the hillsides about the town while a tired sun tried, and failed to bring some light and warmth to the morning. Huddling into their coats the students briskly walked under the gaze of the stone angels and into the reception. Outside the crows settled onto the wings of the angels their droppings desecrating their stone feathers.

Inside, the atmosphere contrasted with the world outside, it was warm, light and airy. High above the students, a domed window filtered the light into the room and strategically placed spotlights highlighted a different world. Turning in a slow circle, Fin took in the walls; each one featured a magnificent pre-Raphaelite painting.

Before Fin could take them all in, Birdie began to

speak, 'Today I am going to introduce you to the history of the world according to Walter Cranmer. You will not see anything about the creation of the world, or the birth of human beings, as a devout Christian he accepted the Bible's account as true. Not in any blind fundamental way, nor as science, but as... how can I put this? He accepted that God created the world but that the how is up to us to discover. Upstairs, in the library, there is a record of all that he discovered, the fall of humanity, the rising of the birds, the ten-thousand year old war and greatest lie ever told.'

No one had heard Birdie speak so eloquently and his voice had power and authority.

'In this place you will see, birds that frighten you, warriors that inspire you, wars that will disturb you and mythical creatures that will amaze you. Yet, they in themselves will not challenge you in any way as much, as the knowledge that Walter Cranmer believed he was painting the truth.'

Outside the crows began making a racket so loud it that echoed around the domed reception. Birdie began to look uncomfortable yet Fin was convinced he saw a streak of stubbornness creep into his eyes.

'There are some who believe what I am telling you is a secret, a secret that you should never, under any circumstances know. What is that secret? The truth of who you are and what you represent, I do not hold that view. Therefore, I am going to tell you and bugger the consequences! Before written time as we know it began, when history was passed on as an oral tradition from father to son, the world fought a war that has since echoed in eternity. I believe that some of you, not all, are part of that story and that you have yet to discover your power and authority,' pausing Birdie looked at them, 'some of you, in years gone by would have been called, in ignorance, gods. That is of course nonsense, you are not and never will be gods, but some of you will be amazing.'

'He's bloody nuts,' whispered Ash, 'he's off his rocker...'

'Do you have something to share with the group Bobrov?'

'No Sir, sorry Sir,' grovelled Ash.

'I risk my life to share this truth with you, nevertheless, take your time, look, read and digest what you see in the pictures,' walking to the entrance doors Birdie stared at the crow's perched all around the entrance, 'I will guard the doors until you return.'

In stunned silence Fin, walked with the others from room to room, it seemed each room told a fantastic story and if it had not been for Jenny's revelation, a few weeks earlier, he would have discounted it as nonsense. Finally, they ended their journey in another large domed room. This room was full off paintings, some unfinished, of mythical creatures. Jenny, who had taken her hair down so that she could see the exhibition, was standing in front of a picture of Methuselah, her snake like hair moving in an unseen wind.

'One of my ancestors,' said Jenny, 'he's got the basics right but the details wrong,' raising her hands to the room, 'if he got me right, what is to say he didn't get all these right too?'

Getting out his notebook, Fin walked around the room jotting down what he saw: As well as Methuselah, the Minotaur, the Griffin, the Phoenix, a Mermaid, Pegasus, a Unicorn, the Ice-Queen, Sphinx and Dryad, there were many he had not seen before.

'There are so many of them,' muttered Fin aloud, 'we need to sketch some of these down.'

'Already doing it,' said Ash flapping his sketchbook up in the air.

Outside the room, the cries of the crows grew louder and more aggressive. A harried Birdie stumbled into the room, 'Please finish off, I am growing tired and I can't hold them back much longer.'

Watching Birdie leave the room Fin turned to whisper to the others, 'He looks exhausted,' but only Jenny was in the room with him.

'They've run back to the different rooms to see if they have missed anything.'

'Well they'd better be quick, Birdie's struggling.'

Within moments, they all returned with even more sketches on their pads. Fin began to explain about Birdie's warning, when out of the silence the fire alarm screamed and shutters began to descend sealing them in. Smoke began to pour under the door and they all started coughing. Outside the door to the room Fin could see Birdie struggling to raise the shutter, but it was too heavy.

Taking the initiative, Sed called the others, 'He cannot do it on this own.'

Knowing she was right Fin wanted to help but he was so cold he could not stop shivering. Jenny grabbed his arm and dragged him to the shutter.

'All at once, heave,' yelled Sed.

Shaking off the shivers Fin joined the others and between them all lifting together the shutter began to rise. Birdie indicated that Jenny should slide underneath first. She did and then took her place holding the shutter up. Smoke now filled the room, it was getting hard to breath, only Fin, and Ash remained on the wrong side of the shutter. The shutter began to descend but none of them, now weakened by the smoke, could keep it up. Within moments, Fin and Ash were trapped.

Feeling sick Fin began to lose consciousness, he struggled with the bars of the shutter to no avail. Out of the corner of his eye, Fin watched Ash slide to the floor, as he watched him fall, Fin's vision failed and he too slumped to the floor.

CHAPTER 6 - CHRISTMAS AT RAVENSWOOD

Coughing and spluttering Fin woke up in an ambulance, at first he struggled with the oxygen mask, but was too weak to move it.

'Ash?'

'In another ambulance but he's going go be okay.'

Turning to face the paramedic, Fin found himself face to face with Detective Inspector Jones.

'We meet again.'

'How did we get out?' he asked trying to sit up.

'The Fire Service arrived and extracted you.'

'It wasn't me.'

'I know you were in sight of Mr Byrd all the time,' said D.I. Jones, 'you and the Ash boy saved the girls lives.'

'No, we all fought together.'

'I'm still impressed; do you feel up to introducing me to your friends?'

Helping Fin to stand up D.I. Jones led him to the others who were standing by a very pale Ash. Looking up Fin watched the Fire Service struggle in vain to save the gallery.

One weary officer came over to them and gave D.I. Jones three crow feathers, 'It was as you suspected, the source of the fire was as hot as hell, but these feathers were there.'

'Do me a favour and keep this from the reporters, there has been enough panic mongering about the Firebird already.'

'Will do, but it will come out in the report.'

'I would expect nothing else.'

The rest of the day passed in a jumble of activity but in the end they were allowed to board the coach and go home. None of them remembered the journey back as they were all asleep within moments of setting off.

Two days after the fire at the gallery police officers, led by D.I. Jones, arrived at Ravenswood and questioned everyone who had been there. The interviews took place in the old house and Fin was pleased to find the Detective Inspector himself was questioning him.

'It's good to see you have recovered from the fire.'

The words were meant to be assuring but Fin could not help thinking there was an edge to them.

'I took a statement from Mr Byrd on the day of the fire and his account describes you and Jenny as being in the same room when it started, is that right?'

'Yes Sir.'

'Fin, please call me David,' he said smiling, 'we are well beyond such ridiculous formalities.'

'Yes Sir, sorry…, David,' said Fin stumbling over the newfound name, 'we were all trying to collect as much information as we could before we had to leave.'

'From where you were could you see any of the other groups in the gallery?'

'No, we all took different floors to begin our exploring; the idea was that we would not be falling over each other.'

'Mr Byrd's account, describes Ash, Sed and Eiry rejoining you just before the fire alarm went off.'

'As I said before, we had split up to make sure we did not miss anything.'

'Did you see the three of them leave?'

'No, I was concentrating on sketching a rough impression of a painting.'

Pausing for a moment, David considered his notes, 'Did they all come back together or separately?'

'Sed and Eiry came back seconds before Ash.'

'So Ash was on his own?'

'Are you asking me to imply that Ash started the fire?'

'Did he?'

'They were all gone for only a matter of minutes, I don't see how he could have and Ash had nothing on him that could have started that blaze.' a thoughtful look crossed Fin's face, 'I'm guessing it's the same as all the other fires, three feathers and the usual mysterious accelerant. That would have taken planning and preparation, something impossible for those of us stuck inside here.' Fin looked David in the eyes, 'Have you asked Ash did he start the fire?'

'Yes.'

'Did he give you a reply?'

A rich, deep laugh emitted from David, 'Yes he did,' he picked up his notes, 'and I quote, "that's a load of bollocks, unless you're saying I started the fire with my own bare hands!"' Closing his notepad they both laughed.

'One last question, did you see anything else strange that day around the gallery?'

Trying his best to be brief, Fin found himself pouring out all of his memories of the crows' behaviour, the way they scared and intimidated Birdie. Then without realising it he started sharing the weirdness of Ravenswood, he only just managed to stop himself from mentioning Jenny's secret.

Listening with an intent expression on his face, David took in all that Fin told him. It was only afterwards that Fin remembered how unsurprised he was about his revelations.

As Christmas approached, the weather changed dramatically and the grounds at Ravenswood became white with snow. Lessons continued as normal but it soon became harder to get between buildings. For the first time since Fin shared accommodation with Eiry she stopped feeling too hot all the time, he on the other hand could not get warm, unless he was sitting in front of the roaring log fire. Apart from Fin, everyone enjoyed the snow and everyday ended with a snowball fight.

Returning from the last lesson of the day with Birdie, Fin struggled through the snow, its cold eating at his bones. Dithering, he longed for a seat in front of the log fire and a cup of steaming hot chocolate. Bracing himself against the cold evening wind, he came around the corner of the old house and bumped into Smith and Fount. Smith skidded on the ice and clattered into Fount, the pair of them collapsed into a heap in a snowdrift. Faring little better, Fin slid on the ice and landed on top of them, pushing Smith's face so far into down that he ended up with a mouthful of snow.

The first to get up was Fount, who grabbed Fin by his coat lifted him up and threw him into another snowdrift. As Fin fell, he felt Fount kick him in the ribs, he cried out in agony. Lashing out with legs, Fin tried to topple Fount but failed; meantime, Smith had managed to regain his feet and started kicking Fin too. Helpless, unable to get traction under his feet, all Fin could do was try to huddle into a ball to try to protect his head and ribs. The kicking seemed to go on for ages, and only stopped when he heard a familiar voice cry out.

'Cowards,' cried an angry Ash, diving into Smith and Fount and they went flaying into the snow. Pulling Fin up, Ash looked into Fin's face and saw two black eyes and blood trickling from his nose. What worried Ash the most was the way Fin was shivering, he decided to quit the fight and get Fin home. However, Fount had other ideas and used his massive body to block their exit.

'I owe you one,' he growled at Ash.

Having successfully blocked their escape route, Fount waited for Smith to join him. As Smith regained his feet, Ash realising that they had one chance to get away swung his fist upwards towards Fount's jaw. Meanwhile, in desperation, a battered and bruised Fin kicked Fount between the legs. Doubling over in agony his head dropped into the path of Ash's uppercut, which caught perfectly on the chin and he fell backwards straight into Smith.

Leaving Smith and Fount in a pile of yellow coloured slush, Ash helped a limping Fin home and into a seat in front of their log fire. The girls took one look at his face and his dithering body and acted. Jenny found a blanket, Sed the first aid kit and Eiry a hot water bottle.

Meanwhile, Ash seemed rooted to the spot, an internal argument fighting inside his head, 'Sod it,' he said looking into Fin's eyes, 'you're going to have to trust me.'

The girls stopped what they were doing and watched.

'I'm sorry I should have told you before I can do this,' he said laying his hands on Fin's shoulders, Ash doubled over in pain, as he did so the bruising left Fin's face and the pain ceased in his chest. Turning grey with pain Ash smiled at Fin, 'I can heal injuries but I don't like doing it because while the healing takes place I feel everything you feel.'

Pain free, Fin sat up, 'You did that for me!'

'Isn't that what friends do for each other?'

'How?'

'I have no idea, but there are a few things I can do, maybe, one day I will show you!'

A stunned silence fell over the room as Fin and Ash gave each other a high five. Afterwards, Fin was convinced all the girls were crying, but he had no idea why and guessed it was just his imagination.

Over the next few days, Fin was grateful that Smith and Fount were in a different academic year from him, since every time they passed him they whispered threats in his direction. Threats aside, nothing could dampen Fin's enthusiasm; Ash's acknowledgement of friendship had lightened everyone's mood and Fin, for the first time in ages, began to feel happy.

A week before Christmas all lessons stopped, the main house and the lodges were arrayed with Christmas decorations. A giant Nordmann Fir touched the ceiling of their living space and when Fin returned, covered in snow, all three of the girls were decorating its lower branches. Ash was leaning out over the boys' balcony arranging a star on the top.

The front door burst open in a cloud of wind and snow and Elizabeth entered. 'If you are up for it, I have arranged for us to join Dr Swan, and his group, for a little Christmas shopping trip to Huntley and Wart,' said Elizabeth laughing at their surprised faces, 'I know you don't have much money so I would understand if you didn't want to go.' The excited look on everyone's faces gave Elizabeth the answer she required. 'Be ready after breakfast tomorrow.'

After breakfast, they all met at the front of the house and climbed into the old bus. The trip to Huntley and Wart took about fifteen minutes and they parked outside the Raven's Claw pub. On the back row, a serious discussion was going on between Fin and Jenny.

'What if they recognise us?' asked a fearful Jenny.

'Tie your hair back tightly and they won't recognise you at all.'

'What about you?'

'I will have to risk it,' replied Fin, 'but it was months ago, they are hardly likely to remember me. If they do I will try to hide in the group.'

The school party split up and drifted through the shops, Fin and the rest kept together and only separated to buy each other and Elizabeth little presents. In the Chandlery shop Eiry and Ash went off together, Sed joined Fin and a frustrated Jenny in the newsagents.

'I can't see anything, I so want to choose my presents myself.'

Sed and Fin tried to dissuade her but Jenny was adamant that she let her hair down. Together they walked around the shop, discreetly making their choices. There was a clang of the doorbell and two old women and Elizabeth walked in, Fin instantly recognised them but was too far away from Jenny to warn her.

Turning to Elizabeth one of the women pointed at Jenny, 'There she is, me and Gerty have seen her in the village before and we never forget a face!'

'I don't see how,' said a perturbed Elizabeth, 'the young people at Ravenswood are unable to leave without supervision.'

'It's definitely her, I tell you,' exclaimed Gerty, 'and she was with some scruffy looking lad, wasn't she Prude?'

'Fin will you get Jenny and come over here please,' called Elizabeth.

Walking across the room to the couple, Fin and Jenny knew they were in trouble.

'How can we help you Miss Gosling?' asked Jenny.

'These ladies believe that they have met you and Fin before, do you think this is possible?'

Reaching up to her wild hair, Jenny tied it back revealing her scarred face to the women. 'I don't see how, Miss Gosling I can't really get around on my own.'

A sympathetic look crossed Elizabeth's face.

Addressing the women directly Jenny said, 'I am blind and if we had met before I am sure you would have remembered this face.'

A look of horror crossed the women's faces as they saw the deep scars embedded in Jenny's face.

'Why are you so sure it was me?'

'Well you hair is so distinctive,' said Prude looking the smartly dressed Fin up and down, 'and the other boy was so scruffy, not like this young man at all.'

'I know my hair is wild but there must be many others with a similar look,' said Jenny trying to turn her face to exactly where the women were standing, 'and the only boy you would see me with is Fin, as he helps me to get around.'

Suddenly lost for words, Gerty stumbled out an apology, 'I am sorry my dear, the girl I saw looked just like you; she was examining torches in a charity shop.' She stared at Jenny's damaged face, 'I see now that I was mistaken.'

'Come on Gerty,' said Prude, 'My Albert wants me to get some nice pork chops from the butchers.'

'I don't understand it,' said Gerty as they left the shop, 'we've never been wrong before.'

'If everyone's finished,' a confused Elizabeth said, 'then I think it is time for us to return to Ravenswood.' Taking Jenny to one side she whispered, 'I'm sorry to have put you through that, but some of the people here in Huntley and Wart are very strange.'

Returning to the old bus, Fin was convinced that he saw Eiry and Ash holding hands as they gathered together with the rest. While he was staring, Jenny pushed him hard in the back.

'Fin, just get in!' then speaking to Sed exclaimed, 'Boys!'

On Christmas Eve, Elizabeth arranged for them all to join her in the local church for the midnight communion service. Saint Hubert the parish church of Huntley and Wart, stood tall and strong at the top of the hill above the village. Fin had a wonderful time singing carols and sharing hugs as the bells rang in Christmas Day. Even seeing Gerty and Prude dressed up in their Sunday best did nothing to dampen their festive spirits. On their return, they all placed their presents for each other under the tree and retired to bed exhausted.

Christmas morning arrived in a blizzard of snow and wrapping paper. Sitting around the tree they each opened their presents. From Ash, Fin received a wooden box full of artist's paints and brushes, from Jenny, a scarf and a pair of thick, thermal lined gloves. In a parcel wrapped up with so much clear plastic tape it was almost impossible to open was a hot water bottle from Sed and in a small presentation box was a snow globe and a bar of chocolate from Eiry.

'Oh, thank you, thank you,' yelled Jenny waving a new hairbrush, elastics and chocolate that Fin had given her. Jumping up she ran up to Fin and gave him a big hug and a kiss on the cheek.

The room suddenly felt much warmer than Fin thought it was at first. Fortunately, the door opened and Elizabeth came in with a pile of presents, including a Christmas stocking for of each them.

Inside the stocking, Fin found a tangerine, a plastic wrapped mince pie, a chocolate in the shape of a Christmas pudding, a pencil and pencil sharpener and a little led torch. Looking around he noticed that all the stockings were the same, apart from Jenny's who, instead of a torch, received a headband that controlled her hair but allowed it to fall free.

'I though you might find a use of those while the nights are dark.'

A slightly embarrassed silence fell on the room as they all wondered if Elizabeth new of their secret intention to go exploring. The moment did not last long and Ash hunted out Elizabeth's gift from under the tree.

They had all grouped together to buy Elizabeth a present and she was delighted with the petite bottle of perfume.

'This is my favourite,' she exclaimed, 'how did you

know I had run out?'

'I saw you use the last of it the other day,' said Eiry, 'so we thought we would replace it.'

'Oh guys,' said Elizabeth starting to cry, 'that is so kind of you,' pausing to wipe her eyes, 'Please open your presents.'

Once again, they all received the same type of present but each was slightly different in colour and shape.

'I thought you all needed some new clothes but I did not know what to get you, so I decided to buy you each a fleece that matched the colours you normally wear.'

'They are perfect,' cried Sed, jumping up and twirling around with her fleece, 'Thank you.'

The rest of day passed by in a blur of fun and activity, in the late afternoon, with everyone else at Ravenswood they met up for the grandest Christmas Day meal Fin had ever had.

Later in evening, they all sat with the lights off around the log fire.

'If I eat any more I am going to burst!' groaned Jenny, 'The kitchen staff deserves their day off tomorrow!'

'Chocolate,' said Fin offering a piece to Jenny.

Laughing aloud Jenny took the chocolate, ate it, and then groaned again. 'I'm too full to do anything tonight, but tomorrow let's get the map out and go exploring.'

'Sounds like a plan,' Ash replied, 'it's the best chance we will have in ages, all our meals are here tomorrow so we won't be missed.'

'I need to get some fresh air and work a bit of this food off,' said Eiry standing up.

'Yeah, I'll join you,' replied Ash.

Fin was just about to say that he wanted to go too when both Sed and Jenny poked him and indicated he was to stay where he was. Not quite understanding their hints, Fin sat back and watched them leave.

'You have no idea what's going on around you, do

you?' stated an amused Jenny, 'They like each other and…'

'I like you,' interrupted Fin.

'Do you?' a smile crossed Jenny's face, 'they want to be alone under the mistletoe.'

'Why?'

'You are kidding?' said Sed, rolling about in laughter, 'he hasn't a clue!' turning to Jenny she sighed, 'Show him while I go and make us all a hot chocolate.'

'What is she on about?' asked a confused Fin.

Standing up, Jenny led Fin to a piece of mistletoe hanging from a doorframe, 'You see it's like this, when a girl likes a boy they like to do this.' Pulling Fin towards her, she reached up and kissed him.

A startled Fin was taken by surprise, he had never been kissed before but he got the idea very quickly and returned the kiss with an enthusiasm he did not know he had.

'And breathe!' a laughing Sed shouted, returning from the kitchen with the mugs of hot chocolate, 'Yeah, I think he's got the idea.'

Holding Fin's hand Jenny led Fin back to the fire and they sat down, 'And mistletoe is not always necessary.'

Saying nothing, Fin felt fire run through his veins, so much, so he was convinced that his hands were glowing, gently he put his arm around Jenny and she cuddled into him. The door swung open, before they could separate, Eiry and Ash came back in, removed their coats and joined them by the fire. The five friends then chatted deep into the night and only parted when Jenny started to snore.

The following morning after a quick breakfast, they all gathered around the map.

'Mr Chough's office is out for now,' said Eiry.

'So is the main entrance hall you used before, there's a Christmas tree covering the entrance,' explained Sed.

Pointing his finger to the corridor outside the library, Ash said, 'There seems to be an entrance here,' moving his hand further across the map, 'another one here at the back of the old stable where the wood store is.'

'Let's try the wood store first,' said Jenny, 'there is hardly anyone ever there and we would have time to try to find it.'

'Jenny's right,' continued Ash, 'look that passage joins up with another one that goes deep down.'

'I can't make it out,' a puzzled Fin commented, 'it all seems at bit vague.'

'There was a stain on the original plan and that whole section is only guesswork,' admitted Ash, 'but we have to start somewhere, and this is a good as any place else.'

'Jenny and I got quite dirty in the other passage way,' said Fin, 'so I suggest we wear old clothes and boots when we explore.'

Half an hour later, they were all at the wood store, with their torches and in their old clothes. Scrambling around the wood store, they could see carvings in the wall but most were well hidden beneath a mountain of logs. It was hard sweaty work rearranging the piles but eventually they cleared a space.

Sliding carefully into the empty space Ash found a similar carving to the one they had found earlier in the woodwork. The mechanism, however, worked in the same way and the door creaked inwards revealing a stairway that disappeared down into the darkness. Slipping inside, Ash closed the door and then reopened it from the inside.

'Well at least it works both ways.'

'That's good,' replied Eiry, 'but we would be trapped if someone moved the logs or one of these piles fell over. I think we should make it safe and hide it at the same time.'

On the far side of the room, there was a selection of old wooden pallets waiting to be broken down. Finding a few coils of old rope Fin suggested that they rest the pallets against the wall, create a tunnel and then cover it with a mound of logs. Placing and binding the pallets together seemed to take an age but when they had finished the entrance to the staircase was hidden and the entrance to their crawl space was lost in the darkest corner of the room.

'It will be spring before anyone gets through that pile of logs,' said Fin admiring their work.

Crawling along the space they had created they all entered stairwell, turned on their torches and headed down. Jenny insisted that she went first as she could see more with her hair then they could with their torches. Fin, Sed and Eiry followed, and Ash after closing the door behind them, brought up the rear.

The staircase was filthy and in a matter of moments, a layer of cobwebs and grime covered them. After an age, they reached the bottom of the staircase to discover five tunnels going off in different directions. Producing a piece of chalk from his pocket, Ash numbered them.

'I was concerned that we might get lost so I brought a piece for each of us,' he said handing them their chalk, 'I suggest we all go a short way down a different tunnel, mark where we stop, and come back and we can discuss which one we explore.'

'Okay, but let's keep talking as we walk, if anyone goes quiet we all return to look for them,' reasoned Sed.

After only a few moments Jenny shouted, 'The ceiling has collapsed here so I'm heading back.'

'Mine's a dead end,' yelled Ash, 'no, hang on, it's a wall around a drop, there are spikes knocked into the side but I don't fancy going down without a rope.'

A scream came from Eiry and then laughter, 'My tunnel has just expanded out and I've come to what looks like a lake but it could be just a rock pool. Sorry about the scream but the water caught me by surprise.'

Strange rumbling noises echoed up randomly from the passageway Fin had chosen, the further he moved down the passage the louder the sound and the more he felt the vibrations. Marking the wall, he returned to the meeting point.

Anxious looks on everyone else's face made him realise

that he had not heard from Sed in ages.

'Bloody typical,' moaned Ash as he followed Sed's route, 'I knew I shouldn't have suggested splitting up!'

'Sed!' Eiry yelled.

'Shhh,' whispered Sed as she rejoined them, 'there are lights down there and I could hear people talking.'

In silence, they all followed Sed along the passageway; in the distance, beams of light pierced the darkness.

'They are like the spy holes I saw into that creepy room,' said Fin quietly.

Finding different vantage points, they all looked through the spy holes, all off the rooms were empty, painted a clinical white, furnished with a bed a wash basin and a toilet.

'What is this place?' a worried Sed ask, 'They look like prison cells.'

'I have lost all sense of direction,' replied Eiry, 'but I don't think we are under Ravenswood.'

'Wherever we are we are deep underground!' gulped Fin, 'They places give me the willies…'

A stronger expletive came from Ash, who immediately was punched by a shocked Eiry, 'Ash!'

'I though you said you heard voices?' said a disturbed Fin.

'I did but I'm not sure where from.'

'Well it can't have been from this tunnel it's as filthy as all the rest. Whoever built those rooms knew nothing about these passage ways,' reasoned Fin, 'let's see where it leads to.'

Quietly they continued their exploration; Jenny stopped and pointed to a release mechanism by a spy hole.

'I can't see through this one,' said Jenny.

Slipping his arm around her, Fin gave her a hug and then looked through the hole.

'There's a corridor below us and this entrance is half-way up a wall. I can see what looks like the outside doors to those cells.'

Behind Fin the others all started talking at once, motioning with hand Fin silenced them.

'Someone's coming,' he whispered, 'there's two of them, they are wearing white lab coats, they look like brothers they've got the same sharp nose.'

The two men stopped and went quiet as if they had heard Fin speak, hearing nothing more they went on their way.

'That was close, they heard me, come on let's keep going.'

The passageway began to climb up a long slow hill until it stopped at a spiral staircase.

'We've come this far,' panted Sed, 'we might as well go the whole way.'

The climb up was not as high as everyone expected and soon reached the rear of a secret door. Looking through the spy hole Fin could see nothing. Opening the door carefully they all entered what appeared to be cellar. Finding a light switch Sed flicked it on and illuminated the room. On the wall was an old framed picture of a saint.

'It's the life story of St Hubert; it says here that he loved hunting and that Jesus spoke to him on a Good Friday when he was on a chase.'

'Then we are in the parish church,' said Fin, 'how strange.'

'Not really,' countered Ash, 'this church is as old as Ravenswood; it was probably an escape route.'

Rattling the door of the room Fin turned, 'Well it's locked from the outside.'

'No point staying here,' said a frustrated Eiry.

'Hang on what's this?' said Fin standing next to a filing cabinet marked Ravenswood. They all gathered around as Fin opened it, inside it was stuffed full of paper wallets each one with the name of a student on it. 'Some are marked in red and others are just plain.'

'Are our names there?' asked an inquisitive Eiry.

'We all are, but only Ash's is red. What does it mean?'

'We'll soon find out,' said Ash snatching at his file.

Before Ash's hand even touched the file, they heard a key turning in the lock of the door.

'Crap, there's someone coming.' Ash said closing the draw, 'everyone out, now!'

There was mad scramble for the door and they all squeezed in, as Ash pulled the door shut he saw the other door open and two people walk in.

'It's not locked and I'm only holding it closed. I'm frightened it will make a noise,' he whispered, 'Can you see anything?'

Looking through the spy hole fin watched a man and a woman go to the filing cabinet, take a file out and attached a red flag to it.

'Are you certain?' asked the man.

'Absolutely, he's definitely a Minotaur, the crows saw him transform in the woods.'

'I've never trusted the crows, their intelligence is so limited.'

'Well Raven believes them, if I'm honest I believe them too and you don't often see a half-man half-bull combination. The crows do not have sufficient imagination to make that all up.'

'True, so Fount is a definite!'

'Will he turn?'

'He's a thug, he already has.'

'And Smith?'

'We still don't know, but it's more than likely, Minotaurs tend to operate in pairs.'

'When do we get to keep them?' the man asked.

'The usual, when they turn eighteen,' the woman replied, 'but I do hate loosing them.'

'Better to loose them now when they don't turn,' he said, 'than them growing up hating us. It's a shame they take so long to find and grow, you can get quite attached to them.'

'I know,' she replied sadly, 'I will update the files. Will I see you later?'

'More than likely,' said the man leaving the room and shutting the door, 'don't forget to lock the door the vicar is getting curious again.'

The woman sat down with the files and started making variety of entries in of them. Meanwhile, in the passageway they all waited in silence for her to finish.

'My arm's growing numb,' groaned Ash, 'I'm going to have to shut it.'

They all held their breath as Ash clicked the door shut; the woman turned around startled by the noise. Standing up she crossed the room and touched the wall. Inside everyone remained silent, keeping as still as statues until Fin indicated she had returned to the desk.

The journey back was a solemn one; no one wanted to speak until they were safely at the five-way junction.

'Something sick is going on here,' complained Eiry, 'I really don't like it; we need to get a look at those files.'

Apprehension filled Fin's face as he said, 'We need a copy those files.'

'That would take hours,' said Ash, 'and what would we do with them?'

'I don't know yet,' said Fin pausing, 'at the very least we might learn more about ourselves and possibly,' he paused, 'we might have something we can use against them.'

'Whoever they are,' muttered Sed.

'We need a digital camera,' concluded Fin.

'Good luck getting one of them,' groaned Sed.

'Looks like we need another trip out,' laughed Fin, 'but not to Huntley and Wart, they would all recognise us if we went back there!'

CHAPTER 7 – THE BIRTHDAY PARTY

Turning restlessly in his sleep, Fin's subconscious mind registered smoke creeping under the bedroom door, his nose twitched and his eyes flickered. In his dream, the beautiful girl on the sunny beach turned into a fire-breathing dragon, flames licked around his body and he started to scream. He knew he was dreaming but could not wake up, panic covered him with sweat, and the dragon bit his shoulder and shook him from side to side.

'Fin, Fin,' yelled Ash, 'wake up!'

Stirring Fin opened his eyes, 'Was I dreaming?'

'Yes, but the fire alarm is going off,' explained an exasperated Ash, 'can't you smell the smoke?'

'But that's in my dream!'

'No it's bloody well not.'

Jumping out of his bed Fin gathered up his shoes and slipped them on, 'Then let's get out of here.'

'I'm with you.'

Grabbing the door handle Fin turned and pulled, nothing happened, 'It's locked!'

Together they yanked and kicked the door but it would not budge. Behind them flames crept up the wall and rolled along the ceiling.

In desperation, they tugged at the door. Unexpectedly,

the door burst open sending them flying, there in the corridor stood Jenny, her wild hair flying in the super heated air, fear in her eyes.

'Don't just lie there; let's get the hell out of here!'

Following the exit signs, they ran down the corridors until they could see the fire exit. There was a massive explosion and the ceiling collapsed all around them. Throwing his arms out, Fin created a protective bubble around them. Jenny screamed out in pain, as a dark figure hit her across the face with a clawed hand, blood ran from behind her fingers and her cries of agony ripped through Fin's ears.

Turning Fin looked into the face of her attacker, instantly recognising her, shocked he cried out, 'Ash!'

'Fin, Fin wake up mate,' cried Ash, shaking Fin awake, 'you're dreaming again!'

Opening his eyes Fin stared around the room everything was back to normal.

'Was it the same dream?'

Fin nodded dithering with cold.

'You called out my name, 'Ash said returning back to his own bed.

'You were there too.'

'No way mate,' said Ash shaking his head, 'that's impossible.'

'I know, but this time I saw the face of Jenny's attacker,' said Fin as he tried to remember his dream, 'I recognised who it was.'

'Who?'

Suddenly standing up in anger, Fin punched the wall, 'I can't remember it's gone again,' groaning he considered his bleeding knuckles.

'Did he look like me?' asked a nervous Ash.

'No, I don't think, each time I have the nightmare I remember a little bit more,' reasoned Fin shaking his sore hand, 'why do you ask?'

Walking over to the bedroom sink Fin ran cold water over his bruised knuckles.

Sitting on the edge of his bed, a distraught Ash began to explain, 'When I was younger and before my father died strange things used to happen. Fire seemed to follow us around. He once told me it was our duty to protect people and use our powers wisely. I asked him what he meant by that and he said he would teach me one day, but he never did. Still he warned me about the danger of fire and not playing with it.' Ash paused and looked close to tears, 'Once when he was poorly, he cried out about the sons of the Dragons and his hands burst into flames, he thought I hadn't seen them, so I never said anything. I was worried my dad might have been the man you saw in your dreams.'

'I can't really remember, the more I try the worse my memory gets,' said Fin, 'he sounds very special, how old was he?'

'He once told me he was five-hundred years old and had been married six times; the last time was to my mother,' Ash said sadly looking at the floor, 'You should know I'm dangerous.'

'Why's that?'

'I haven't told anyone before, but when he died, I ran off by myself and wept.'

'That's understandable; I wept when my mum and when my foster parents died.'

'Yeah but did your hands burst into flames as my dad's did?'

'No.'

'That was the start of me discovering I had a few special powers.'

'Like healing me,' replied Fin, 'amazing I wish I was someone special like you,'

'If Jenny and your dream accounts are true then you might be,' suddenly laughing Ash continued, 'nothing personal mate, but you stink of sweat, your hand is bleeding and you need a shower!'

As April approached the shock of nearly being caught at Christmas and the February midterm exams had put a stop to the group's exploration plans. Instead, they decided their most urgent priority was to get hold of a digital camera. In all their spare time they roamed Ravenswood, looking in cupboards, opening draws and searching every nook and cranny for a digital camera. They got excited when Sed found a camera but on closer inspection, it turned out to be an old film version. A quick trip to the library dampened their excitement the film was obsolete.

'It says here that this 126 film used be popular and was created in 1963 but is no longer made and no one processes it anymore,' groaned a frustrated Sed.

'Told you it was crap,' said Ash.

This remark earned him a dirty look from Eiry.

Shrugging his shoulders Ash complained, 'But it's true.'

'I'm afraid he's right,' agreed Sed, 'totally tactless, but right. We are going to have go exploring again outside the grounds.'

'Is there another village out there other than Huntley and Wart?' asked Eiry.

A quick search of the library revealed a 1960's road atlas.

'If we exit at the well and head north across the fields about five miles there's a small market town called Howden upon Tear,' said an exited Sed.

'Can we afford a camera?' asked Fin, 'because I'm broke!'

They pooled together all their money and produced enough to buy a cheap camera.

'Look guys,' said Eiry, 'I think I should go on my own this time. We can tell Elizabeth that I'm not well and in bed with a hot water bottle. That should get me a day, especially if Sed and Jenny cover for me.'

'Hang on,' said Ash.

'No seriously, Fin and Jenny can't afford to be

recognised again, Sed needs to cover up for me and no one would believe that you were ill enough to sit in bed for the day.'

'Really and why do you think you can get away with it?' grumbled Ash.

Raising her eyebrows Jenny stopped Fin from agreeing with Ash, 'Unbelievable, hot water bottle, staying in bed, you really have no idea either of you do you?'

Fin returned Ash's blank look.

'Boys,' cried an exasperated Jenny leading off a giggling Sed and Eiry.

The plan was simple, early in the morning, before breakfast, Eiry guided by Ash would enter the passageways via the entrance hall, and together they would head towards the well. Eiry would exit and cross the fields, find the shops and buy a camera and Fin would return to the house and go back later to meet up with her. However, the reality was somewhat different. On arriving in the entrance hall, Fin and Eiry had to dodge the cleaners, that was simple enough but just as they were opening the door, they heard footsteps and had to hide in a cupboard.

'You're squashing me,' Eiry complained while unintentionally poking Fin in the ribs with her elbow.

'It's not like I have a lot of choice,' whispered Fin, 'and move your hand I'd rather not be squeezed there.'

'Sorry,' said a blushing Eiry moving her hand, 'can you see?'

Outside the cupboard, a cleaner produced a duster and started dusting the tops of the pictures.

'I've got pins and needles in my arm,' said a trapped Eiry.

'Yeah, well I'm getting cramp in my leg,' moaned Fin and then started to giggle.

Soon they were both trying not to laugh aloud and tears poured down their faces. Finally, the cleaner finished and they fell out the cupboard and hobbled across to the passageway entrance, turned the carving and entered. The journey to the well was uneventful and relatively quick.

On reaching the wall spikes, they climbed to the top, slid open the bolt and started to push the frame open when they heard voices. Carefully they lowered the cover and waited, two people wearing florescent coats and hardhats appeared. One of them lit up a cigarette and threw the match down the well; it landed still burning on Eiry's arm and singed it. Tears welled up in her eyes and it took all her will power not to scream.

'So what do you think of this job?' asked the smoker.

'I've had worse and that farm house will look fantastic when we've finished it,' said the workwoman next to him, 'What have you got to do first?'

'When I've finished this cigarette I'm going to weld this cover permanently onto the well, it's really not safe and the boss wants it done immediately. He said something about a special school being not far away and building sites to those kids are like wasps to honey!'

Fin and Eiry did not have to hear anymore, they headed down and shut the secret door behind them.

'We'll just have to go back and try to find another way out,' Eiry whispered.

Frustrated they walked back in silence down the old tunnel; as they walked, they examined the walls in more detail.

'It's no good,' said Fin, 'I've already checked all the walls for passageways.'

Stopping in her tracks, Eiry lifted her face and turned around on the spot.

'What is it?'

'Turn your torch off and close your eyes,' suggested Eiry.

Doing as he was told Fin closed his eyes.

'Can you feel that breeze?' asked Eiry.

'We noticed that when we first came down here,' replied Fin, 'the staircase and passageways were so stuffy and you could feel the air freshen up.'

'But where does it come from?'

Turning back on their torches Fin and Eiry searched the tunnel. Fin could see that Eiry had found something because she was shining her torch into the ceiling above a narrow bend.

'It looks like a ventilation shaft,' said Eiry, 'there are spikes in the wall, hang on here while I check.'

Jumping up Eiry caught the first spike and climbed up the chimney, on reaching the top she discovered that it ended in the remains of a shepherd's stone cottage.

'I can see the perimeter wall of Ravenswood House,' she called down, 'but it's a five minute exposed run across an open field.'

Dirt fell in Fin's face as he stared up the chimney, a moment later Eiry dropped down beside him.

'Let's head back to the others and try to think up another plan,' said Eiry, 'this way's a waste of time.'

By the time they had both returned to the top of the stairs they were feeling completely disappointed and fed up. However, when Fin tried to open the door it would not budge. A quick inspection through the spy hole revealed the source of their problem, jammed against the door was a decorator's scaffolding tower.

'We're trapped,' groaned Eiry sitting down on the top step, 'I've got an hour or two but you need to be back.'

'That scaffolding tower will take at least two of us to move it,' groaned Fin, 'and we can't do that trapped in here!'

'Somehow we need to get a message back to the others.'

'I think our only option is to go up that chimney and try and get in over the wall.'

'I don't think that's such a good idea,' said Eiry making room for Fin to sit next to her, 'the ravens will see you.'

'What choice do we have we can't sit here all day,' argued Fin, 'no-one will suspect you of being involved in anything silly as you are tucked up in bed with a hot water bottle but I need to get back.'

Reluctantly Eiry agreed and Fin left her at the top of the steps.

'Whatever happens I will make sure the others know you need rescuing, but it may take them a while.'

The old stone cottage was derelict and Fin climbed up and out of the shaft into a space hidden between two walls. Carefully he hid the entrance with some old timber and rock. Satisfied it was concealed he walked out into the shadow of the house. Overhead the sky was grey and blustery, wind whipped the trees in every direction and rain was starting to fall.

Watching the wall for the moment to run, Fin noticed that the crows overhead were flying in patterns, counting he worked out that he would have only minutes to sprint to the wall. Testing his theory Fin counted the seconds and watched, he reckoned that he could just do it.

The moment came when the birds flew away from where Fin was hiding and he ran for the wall. Legs pumping arms swinging, he sprinted for the wall; it was getting closer and closer. Yes, he thought, I can do this and then his foot slipped in the mud and he went sliding, out of control across the grass towards the wall. The air was full of the noise the returning crows as he stopped, out in the open, only yards from the wall.

In moments, the angry flock of birds spotted him and attacked. Overwhelmed by a mass of birds pecking, clawing and ripping at his skin his clothes became torn and he began to bleed from countless cuts.

A murder of crows, Fin remembered, not a flock, and despite the pain started to laugh. The more he laughed the better he felt, tears of laughter rolled down his face and his mouth began to ache. As he laughed, the birds rose up in the air, ignored him, and resumed their search pattern.

Struggling to his feet, Fin walked to the wall, climbed

over it and headed for the lodge. His euphoria began to ware off leaving him exhausted, tired, and puzzled by the crow's sudden change in behaviour.

Once back with Ash, Sed and Jenny, Fin shared Eiry's predicament. They all agreed that they had to move the scaffolding but that they could not do so until early evening when the staff and other students were eating.

The day dragged on slowly, Ash dealt with and healed Fin's many cuts and bruises. Fin binned his old clothes but the pressure of not being able to help Eiry frustrated them all. As usual when things did not go the way Ash wanted, he started to argue with everyone, that was until Fin took to one side just as he was about call Elizabeth an old hag. A few well-chosen words quickly told him that he was not helping Eiry and it was time to shut up and behave. To everyone's surprise, including Ash's, he listened and calmed down.

When the majority of the staff and students were eating their evening meal, they rushed across to the entrance hall, moved the scaffolding and released a very bored, cold and miserable Eiry. Grumbling Eiry retired to bed with a hot water bottle.

That night when they had all retired there was thunderstorm, the rain battered the windows, the night was lit up with jagged lightning and thunder rattled the doors. No one slept and at half past four they all came downstairs, Eiry was the last to arrive clutching her hot water bottle.

'I just can't get warm,' Eiry complained, 'I don't understand it, normally I'm too hot.'

Putting another log on the smouldering fire Ash blew repeatedly until it burst reluctantly into flames. Everyone was cold, but it seemed to affect Fin and Eiry the most. Outside the rain turned to sleet and then snow. It was the wildest storm Fin had ever seen or heard. Infuriatingly the fire continued to refuse to burn properly and give off any proper heat. Struggling with the cold Fin tried to help Ash with the fire but his hands felt numb. Next to Fin, Eiry's face began to turn blue; Jenny covered her with a blanket while Sed refilled the hot water bottle.

Outside the snow fell heavily and mounded up around the lodge. Inside the pitiful fire was doing nothing to help keep them warm. Frustrated, Ash shoved his hand in the fire. Sed screamed and tried to pull his hand out but Ash gently held her away with his spare hand.

'It's okay I know what I am doing,' he explained as the fire burst into life and the flames rushed up the chimney, 'I can make fire at will.'

Removing his hand from the fire Ash sat down next to Eiry and hugged her, heat flowed from his body into hers and her skin colour returned to its normal white.

'Tha... tha... thank you,' she shivered, 'I was so cold.'

A stunned silence filled the room as the freak storm outside turned to heavy rain and began washing the snow away. Sed and Jenny checked Eiry over but she seemed fine now but was happy to remain cuddled into Ash's arms.

Watching from the side, Fin felt an overwhelming sense of anger overtake him. Standing up angrily he stared at Ash, stormed off up the stairs, and slammed his bedroom door behind him.

The following week Fin ignored everyone, ate his meals on his own and refused to talk. If Ash entered a room, he left it immediately and at night, he left a chair blocking his view of Ash's bed and slept with his back facing towards him. On a number of occasions, Jenny tried to talk to him but all he could do was mumble something inaudible and walk off. Fin had never been so angry in all his life but try as he might he could not put it into words. Once again, he felt as if he was in a deep dark tunnel with no way out, betrayed, disappointed and let down by a friend who he was just starting to trust.

Each of his friends watched him, not knowing what to

say or do. Feeling slightly guilty, Ash avoided Fin as much as he could. Sed and Eiry kept trying to include him in things but Fin would have none of it. Secretly, Fin was delighted that Eiry was better but he was annoyed with her because she kept sneaking off with Ash. He could see them walking around the grounds, talking, holding hands and kissing when they thought no one could see them. Finally, Jenny decided it was up to her to deal with it.

'Fenix Butler,' she snapped, when he tried to leave when she started talking, 'we are quite alone and I have had just about enough of this!'

Stopping in his tracks, Fin noticed Jenny for the first time in days saw the look on her face and decided that running away would be the best option. Instead, he shut the door and walked over to her.

'What is the matter with you?'

Taking a risk, he reached out, took hold of Jenny's hand, and held it.

'I am sorry, if I am hurting you,' he mumbled, 'you have been and are my best friend.' Pausing he held her hand tightly, 'I have been followed by arson all my life and I am still hurting because I miss,' a tear rolled down his face, 'both my mums.'

Seeing the tears Jenny pulled him into a gentle hug.

'I have never known, who are what caused the fires that killed them, but I have always blamed myself. Maybe if I could have warned them, rescued them, I could have saved them. Maybe it was me that started the fires and I don't remember,' seeing a shocked look in Jenny's face he continued, 'I am the common factor. I have always thought it was impossible just to start a fire with just your hands. Now I know I was wrong... if Ash can do it maybe anyone can.'

Shaking her head slowly, Jenny said, 'Ash is special, it is a gift he alone has.' Seeing the doubt in his face, Jenny kissed him briefly on the cheek and held him tight to her.

The door opened and Sed looked in and immediately

left, smiling she hoped that this would be the start of life returning to normal. When the door clicked behind her, she burst out laughing at the thought of Ravenswood ever being normal.

That evening Jenny and Fin's relationship was back to normal. Unfortunately, just as Fin was calming down Eiry and Sed announced that they had discovered, from a reluctant Ash that the next day was his birthday and he would be fourteen. In no mood to consider Ash's birthday Fin went to bed without speaking to anyone else. As he left the room, he heard Jenny apologising for him to Sed and Eiry and he wanted to return and say sorry for himself, but the moment passed and he went to bed.

At the stroke of midnight, Fin woke up in screaming agony and fell out of his bed, writhing around on the floor his hands felt like they were on fire. The initial spasm of pain wore off and he sat up to see Ash rolling about in agony on his bed.

Making eye contact across the room he screamed at Ash, 'Stop it... your stupid powers are killing me.'

'I'm not doing this,' groaned Ash doubling over in pain.

'Liar, you're a bloody liar!' panicked Fin, 'It has to be you!'

'Don't be so stupid!'

'Stupid am I now,' fired Fin at Ash, 'stupid for trusting you, stupid for thinking you were my friend.'

'Of course you bloody are, 'spat Ash, 'if it was me doing this would I be doing this to myself?'

Crawling to his bed, Fin heaved himself up, staggered across to Ash, and grabbed him.

'I will punch you through the wall if you don't stop it,' he yelled throwing Ash backwards.

In agony and surprise, Ash threw a hand out at Fin and a ball of flame flew at him. Fin caught it as it reached his chest and threw it back. Falling away from each other, they started throwing fire around the room. Balls of flame ricocheted off the walls but left no singe marks. Shouting and swearing at each other they fought sometimes punching, kicking, and eventually wrestling with whips of fire.

The boys' bedroom door burst open and an angry Elizabeth stood there with her hands on her hips. Fin and Ash fell back exhausted, the room was a mess but there was no sign of fire damage, amazed they both looked at Elizabeth and then each other and burst out laughing.

'It's not a laughing matter,' shouted a confused Elizabeth not quite sure what had happened.

Thinking quickly as he stood up Ash tried to explain, 'I am sorry Elizabeth, at midnight it was my birthday and I got all excited and woke Fin up, and we started to play fight,' looking around the room, 'I'm sorry we got a bit carried away.'

'I thought you were killing each other,' snapped a frustrated Elizabeth, 'and yes Ash I do know it's your birthday! Now go back to sleep and let me go back to mine. If I hear anything else, you both will be on detention. Is that clear?'

In unison they both replied, 'Yes Elizabeth.'

With a deep sigh, Elizabeth closed the door and left the two of them standing in their room. Looking at each other they both laughed.

'What was all that about?' asked Fin.

'It's a long story,' he replied opening the bedroom door and looking downstairs at the shocked faces of the girls, 'I might as well tell you all.'

Sitting around the kitchen table each holding a mug of hot chocolate Ash began to explain.

'You all already know that I have some special powers, I can create fire at will and I can heal people of most injuries,' Ash looked around the group and continued, 'Before he died my father told me that he was five hundred years old and the Phoenix. He explained to me that there can only ever be one phoenix at a time but something strange happened that had never happened before, his wife had twins.'

Outside the lodge, it started to rain and the wind blew through the treetops.

'As a result he was not sure which of us would inherit his abilities. I was the older son and when one day my hands burst into flames they both thought it was me, so my mum took my twin and they separated.'

'That's so sad,' said Eiry, 'I never met my dad and my mum never spoke about him. Were they in love?'

'My dad said it broke his heart to leave her but they knew that the Dragons and the Flock were after them so they tried to disappear, I don't even know my own true name.'

Standing up from her kitchen stool Eiry walked over to Ash and put her arm around him.

'My dad told me two important things, one he was certain about the other was a guess. He said that when I was fourteen, like clockwork, at the stroke of midnight I would inherit his powers. When Fin woke up and saw me in agony he witnessed that awakening.'

'So you are the Phoenix now.' stated Fin.

'The clockwork phoenix,' laughed Sed.

'I still don't know,' said Ash shaking his head, 'the second thing my dad said was that it was possible that the power of the phoenix would be split between the living twins and that neither of them would be complete without the other.'

Pushing back his stool Ash stood up, walked around the table, and put his hands on Fin's shoulders, 'At the stroke of midnight I was not the only one to experience the awakening, I watched you erupt with power too.'

Silence filled the room as one by one they each realised the implications of what Ash was saying.

Breaking the silence Fin spoke up, 'That can only mean one thing, that I am your twin brother.'

'Yes, and like me you have semi-dormant powers like when you saved Jenny from the fire.'

'I don't remember,' reasoned Fin.

'Earlier you instinctively caught the fire I threw at you, but more importantly you can control the fire I can only make it.'

'What makes you say that?'

'Well the fact that our room was not burnt to the ground, that wasn't me, I can only destroy,' said Ash shrugging his shoulders, and then speaking more seriously he continued, 'However, my dad also reckoned that one of us might have to die for the other to have all the power.'

'I don't like the sound of that!'

'Neither do I.'

'But together we are strong!' said Fin, 'Then that's how it will be, I thought we were going to be friends, a friendship forged in fire, but now I find we are brothers. I have never had a brother before; I think I might get to like it!'

The two brothers stood up, faced each other, and exchanged an immature, half hug. The girls not wishing to miss out surrounded them and turned their embarrassment into a group hug.

A large smile crept over Fin's face, 'That means that today is my birthday; I have never had a birthday before.'

'Never?' asked Jenny still maintaining the hug, 'Are you sure?'

'Not that I remember,' answered Fin, 'we always celebrated my birthday on the last day of the month. What is today's date?'

'Today is Thursday the thirteenth of April,' laughed Sed, 'happy birthday Fin.'

Exhausted they all went back to bed, Fin and Ash's room was still a total mess, but being boys they ignored it and went straight to sleep.

CHAPTER 8 – THE INSPECTION

On the morning of the twin's birthday, they all gathered in the kitchen and agreed it would be safer to keep Fin and Ash's family relationship a secret. Overnight the girls managed to create birthday cards for them both, give Ash a massive bar of chocolate and then sing a raucous version of happy birthday. Laughing they all went over to breakfast. On the way, Eiry confessed that the girls were slightly embarrassed that they had no present for Fin, but he thought having a brother was present enough.

'Happy birthday!' said Ash to Fin as they sat down and then surprised everyone by breaking his chocolate bar in half and sharing it with Fin.

'Thanks,' said a surprised Fin and then whispered, 'Who are you and what have you done with Ash?'

'They came and took him away in the night!' laughed Ash.

Noticing Ash's kindness, Eiry whispered to Sed, 'I have never seen Ash so happy.'

'Long may it last!' giggled Sed.

Following breakfast, all the students gathered for their

weekly assembly, after listening to the usual thought for the day and a moment's enforced reflection to a selection of classical music, Mr Chough stood up.

'Good morning,' began Mr Chough, 'in the course of this next week IEISTED, the Independent Education Inspectorate will be inspecting our facilities. The Governors and staff expect you to behave well and treat our visitors with respect.' Mr Chough paused as if daring anyone to argue with him, 'If you are asked a question by IEISTED you will answer clearly and truthfully. However, we will not tolerate any misbehaviour whatsoever, this inspection is important to the future of Ravenswood. All of us, our private sponsors, Governors and staff want this visit to go well and we expect you to play your part.'

A sudden murmur of voices echoed across the room, whispered questions hung in the air, Fin felt the hairs on the back of his neck rise, something was not right.

'Silence!' barked Mr Chough, 'IEISTED is made up of educational specialists, members of a Government Select Committee, the police and our private sponsors.' Standing to his full height Mr Chough's expression grew extremely serious, 'This inspection has come as a surprise to all of us, Ravenswood prides itself in being cut-off from all extraneous influences and not everyone understands our ethos. You will do everything you can to help our cause, should we fail the inspection Ravenswood will close, dismissed!'

It seemed to Fin as if an air of panic had descended on Ravenswood, all lessons were cancelled and the students given all kinds of tasks. Fin and Sed were asked to remove some old and peeling corridor artwork while Eiry and Ash created colourful replacements. Passing Elizabeth in the corridor Fin tried to catch her attention but she muttered something about having to review her students' Personal Educational Plans.

It became apparent quickly to them all that they needed

to get out of the way of all the panicking teachers and so they headed back to their accommodation. Leaving by the main entrance, they only just avoided crashing into Mr Chough.

'And where do you think you are going?' he growled at them.

As quick as a flash Sed replied, 'Sorry Sir but we are off to get our course work books up to date in case they are inspected,' Sed smiled, 'we wouldn't want any of our teachers to be embarrassed should they be not up to standard.'

'Humph,' he replied, 'carry on.'

Returning to their kitchen they all gathered around the table.

'That was quick thinking Sed,' praised Jenny, 'that placated Mr Chough, but we are all up-to-date anyway.'

'Yeah, but he doesn't know that.'

'I don't care,' said a joyful Ash, 'it's my birthday and all lessons have been cancelled!'

'While everyone is distracted,' suggested Jenny, 'why don't we go explore the tunnels again and see if we can find another way out.'

Everyone liked the idea digging out their torches and old coats they set off for the wood store. Their excitement dissipated once they got there for there was a large sign written on the door of it. "OUT OF BOUNDS, Because of lightening damage to the structure this area is out of bounds to all students and staff."

'Garbage,' groaned Ash and pushed the door open, 'let's see...'

As the door swung open, there was an enormous crash as part of the ceiling fell in. Clouds of dust and debris scattered everywhere and covered them all in a white powder.

'Maybe,' coughed Ash, 'that was not such a good idea.'

'No kidding superman,' mocked Eiry.

Disappointed they all trooped back to the lodge, threw off their coats and washed. Once back together again they dug out the map and examined it for another entrance.

'The way I see it,' said Ash holding the map to the light, 'Mr Chough's office is our only other option.'

'You are kidding?' snorted Jenny, 'They are all running around like headless chickens, how do you think we are going to get in and out without being discovered?'

'No I'm serious,' continued Ash, 'Mr Chough is often off site and today I bet today they will be having an extended staff meeting. They normally last about two hours that's long enough for us to have a quick look around.'

Silence fell over the room as they all contemplated the consequences of being caught.

'Listen guys,' said Jenny interrupting the silence, 'I really don't want to get caught, some of the staff here scare me silly, but something is going on and we've been avoiding trying to find out what.'

'We've had exams,' said Eiry.

'Since when have exams been more important than our lives and who we are?' responded Jenny, 'We've all been dodging it, if we can't get a camera I say we go and steal the files.'

'What?' groaned Ash, 'Then they would know someone has seen and taken them.'

'I didn't say that it would be my first choice.'

'What would we do with the files?'

'Leave them in the tunnels,' explained Jenny, 'they know nothing about them and it wouldn't take long to shift them.'

'Okay,' said Fin joining in the debate, 'if we can we explore Mr Chough's office today.'

'All of us!' said Jenny, 'We all go this time.'

'No way,' replied Fin, 'it's not safe.'

'All or none,' snapped Jenny, 'if we get caught we all share in the consequences.'

'I agree,' said Eiry and Sed simultaneously.

Ash nodded, Eiry, Sed and Jenny looked defiant. 'Okay, we need to find out the time of the staff meeting.'

'Two o'clock,' stated Sed, 'I heard Elizabeth moaning about it early.'

At two o'clock they all stood outside Mr Chough's office, it had all been much easier than they expected all the staff had gone early to the meeting. Just in case Jenny knocked at the door, there was no answer, she opened the door and went in.

'All clear.'

Quietly they all went in and Ash opened the map and pointed to the fireplace surround. The overly ornate carvings were highly polished, dust and ash free. Ash pointed at the now familiar carving at the top right corner of the fireplace. Twisting it Fin opened the door, it swung open silently and the passage was clean and well used.

'I don't like this,' remarked Fin, 'all the other passageways were unused and this one is used regularly.'

'Mr Chough has to know about,' said Jenny, 'it must be his entrance.'

'His entrance to what?'

'There's only one way of finding out,' said Fin walking down the corridor.

The passageway was long and straight, spotlessly clean and easy to travel down, at its far end there was a staircase heading down. They trooped silently down the stairs and came to a big old wooden door.

Pushing the door open Ash entered into a corridor of doors, some were obviously well used others not, all of them were locked.

'The keys for these doors must be enormous,' he said testing each door as walked along, 'you couldn't hide them in your pockets!'

Shivering, Fin began to feel cold, 'I really don't like this.'

Reaching the end of the corridor Ash opened the final door, as he did so, light streamed out into the passageway.

'Crap,' he moaned, 'there's someone down here.'

Standing still, they froze but no one came out the room and challenged them. Reluctantly Ash pushed the door open and entered the room. It took a moment for his eyes to adjust but when he had, he waved everyone in.

They entered a candlelit room, their shadows danced along the walls as the candles flickered in the air. A big oak table dominated the centre of the room, chains hung on the walls and water dripped down and gathered in dark puddles. The room stank of damp and mould, or sweat and fear. Fin was uncertain but he could taste the air at the back of his throat. The room was warm and yet the cold ate at his bones.

'This place gives me the creeps,' whispered Eiry.

The room smelled of fear, they could all feel it; it was as if someone had died and the echoes remained. Carefully and without touching, they examined everything. Looking around, Fin took in the chains and the ancient torture equipment and realised he had seen this room before from the secret passage. The table, stained with what looked like recent blood, the chains sticky with a skin like residue, appalled him.

They all jumped when one of the hanging chains moved in an unseen draft and grated against the wall. Eiry, looking at a stone shelf, screamed when a pair of rats fighting over a morsel of unrecognisable meat, ran across her hand.

'We are not going to find anything in here,' said Fin, 'one of those locked doors we passed earlier might be an exit, but I really don't like this, this is an evil place. Let's get out of here!'

No one argued. Taking a last look around and shuddering, Ash closed the door behind him. The sinister room had changed all their moods and they quickly headed back to Mr Chough's office. Thankfully, it was still empty and they left the building quickly and quietly.

Crossing the pathway back to their accommodation, Jenny whispered, 'Look there's Mr Chough heading back to his office.'

Looking at the house clock, Fin replied, 'The staff meeting must have finished early.'

'I think we should avoid that entrance to the passageways,' said a frustrated Fin, 'they are too well used.'

'Not to mention bloody weird!' swore Ash, 'Why would you have a meeting room in a torture chamber?'

'I'm not sure I want to know,' whispered Eiry.

'Did you all see the blood stains on the table?' said a scared Jenny, 'Something bad has happened there recently and Mr Chough is part of it.'

'That's hardly a big surprise,' said Ash, 'he's always been a bit of git.'

As Mr Chough disappeared into the main building, their narrow escape began to affect them and they started to laugh. However, it was only later over their evening meal that they started to feel really better, and for Fin to feel warm again. They tried not to talk about it while they were eating and other students were around, but they could not help themselves.

'Shut up!' snapped Jenny as she kicked Fin on the shin, 'All of you shut up, you think you are being quiet but all you're doing is attracting attention!'

Shamefaced they all fell silent and it was only when they returned to their common room that they discussed it again.

'The wood store is not safe,' reasoned Sed, 'Ash proved that for us, Mr Chough's office is completely out.'

'Unless we can find the keys to those passages,' responded Ash.

'Like they are going to leave them lying around,' snarled Eiry while giving him a glare that could strip paint, 'Dingbat!'

'That only leaves the one in the main entrance,' Sed

continued, 'but we have to be careful to make sure we can get out once we go in.'

'Dam right,' exploded Eiry, who had not forgotten being trapped in it, 'but there were other passages on the plan.'

'I know,' said Ash, 'but I haven't figured out how the two plans overlap yet.'

'Maybe we should search all the buildings for the carvings,' suggested Eiry, 'but that would take ages.'

Slightly frustrated they moved to the kitchen and made themselves fresh drinks. Pulling up a stool to the table Fin made a suggestion.

'I have been thinking,' he explained, 'we have three choices; we search for fresh carvings, we try to make the wood store entrance safe or we use the one in the main entrance.'

'The first will take too long,' said Ash.

'I agree and the idea of making the wood store safe is too dangerous when we have another option.'

'Okay,' said Eiry, 'I agree, but next time I am not going to be the one left behind.'

'The inspection is going to begin at nine on Monday morning,' explained Elizabeth, 'Mr Chough and the Governors are meeting this afternoon in his office and an in-service training day has been arranged for all the staff.'

A confused look crossed all their faces.

'That means you have a day free of lessons and we will be lectured on how to treat the Inspectors,' sighed Elizabeth, 'I understand the accommodation is going to be inspected,' she paused to look around their untidy dwelling, 'that means I want this place spotless. Today is Friday and you have until Monday to clean it up.'

Suddenly the cheerful thought of no lessons vanished and was replaced with a look of despair.

Noting the change in the room Elizabeth smiled, 'Mr Chough has authorised a few special favours if you oblige and are helpful. Is there anything you would all like as an incentive? I warn you the budget is small!'

Suddenly a smile crossed Ash's face and his countenance lit up, 'There is one thing Elizabeth that we would all like, but it may be against the rules.'

'What's that?' asked a cautious Elizabeth, 'This I must hear!'

'We are all orphans,' began Ash, 'and we have become family to each other. You must have noticed the change between Fin and I, we are brothers now.'

'And we are all sisters,' said Jenny catching on to Ash's idea, 'our home here has become so special.'

'Go on,' said Elizabeth expecting the worst.

'This family of ours won't last long and when it goes we will have no physical memory of it,' continued Ash, 'we have been talking and we would love a camera to take photographs of our life here and have a simple way to keep them.'

A relieved but sorry look crossed Elizabeth's face, 'I'm sorry to disappoint you but digital cameras and computers are not allowed in Ravenswood.'

Realising finally what was going on Fin joined in, 'Before I came to Ravenswood my adopted parents had a Polaroid instant camera, if we could have, even a second-hand one of those and a few films that wouldn't involve any computers at all.'

Elizabeth smiled, 'At Christmas I saw one of those in one of the second-hand shops in the village, and I'm sure the pharmacy still stocks the film.' Looking around at all their excited faces she continued, 'Okay here's the deal, I will get you the camera and film if you make this space look perfect, and I mean perfect. However, I'm sure Mr Chough would frown on the idea or take the camera off you if he knew,' she paused, 'so you must keep it our little secret.'

'Thank you Elizabeth,' said Jenny, 'I won't be able to see the pictures but I know it will make all the others very happy.'

As Elizabeth left the room, Fin was convinced he saw a tear in her eye. As the door shut, he turned around and looked at everyone and burst out, 'You lot are brilliant!' Then noticing a look on Ash's face he asked, 'What's the matter?'

'It means,' said Ash looking around the room, 'we are really going to have to clean this place up.'

After a quick council of war, they all agreed, if somewhat reluctantly, that Fin and Jenny should explore the main entrance passageway while the rest tidied up.

Eiry summed up the conversation neatly, 'Jenny's room is always tidy because it has to be, Ash you can do your room as that's the worst room in the house!'

'Come on,' moaned Ash, 'half the mess is Fin's.' Then seeing the look Fin gave him he conceded, 'Okay it's mostly mine,' and then looking around the living space, 'and this is too.'

'I will do down here, Sed is doing our room and when Jenny and Fin get back, we can all clean and polish,' said Eiry picking a plate up off the floor, 'Ash if you leave another dirty dish under the sofa I'm going to break it over your head!'

Seeing the start of another squabble Fin and Jenny ran and collected their things and headed over to the main house. As they approached the entrance, they noticed a group of shadowy figures standing chatting.

'It's strange,' said Jenny with her hair flying in the breeze, 'I can't see their faces and it's as if there is a haze hanging over them.'

'I can't either,' replied Fin, 'they all have their backs to me or their collars and hoods up.'

As they watched, Mr Chough opened his study door and invited them in before closing the door behind him and hanging up a sign.

'Can you read what it says?' asked Jenny.

'Not from here.'

Now that the coast was clear, they headed into the entrance hall, Fin stopped at the door.

'It says: Strictly no admittance Governors Meeting in progress.'

Not wishing to be caught snooping outside Mr Chough's office they moved quickly to the secret entrance and after a one last check that no one was around they opened the door and headed down the long spiral staircase.

The journey down was easy than expected but Fin started to feel cold and shiver as they approached the corridor.

'What makes you think they are having their meeting down here rather than in Mr Chough's office?' asked Jenny.

'I don't know,' replied Fin, 'but there was something odd about the way we could not see who they were. If the chamber is empty we can look to see if there are any other routes we may have missed.'

'We've been that way a few times and I haven't seen anything.'

'Neither have I but we could always look.'

As before, the passage off the staircase to the chamber made them feel uncomfortable; Fin was dithering with the cold and Jenny's hair was moving wildly. Reaching one of the spy holes Fin looked in but the chamber was empty.

'Looks like I was wrong,' he muttered, 'there's no one there.'

'What's at the end of this corridor,' asked Jenny, 'we never went passed the chamber last time?'

Leaving the chamber spy holes behind them, they explored further the passageway and the ominous sense of dread they had been feeling eased as they progressed. At first Fin felt that they had arrived at a dead end but when Jenny walked passed him and stopped and then turned sharp right, he realised it was just a corner.

'There's another spiral staircase,' said Jenny as she

began to go down the steps, 'it's just like the other one, only the air feels fresher.'

Proceeding carefully they trailed their hands along the sides of the wall and a breeze was blowing up towards them. Ahead of them, a pile of rocks lay across their path, shinning his torch at the pile Fin could see that while the passageway was blocked the fall had revealed a parallel tunnel.

Stepping out into the new tunnel the atmosphere changed, the air was fresh and tunnel was brick lined.

'This is not as old as the secret passageways,' Fin said aloud, 'these are more like canal or railway tunnels, the air is too fresh and the dirt is not so thick.'

Jenny's hair flew wildly in the wind, 'It looks to me as if this tunnel was excavated without anyone knowing just a few feet away there was another passage. The collapse looks quite recent and it's exposed the secret way.'

'Even so, no one has been down here for years,' grumbled Fin, 'it's just another waste of time!'

'Don't you dare grumble, Fin Butler,' growled Jenny, 'this is new to us and the air is fresh, so quit moaning and walk!'

Muttering under his breath Fin began to walk down the tunnel, stopping suddenly Jenny bumped into him.

'What now?'

'There's an opening and listen I can hear water and an engine.'

The sound of water dripping was gradually drowned out by the noise of a slowly chugging diesel engine. Carefully they looked around the corner and Fin was blinded by a bright spot of light, still in the distance, but blazing in the dark.

'Let me see,' said Jenny moving Fin out of her way and allowing her hair to move in the tunnel, 'it's a narrowboat.'

'A what?'

'A narrowboat, a canal boat, this is a canal tunnel.'

In what seemed an age the light grew brighter and the

noise of an engine became deafening. Hiding back out of sight they watched a traditional narrowboat chug passed them and disappear off into the darkness.

'Well I'm not swimming out of here,' said Fin.

Changing direction, they returned the way they came and arrived at another opening. Just about to speak Fin was silenced by a noise so loud and approaching so fast that he fell back into Jenny. The pair of them tumbled to the floor as the ground shook and an express train roared passed them. Dumbstruck they lay in silence.

'So that way's out too!' said Jenny suddenly laughing, 'I don't mind getting wet but I certainly don't want to get run over by a train!'

'Well at least we know what these tunnels are here for,' said Fin helping Jenny up off the floor, 'servicing the canal and railway tunnels.'

Frustrated once again they headed back, reaching the top of the steps they stopped, in the distance they could hear voices. Quietly they crept along the corridor and looked through the spy holes. Inside the room was full; a sense of fear and loathing gripped the watching Fin and Jenny. Doubled over in cold and pain Fin had to concentrate to stand up and pay attention.

Sitting around the oak table dark figures whispered angrily with each other, Fin tried to see their hidden faces lost in the shadow of their hoods, but failed. An empty chair sat at the head of the table, every now and then, a hooded figure would look at it, and another explosion of whispers would begin.

The door burst open and a cloud of mist poured into the room, silence fell and a cloaked figure limped in and sat down. A glint of red eyes flickered from underneath the dark hood and a fist fell with a thump on the table, everyone jumped even the watching Fin and Jenny.

'The Council of Crows is in session,' a gravelly voice croaked, 'welcome councillors and of course Governors.'

As the meeting began, Fin began to feel colder, Jenny's

hair was standing on end and they both felt they were in the presence of pure evil. Without realising it, Fin put his arm around Jenny and held her to him, immediately they both began to feel warmer.

'Thank you,' whispered Jenny.

'To business then, why have you called a Council of Crows?'

The tone of the gravelly voice caused everyone to shiver except one figure in an ornate black cowl.

'I, Corneille and my colleague Corbeau are here because our Lords in France do not like what they are hearing,' said Corneille, 'they are most dissatisfied with your progress.'

'Since when does our French flock care about what happens here?' snapped the Crow.

'Since your experiment has proved a failure and your ineptitude to make progress embarrasses us all.'

'You dare to pass comment in my own nest?'

'My Lords insist upon it.'

'Then explain,' the menace in the Crow's voice grew palpable, 'what it is that has embarrassed you.'

'Certainly,' said a smug Corneille, 'your school here is a failure and has produced nothing good.'

'My Lord, I must object,' objected Raven, 'they insult you in your own nest, and their ignorance of our findings...'

'Silence, Raven,' snapped the voice, 'Do not let your enthusiasm for my cause make you a fool!'

'Lord!' snivelled Raven, 'I only care about your interests.'

'You cannot even handle the disappearance of a child, what was his name, Greg Matthews,' said Corneille, 'and now you are due an inspection from your so called authorities.' Pausing Corneille smiled, 'You have even attracted the attention of the Royals, and your oversight has been pitiful, what message do you wish me to take back to my Lords?'

'Only this,' whispered the Crow.

The Crow's eyes flashed red and Corneille flew up into the air crashed high into the wall, the hanging chains wrapped around him and began to crush him.

'You come into my nest and insult me,' cried the Crow, 'you show no respect to me or my flock, you will be my message.

Fin pulled Jenny away from the spy holes so they could not see, but the cries of pain ripped through their skulls, when it was too much to bare they suddenly stopped. The Crow's voice echoed around the chamber.

'Corbeau, do you have anything to say to me?'

'No my Lord,' responded a fearful Corbeau, 'I understand your message and I believe my Lords will too.'

'Good,' sneered the Crow, 'I have wasted enough of your valuable time and I have things to do.'

The chamber filled with the noise of people exiting and Fin and Jenny once again looked through the spy holes, the room was empty except for a body hanging from the wall chains. Stunned into silence by the sight of the discarded Corneille, Fin and Jenny escaped the passageways and returned to the others.

'The Crow Lord just killed him with a look?' asked an astonished Sed.

Unable to speak Fin and Jenny just nodded.

'Did you recognise anyone?'

Nodding again, Fin managed to respond, 'I think the one called Raven is Mr Chough.'

'Of course he is,' said Jenny regaining her voice, 'but he was scared stiff of this Crow Lord and I can see why.'

'It seems that this war of the birds that Jenny spoke about is real and we're stuck in the bloody middle!' swore Ash.

'Eloquently put dear,' laughed Eiry, 'but Ash is right this is Jenny's war.'

'Hey, don't blame me for it!'

'Sorry, poor choice of words,' apologised Eiry, 'but what do we really know?'

'Fount and Smith are Minotaurs,' began Fin, 'Jenny is a Gorgon, Ash and I am half Phoenix. I have no idea what talents they think Sed and Eiry might have but they must suspect you of something.'

'If Greg had powers he never told me,' said Ash.

'Maybe they tried to tame or convert him to their cause,' added Eiry.

'Well they obviously failed or he would be here still,' said Jenny.

'I think it's really important,' said Fin, 'the less they know about us the better.'

'Yeah,' said Sed, 'but it would help if we knew what our gifts are.'

'Everything comes back to those hidden records,' said Eiry.

'We need to get hold of them,' said Ash, 'because I for one want to know what they've got on me!'

'Then it looks like we are going to have to risk the log shed and go and have a look,' said Fin putting his arms around Jenny, 'we have just witnessed a murder and everyday we wait we risk something else awful happening to us.'

CHAPTER 9 – THE SECRET FILES

Tossing and turning in his bed Fin was lost in another nightmare. Awake and yet asleep he struggled to open the door to his room. Why was it locked again? Again, why again? Smoke filled the air and he began to struggle to breathe, falling to the floor he felt his consciousness begin to leave him. Why hasn't Jenny kicked the door open? Why would she? Reality crept like smoke into his mind, I'm in a nightmare. Fin's subconscious brain fought against the dream. Then he heard laughing and once he had heard it, the laughter echoed around inside his head.

'Clever boy,' a familiar voice chided him, 'you are beginning to remember, but you don't want to, so burn!'

Flames scorched Fin's body and he tried to scream but all that came out was silence. The chains that hung around his body grew tighter and began to cut into his skin.

'I know who you are!' Fin cried knowing and forgetting in an instant.

'Not yet little man but when you do remember it will change everything,' laughed the voice, 'but until then you will have to wait.'

'Fin wake up,' Ash shook Fin's sleeping body, 'come on it's just a dream.'

Suddenly wide, a wake Fin grabbed Ash's arm, 'I know who it is in the fire!'

'Who?'

Struggling to remember Fin started to mouth the name, then stopped and shook his head, 'It's gone.'

'Can you remember anything?' asked Ash.

'It was different this time, I knew I was dreaming and I saw her, but it's all gone now,' frustrated Fin got and up and fetched himself a drink of water.

'You said she,' said Ash.

'Did I?' replied Fin, 'I have no idea it's all disappeared.'

'It'll come back,' reasoned Ash, 'each time you dream you remember a bit more.'

'That's true,' conceded Fin, 'but the dreams are getting further apart, what if I stop dreaming, it's not as if I want to have these nightmares.'

'Maybe you should!'

'You're kidding they rip me apart.'

'I don't think they are just nightmares,' Ash paused and looked intently at Fin, 'I think they are memories, something so terrible that just don't want to remember.'

'That's what she said.'

'Who said?'

'The woman in my dream, she said I didn't want to remember,' struggling to drag the memories out Fin put his head into his hands, 'so she burnt and strangled me in chains like those in the secret chamber.'

'Fin, take a deep breath and relax, you are not going to remember anything by forcing it,' comforted Ash, 'but this is new, you had a little control of what happened in your dream and now you remember this girl.'

'Lady,' said Fin.

'Lady,' said Ash, 'how old was she?'

'I've no idea but it wasn't a girl, it was someone much older.'

After breakfast, they all met and Fin shared this new dream with the girls.

'I just can't retain the faces afterwards,' said Fin.

'But you are certain it was a woman who spoke to you.'

'Yes I think so,' agreed Fin, 'but it's all so vague and I have no idea who it could be.'

'I have an idea,' said Ash, 'but you are not going to like it, there is a way you could remember.'

'I can't turn my dreams on and off like at tap!' retorted Fin.

'There is a way,' continued Ash, 'get sent to the nightmare room.'

This suggestion animated everyone only Jenny sat in silence.

'What's up Jen?' asked Fin.

'Ash is right, the only way for you to remember is to get sent to the nightmare room and stay there until it all comes back.'

'Great idea Ash,' said Fin sarcastically, 'but I don't think so.'

The others tried to continue the conversation but Fin got up and walked out the room.

'I'll work on him,' said Jenny, 'but it may take a while!'

An hour or so later Fin returned but ignored any conversation that leaned towards his nightmares, in the end the others gave up and began planning how they might get back into the wood store.

A week later, a rumour started to spread among the students that there was going to be a royal visit, no one took any notice until strange workers started appearing and everywhere started to look cleaner and tidier. One crew started work renovating the wood store and Ash took the responsibility of watching over and befriending them.

'They're all locals,' Ash told the others after he had spent an hour chatting with the work crew, 'and they hate this place, they told me it gives them the creeps.'

'Is there any chance that they will find the entrance?' asked Sed.

'Nah,' replied Ash, 'the collapse was not as bad as we feared, they are going to jack up one corner and put in new steel supports and then make the rest safe. The old wall is so solid they have no need to do anything to it.'

'Did they say how long it would take?' continued Sed.

'They said something about it needing to be finished in the next two weeks,' said Ash, 'I guess then that the rumoured royal visit is real.'

'Then why haven't they told us?' asked Jenny.

'They had a royal visit in one of my previous homes,' said Eiry, 'and they didn't tell us until two days before.'

'We will know for sure when we get a visit by the police,' said Ash, 'locals first and then Special Branch.'

'We were even visited by Royal Protection,' said Eiry.

'Something else to look forward to,' moaned Ash.

As the week progressed, the wood store began to look finished and the work crew left. As a group, they decided to make sure that the entrance was accessible and were greatly relieved to see that it was.

'All we need now is the camera,' remarked Sed as they headed back.

Taking Fin to one side, Jenny tried to talk to him about the nightmare room, but Fin was adamant, 'Look Jenny, I know it's a good idea but that's all it is, there is no way I am going back to that room.'

'Why?' asked Jenny seeking to understand, 'We all hate our nightmares but if it was me I would do it.'

'It's not just a nightmare, it's a memory and I hate watching you get struck blind repeatedly,' said Fin his voice croaking with emotion, 'but now I know there's something worse to come. Something so horrible that I don't want to remember, or can't remember. I look at you and I can't think of anything that's worse than you losing your eyes!'

'Oh Fin you silly boy,' cried Jenny and wrapped her arms around him.

Without thinking, Fin put his arms around Jenny and for the first time since Christmas kissed her.

In the first week of May, the expected visit from the local police took place; accompanying the three uniformed officers was a familiar face, DI Jones.

'I thought I would join them,' said David after leaving the uniformed officers to join Fin and his friends, 'I wanted to see how you were all getting on.'

Feeling a sense of excitement that he could not explain Fin greeted David warmly, 'I'm so glad you are here!'

Patiently, David shook hands with each of them, saying their names as he did so. Leaving Sed to last David was more than a little surprised when she jumped into his arms and hugged him.

'I can't be doing with handshakes,' she said laughing at the startled look on David's face, 'and I know that you can't hug me! Where are your family from?'

A confused look crossed David's face, Sed's sudden question catching him by surprise, 'Cardiff,' he replied, 'my father was a sailor in the Royal Navy and my mother was from Kilindini Harbour.'

'The main port for Mombasa,' explained Sed to the others, 'That's where my grandmother's from.'

'That's right,' said David, 'it is Kenya's main international port.'

'How did they meet?'

'Sorry?'

'Your parents,' explained Sed.

'My father was stationed there with British Eastern Fleet during the war,' replied David, 'he met my mother when he was on leave and after the war went back and they got married, I was their only son.'

'Have you ever lived in Kenya?'

'No I was born and raised in Cardiff by my aunt,' said David sadly, 'my father died in a ferry accident just after I was born and my mama was heartbroken and just vanished.'

'So you are an orphan like us,' said Sed sympathisingly.

'That's true,' agreed David, 'that's why I am so interested in all of you.'

'Do you have any children?' asked Sed, then noticing a pained look cross David's face she continued, 'Sorry I was not meaning to pry, it's just that we meet so few people now that I've become really nosey.'

'It's okay,' said a slightly embarrassed David, 'I was once engaged to a lovely girl from Yorkshire and just before we were due to get married, we discovered that she was pregnant and we had a massive argument and she left me.'

'That's so sad,' whispered Sed, 'was it a boy or a girl?'

'I don't know,' said David, 'she disappeared and I have never been able to find her,' then noticing the sad mood that had descended, smiled, 'It was all a long time ago. Look, I'm going to have to join the others officers but it has been great to see you all, now you all be good and don't get into any trouble!'

Laughing he left them and headed back to Ravenswood House. Sadly, David was too busy to chat to them again but he did wave goodbye from the car when he drove off.

Fin was sitting reading by himself while the others were all upstairs when Elizabeth came in.

'Are you the only one in?' she asked. 'I would like to have a quick chat with you all.'

'No they are all in,' said Fin, 'do you want me to get them?'

'Yes please.'

Moving to the centre of the room Fin yelled up the stairs, 'GUYS, EVERYONE, DOWNSTAIRS NOW!'

'If I had wanted to shout I would have done it myself,' said Elizabeth laughing.

In moments, there was the sound of running feet the entire house gathered around Elizabeth.

'As you know, in the next few days IEISTED will be inspecting our facilities. That's got the Governors and staff running around like headless chickens but now we can tell you that immediately afterwards we will be having a royal visit.'

'Which royal will it be?' asked Eiry.

'His Royal Highness Price Hugo, the Duke of Karmania,' she replied.

'Never heard of him,' said Fin.

'Nor have any of us,' said Elizabeth, 'I am told that he is a second cousin, twice removed, of the Queen. Karmania is small part of the Commonwealth; it only has a population of three million, it is situated with Europe one side and the old Eastern Block on the other.'

'How come they are coming here?' asked Fin.

'The rumour among the local police is that the authorities needed to do something to keep him occupied and out of the Queen's hair, he has reputation of being haughty and arrogant.'

'So let me guess, we need to be on our best behaviour and keep the place tidy.'

'You've got it,' said Elizabeth, 'but that's not the only reason I am here.' Pulling open her large shoulder bag, she produced a bubble wrapped package, 'I intend to keep a promise, I am really pleased with how tidy everywhere is, so here is the Polaroid instant camera I agreed to get you.'

'Oh thank you,' cried Jenny as Eiry and Sed jumped up and hugged Elizabeth.

'Now remember,' Elizabeth warned as she handed over a few packets of Polaroid film, 'this is our secret.'

The day of the inspection arrived, Ravenswood now clear of maintenance workers looked in pristine order. To Fin's disappointment normal lessons took place while the Governors met with the Inspectors. Then through the morning, Inspectors sat at the back of lessons, watched, and wrote copious notes. Nervous teachers highlighted the quality of their students' work but the Inspectors neither acknowledgement or commented aloud on anything. Lessons occasionally became chaotic when teachers disappeared to be interviewed and came back seething with anger. At lunchtime, all of the IEISTED team sat together and whispered, quietly passing hand written notes to each other. The atmosphere around the school grew heavy as excitement and nervousness turned to fear and suspicion, Fin began to dread the prospect of his timetabled interview with an Inspector.

'Fin,' said the visitor, 'you don't mind if I call you Fin?' whether Fin minded or not she carried on in the same breath, 'I am Mrs Gillard, please sit down.'

'Thank you,' said Fin politely.

Sitting down Fin struggled to see who was talking, at first all he could see was a silhouette against the bright sunlight streaming through the window. Then as his eyes adjusted to the light Fin saw the strangest woman, he guessed she was in her fifties and she wore ugliest pair of glasses he had ever seen. Her clothes looked expensive but looked mismatched as if she had dressed herself with her eyes closed.

'As you know I am one of the school Inspectors and it is very important that you answer all my questions as honestly as you can,' she purred, 'I would like you to think you could talk to me as a friend.'

Mrs Gillard's voice was loud and overly sweet, Fin felt that she was talking down to him.

'How long have you been a student?' asked Mrs Gillard failing to disguise her lack of real interest.

'Since the end of last summer.'

A look of frustration passed over Mrs Gillard's face, picking up her notes she quickly skim read them and smiled as if remembering why she wanted to talk to Fin.

'Are you happy here?'

'Yes, mostly.'

'What would make you happier?' she asked smiling at Fin.

The smile unnerved Fin more than her tone, a sudden feeling of being trapped overwhelmed him and he wanted to leave.

'Nothing really, I just wish my parents were alive,' answered Fin trying to guess what she wanted to hear.

As Fin looked into Mrs Gillard's eyes, he thought he saw them pull into focus. Here it comes he thought.

'Did you know Greg Matthews?'

'No,' replied Fin, 'he had left before I arrived but I have heard of him as he used to share with my room mate.'

'Does Ash talk about him?'

'Not really,' said Fin.

'Why is that?'

'I don't know,' said Fin curious as to where they were going, 'I think you need to ask Ash that question.'

Mrs Gillard's eyes narrowed behind her grotesque glasses, 'Do you think he has anything to hide?'

'About Greg Matthews?' Fin asked puzzled.

'About anything!' snarled Mrs Gillard then realising that she might have sounded a little harsh, smiled, 'Sorry dear, about anything unusual.'

'No not really,'

'Are you sure,' she continued, 'After all they were roommates for quite a while,' and then with a knowing look stared at Fin, 'and we both know roommates share secrets with each other.'

Starting to dislike Mrs Gillard intently Fin continued, 'To the best of my knowledge Ash has no hidden secrets about Greg or anything else.'

'Are you certain,' asked Mrs Gillard in a sickly sweet tone, 'he is a very strange boy; he may have bullied and frightened Greg into leaving?'

'All I know is what Mr Chough told everyone when Greg left, that he had been moved to a new home to be near a distant aunt. Are you saying that something has happened to him?'

Mrs Gillard's face grew stern, 'I'm asking the questions Mr Butler!'

'Yes Mrs Gillard you are,' smiled Fin, 'but I'm not stupid, and I can tell from the focus of your questions that something has happened to Greg. What really confuses me is why are you asking these questions and not the police? I have spoken to the police on many occasions and when they have a question to ask they ask it. You are not the police, I don't know who you are but you are looking in the wrong direction.'

Shaking his head slowly Fin watched Mrs Gillard, starting at the base of her neck turn red slowly. 'It is clear to me now that something has happened to Greg, now I never knew him but I know he was liked and that he disappeared over night,' continued Fin, 'That begs the question, are all the rest of us here at risk of disappearing overnight and if so what are you going to do about it?'

'Thank you Mr Butler that will be all,' said Mrs Gillard, 'you may leave.'

'The stupid woman was trying to blame me for Greg's disappearance!' shouted and angry Ash, 'Well she can...'

'ASH,' screamed Eiry, Jenny and Sed at the same time, drowning out what he thought Mrs Gillard could do.

'She's clutching at straws and she tried to blame us too!' moaned Eiry, 'Well at least we all know he's missing and not vanished off to some aunt.'

'But why did Mr Chough tell us that pathetic story about him moving to be near his aunt?' asked Ash slowly regaining his composure.

'I can think of two reasons,' said Fin, 'Firstly, he was trying to prevent a panic among the students, because whoever took him removed him from his bed in your room while you were asleep. Or secondly, Mr Chough is the Raven and the Flock wanted Greg for their purposes.'

'It's more likely the latter,' said a subdued Eiry, 'if everyone thinks he vanished after he left Ravenswood they will be looking in all the wrong places.'

'That explains Mrs Gillard's questions,' muttered Sed to herself and then to everyone, 'there is no evidence to link Greg's disappearance with Ravenswood so the police are helpless.'

'Then it's a fishing expedition,' said Fin, 'the Inspectors are looking for anything suspicious, bullying, intimidation, abuse or even abduction. If they find so much as a whisper of impropriety then they will call the police in.'

'Then David wasn't just popping in to see us,' exclaimed Sed, 'he's watching over this place.'

'Or us,' said Fin, 'he's certainly looking for Greg.'

'We don't even know if Greg's alive,' said Jenny thoughtfully.

'But we can check,' said Fin, 'the time has come we have to get to those files.'

That night the sunset late and the twilight took an age to fade away. When finally it was dark Fin checked Elizabeth was in her room, a quick look through her window revealed that she was curled up with a glass of wine and book. Meanwhile Ash double-checked the route to the log shed was clear.

'Crap,' whispered Ash while signalling everyone to stop, outside the wood store half hidden in the shadows were Smith and Fount smoking.

'Smoking is forbidden at Ravenswood,' whispered an indignant Eiry.

'So is sneaking about at night,' countered Sed.

'Shhh!' growled Ash, 'they heard us.'

Smith and Fount dropped their cigarettes quickly and disappeared into the night. Frozen in the darkness they waited quietly but the only noise they could hear was an owl hooting in the distance.

The wood store was deserted and they crept to the far

wall, some of the logs had toppled over but their improvised entrance was still there.

As before, they entered the passageway and travelled towards the church. In silence, they climbed up the long slow hill until they reached the spiral staircase and the gentle climb to the rear of the secret door. Looking through the spy hole Fin could see that the room was in darkness. Opening the door carefully they all entered the cellar. Sed found the light switch and flicked it.

'Let's be organised about this,' said Sed taking control, 'we need to be as quick as possible. Jenny your hearing is better than anyone else you guard the door. Fin and Ash you get out the files and put them away. Eiry and I will photograph them, don't just stand their gawking, unless you have a better plan move!'

Pulling open the top draw of the filing cabinet marked Ravenswood Fin sorted through the files, 'I'm starting with ours,' he said, 'Don't try and read them now,' he said to Ash who was starting to flick through one, 'just pass them to Sed.'

Soon the room was full of the sound of the camera clicking. Frustrated that the first few were unreadable Eiry dragged the table under the light and the quality improved.

From the filing cabinet Fin called to Eiry, 'Put all the photographs into the tunnel now just in case we have to run.' The room was hive of activity but everything was going too slow for Fin's liking, 'What's the hold up?'

'It's not like scanning documents we're doing our best,' snapped Sed.

'Guys will you keep the noise down,' gestured Jenny, 'I can't hear anything other than you.'

'Sorry,' apologised Sed, 'I know it's all taking time and I have lost track of how many we have done.'

'Ash is bringing you the last of our files and I'm now looking for Greg's but I can't find it.'

Rummaging through the draws and wallets Fin grew more and more frustrated.

'Try one of the other filling cabinets,' suggested Sed, 'there are at least five others.'

'But none of them are marked Ravenswood,' groaned Fin, 'which one do I choose?'

'How are they labelled?' asked Sed.

'Three aren't marked at all and the other two are the Farm and The Factory.'

'It's a lottery just pick one!'

Just as Fin pulled open the top draw of the filing cabinet marked, the farm, Jenny signalled them all to be quiet. As the others watched Jenny's hair took on a life of its own and swirled around her head.

'Found it!' whispered Fin.

Ash grabbed the file and threw it to Eiry and they started to take photographs of it.

As quickly as they could they returned Greg's and their files back to the cabinets.

'Shhh,' whispered Jenny, 'I can hear someone creeping up on us.'

Waving his hands to Ash, Fin gestured that they had to put the table back against the wall. The sound of a key in the lock caused panic among them, the key turned and the door began to open. Using her body weight Jenny slowed the progress of the door opening, but it opened anyway and a tall figure entered the room.

Thinking quickly Jenny knocked the light switch to off but it was too late a firm hand knocked Jenny's hand away from the switch and the light came back on.

They all stood, trapped like a rabbits in a headlight and stared at the tall man that entered.

'Don't just stand there,' he said, 'get into the passage the guards are right behind me!'

Not understanding anything they all dived into the passage, the tall man turned the key in the lock and switched the light off. Flicking his torch on he jumped in and closed the door behind them. They all froze behind the door for no sooner had the door shut they heard the key turn in the lock and people come in.

'I told you that bloody vicar was getting too nosey,' said the woman, 'Alright vicar come out we know you are here!'

'Don't be stupid there's no one here,' said a man's voice, 'where could he hide?'

Behind the door, they all heard the crashing of furniture as a quick search was made of the room.

'I told you there's no one here,' said the man.

'Then explain this,' said the woman, 'why is this filing cabinet still partly open?'

'It can't be.'

'Look for yourself!'

'I closed it,' the man said, 'and these files are all in the wrong order.'

'What's that doing there,' snapped the woman, 'that's Greg Matthew's file that belongs in the farm stock?'

'Okay I agree someone's been down here, but whom? It's not the vicar,' reasoned the man, 'don't look at me like that, if it had really been the vicar he'd still be here.'

'Then how the hell has anyone got in here,' asked the woman, 'there's no way it was the church mice.'

'Be reasonable,' the man continued, 'unless there's a secret passage in this room that we haven't found, it's our poor filing.'

'I'm telling the Raven,' said the woman, 'I know this mess was not left by me.'

'It's your feathers,' cringed the man, 'if it was me I wouldn't tell him!'

Everyone stood motionless as the noise of filing cabinets being rearranged and the room being tidied filtered through into the passageway. After what seemed an age the light went out in the room, the door slammed shut, and the lock clicked.

Quietly they all moved off down the passageways and staircases and did not speak until they reached the five-way intersection.

'Who are you?' asked Fin.

'You know who he is,' said Jenny.

'Yeah, but I want to hear it from his own lips,' said Fin.

'You must recognise me,' said the Reverend George Oak, 'I certainly remember you coming to church at Christmas with Elizabeth.'

'What were you doing in the cellar and how do you know about the secret passages?' asked Fin slightly more aggressively than he intended.

'I have been unhappy for a while with the use of the cellars for restricted data storage,' said the Vicar, 'but they paid well for the use of the room and the old crypts.'

'Why the crypts?' asked a puzzled Fin.

'They wanted somewhere relatively dry and damp free to keep their records; they said they didn't trust computers as they are too easily hacked!' The Vicar continued, 'I have been trying to get down here and see what they are up to for a while, but their agreement was for the exclusive use of the space, so they kept stopping me.' the Vicar laughed, 'I thought I'd managed to sneak past them but they obviously heard or saw me. As to the passages, I have known about this one for years, my father was Vicar here when I was a child and I had a friend at Ravenswood before it was a home and we used them all the time. Not that my father knew he would have gone ballistic if he had found out. The secret passage was my way out if I needed to make a quick disappearing act,' the Vicar laughed again, 'imagine my surprise in seeing the passage door open and you standing there!'

'What now?' asked Fin, 'How are you getting home?'

'There is a lake down this passage; above it hidden near the roof is a tunnel to my old vicarage.' the Vicar grew serious, 'If I'm right there's going to be a knock on my door and I will have to attend a pastoral emergency. I suggest you get back before there's any trouble.'

'Could you do us a favour please Vicar?' asked Sed as the vicar was about to leave.

'If I can.'

'Will you contact Detective Inspector David Jones and tell him there are files down here about Greg Matthews,' begged Sed, 'we can't do it but you can.'

'I know David,' said the Vicar nodding his head, 'which file was it in?'

'The one marked the farm,' replied Sed, 'but that's all we know at the moment.'

'If I can I will,' said the Vicar reassuringly, 'but hurry I think there is going to be uproar as soon as the Raven hears of tonight's antics.'

With that, the vicar ran off into the dark. The journey back was uneventful; the wood store exit was clear, as was the trip across the gardens. However, the second they entered their living area all the fire alarms went off, moment's later Elizabeth ran in.

'Oh good you are all ready,' she said breathlessly, 'this is not a drill; move quickly and safely to the meeting point.'

Within moments, all the staff and students gathered in the main courtyard, in the distance the sound of a fire engine drew closer.

'This is not a practice,' declared Mr Chough, 'there will be a full roll call and then you will all wait here until the fire crew give the all clear to return to your dwellings.'

The fire tender arrived and the crew disembarked and began to check all the dwellings. Fifteen minutes later everywhere had been checked and the fire officer reported to Mr Chough that they could all return to their accommodation. It was only as the officer removed her helmet that Fin recognised her as the woman from the data store under the church.

'Stop staring,' growled Jenny, 'I can see her without gawking like you are.'

'What was all that about?' asked Fin.

'Oh come on Fin, think,' said Jenny, 'it's what the vicar warned us about, they are checking everyone to see if anyone is missing.'

'The photographs,' asked Fin.

'They are in the lining of my jacket,' comforted Jenny, 'I figured they wouldn't search a blind girl for photographs.'

Across the courtyard Mr Chough spoke out, 'I have been given the all clear from the fire officer it appears that it was a false alarm triggered by the central control box. You may now return to your rooms, breakfast will be served two hours later than usual and there will be no lessons until first session after lunch.'

Exhausted Fin led the rest back to their accommodation where they all crawled up to their beds too tired to stay up and chat. On her way back to her bed, Elizabeth popped in to check that they were all okay, the downstairs was deserted and the sound of multiple people snoring echoed down the stairs, smiling she left and shut the door quietly behind her.

CHAPTER 10 – SPECIAL BRANCH

Struggling to keep awake over his lunch Fin propped his chin on his hand, looked out the window, and watched a black, sleek Range Rover glide into the courtyard. Tucked away under the bonnet he noticed that it had dark blue lights, an unmarked police car he thought and three men in suits climbed out followed swiftly by the familiar imposing figure of David. Eiry was right, these were no ordinary officers; it has to be Special Branch, he thought, but why is David with them?

As Fin watched, David gave instruction to one of the suited officers; Fin was convinced that the officer nodded his head and replied, 'Yes Sir.' Suddenly paying attention Fin's chin slipped off his hand and as Jenny laughed at him, he told her what he had just seen. Having finished their lunch, they left the table and headed outside only to find David, now on his own, waiting for them.

'Thank you I got your message from the vicar,' he began and then noticing Smith and Fount walking past and showing interest continued, 'Butler isn't it? I hope that you are keeping out of trouble and that false alarm last night wasn't your doing.'

'No Sir, I was in bed and so deeply asleep when the alarm went off that Ash had to shake me awake.'

'Good, good, it wouldn't do to scare the authorities before the royal visit.'

Smith and Fount having heard everything sniggered as they left.

'Sorry guys,' he apologised, 'I just don't trust those two.'

'Well they are Minotaurs,' laughed Sed, 'what do you expect?'

'Really, Minotaurs, that's an interesting way of describing them,' remarked David, 'why do you say that?'

Ignoring the looks of horror from the others Sed looked at David and challenged him, 'Just because we are young please don't treat us like fools. We know that you are more than an ordinary copper, we heard the Special Branch officers calling you Sir. You know dam well that something weird is going on here and I'm pretty certain you and the vicar know more than you are letting on.'

A smile spread across David's face, 'We need to talk but we can't do that here,' he paused, 'I have an idea but you won't like it!'

Before anyone could respond, David walked off towards the Special Branch officers and began to talk to them. The officers stayed around for most of the day and at one point had a heated discussion with Mr Chough, from his angry demeanour he obviously had to concede to whatever their demand was. Elizabeth kept popping in an out of their accommodation so it was impossible to study the photographs. Frustrated Ash starting arguing with everyone until Sed threatened to hold him to the wall by his neck if he said another word. Taking one look at Sed's face Ash decided discretion was the better choice and went to his room.

An hour later an anxious Elizabeth popped in again and told them that Mr Chough wanted to see them immediately. Trouping over to the main house, they quickly arrived at his office, knocked and were immediately shown in. An unhappy Mr Chough sat behind his desk and in the armchairs were the three Special Branch officers.

'Thank you for coming so promptly,' said Mr Chough his face displaying more displeasure than gratitude, 'please sit down.' Then looking across at the officers said, 'They are all yours.'

'Excellent, Mr Chough,' replied one of the officers and then to the group, 'after much thought we decided to pick a house at random and interview the students in some depth. We have chosen your house; however, due to the security nature of the upcoming royal visit, we thought it best to interview you off site. Although, I must inform you that Mr Chough is not happy at all about this but has graciously agreed you may join us and we will return you to the school tomorrow.'

Not knowing what to say Fin sat in silence, aware that Mr Chough was seething with anger but powerless to stop them going.

'In order for Mr Chough to agree to our demands we have had to concede that a member of the school staff joins us too, Mr Chough is too busy so he has indicated that,' lifting up his notes he read aloud, 'a Miss Elizabeth Gosling, your houseparent I believe, would be acceptable.'

Fin looked at Mr Chough and realised that none of this was acceptable but that he could not refuse without questions being asked.

'Please pack a bag for the evening and meet us in the main entrance in ten minutes,' standing up he turned to Mr Chough, 'we are finished here; we will be in touch in due course with our requirements.'

Not knowing whether to go or stay the five young people sat there until Mr Chough indicated with a nod of his head that they should go. Ten minutes later with bags in hand, a fleet of black Range Rovers arrived and whisked them away.

An hour and a half later, they arrived at the outskirts of a city where the traffic was stationary. Out of nowhere, four police motorcycles joined them and the Range Rovers put their flashing blue emergency lights and sirens on and hurtled through the traffic. In the centre of the city they arrived at a five-star hotel and stopped, officers in suits met the cars and led them all up to the biggest suite of hotels rooms Fin had ever seen. Fin and Ash, Eiry and Sed had rooms with two king-size beds in them and Jenny had the same all for herself.

Once they had all used the facilities, washed and unpacked their tiny bags they invited into a private lounge. Opening the door they entered and there laughing and chatting with each other were David and the vicar.

'Where is Elizabeth?' asked Fin, worried that he had not seen her since their arrival.

'She's fine,' said David, 'she's having a shower and will be joining us later, she is under the impression we are meeting in an hour or so.'

'Does she know about you two?' continued Fin.

'Not fully,' said the Vicar, 'I've known Elizabeth for a while but David she has only met recently.'

'Did you get home in time vicar?' asked a concerned Sed, 'The fire alarm went off and the grounds were searched.'

'As expected I was called out immediately to an old lady who was dying,' said the Vicar, 'strangely enough she had a miraculous recovery by the morning!' The Vicar smiled, 'You can't keep calling me Vicar and Mr Oak is too formal, my name is George.'

'Did you arrange all this?' asked Fin looking around the room and addressing David.

'As Sed commented earlier, I am no ordinary copper; I head up a Special Investigation Unit of North Wales Special Branch.'

'How come you are operating in Yorkshire,' asked Sed, 'that's a long way from North Wales?'

'Originally my task force was gathered together from the four Welsh police forces but now it incorporates Special Branch officers from across Britain.'

'Why are you watching Ravenswood and us,' continued Sed, 'it's no accident is it?'

'No,' replied David, 'but nor is it easy to say why or what our suspicions are, we know some of the story but not all. What detail we do know comes mainly from George.'

'It has been hidden from the majority of the population but we have known for a number of years that there are specially gifted people in the world. We believe Ravenswood is used as a place to discover, train and in some cases pervert, those gifted individuals to serve a faction called The Flock.' George's voice drifted into lecture mode but no one complained, 'We have discovered at least three factions, The Birds, Mythical Creatures and some other controlling group that everyone is too scared or afraid to mention.'

'The Royals,' murmured Sed.

'Sorry I did not catch that,' queried George.

'Just talking to myself,' laughed Sed, 'so when did you first discover there was a parallel history?'

'It started from a simple bible study on birds; I saw a pattern forming that began in 1 Kings where Elijah is supplied with food by Ravens, in Psalm 147 that God provides for the young Ravens by name when they call. But what began to disturb me most was Proverbs 30 where we find Ravens appearing and dealing out eternal judgement by killing and pecking out the eyes of their victims,' seeing the look of shock on their faces continued, 'gruesome I know but we believe it is still happening today. In the gospel of Luke, in the New Testament, Jesus tells his disciples to consider the Ravens, birds that do nothing to help themselves but God feeds them anyway, Jesus tells his disciples how much more valuable they are than the birds!'

'The matches much of what I have heard,' said Jenny still be cautious to what she was admitting to.

'Since that simple start I have studied and delved into

history and found echoes everywhere, one reference was in an old unattributed Scottish poem,' closing his eyes George began to recite,

'I heard the child with smoke in its mouth,
I heard the chough on the top of its nest,
I heard the ravens in the thicket beyond,
And I heard the squeal of the bird in a snare.
I saw the bird frighten the crows away,
I saw the blind girl see in the dark,
I saw the trees walk like a man,
And I foresaw that the year would not
Go well with me.'

Opening his eyes George blinked, 'I believe that there is a war coming that is going to affect us all,' George's tone grew troubled, 'I am worried that time is now and that it is not going to go well for any of us.'

'That's where I come in, George and I were at university together and he shared his research with me,' said David, 'What George didn't know was that in my family tree there is a rumour of a mythical element, it appears every generation or so although I've been kept ignorant of what that is.'

The room fell quiet as they listened, outside the traffic muted by the expensive double-glazing, seemed worlds away.

'George knew I was involved with certain clandestine aspects of anti-terrorism.'

'And I can tell you that David took some convincing to believe that a war was coming,' said George, 'but the evidence is there, hidden in plain sight, everyone sees it but ignores it, once you do see it you can't ever ignore it again.'

'Like one of those images optical illusions,' suggested Eiry, 'you know, like the one that could be a candlestick or the silhouette of two faces in front of each other.'

Smiling at the illustration David paused, 'George is right, it is hidden in plain sight but they have also worked hard to eliminate any obvious physical evidence. It is the ultimate conspiracy theory you can say there it is and all can see it, but hard evidence is difficult to find. In essence, that is our problem, how do you defend against a threat that has been hidden and expunged from history and is yet real, immanent and dangerous? Therefore, we watch, wait and follow every lead no matter how juvenile or silly. It was following one such lead about an arsonist, a potential phoenix, that we were led to Fin and then you. We still have no idea if any of you are specially gifted or not, but in watching you we have become certain that many at Ravenswood are.'

'David says that you called two of the students, Minotaurs,' said George, 'it might have been a figure of speech, but I doubt it. We are certain that Mr Chough is not just a simple principle of a school,' added George, 'but a raving lunatic.'

To everyone's surprise Ash burst out laughing, when everyone looked at him he shared his joke, 'He's a Raven lunatic!'

Ash's terrible joke earned him a pained look and a punch in the arm from Eiry. Then everyone laughed, the pun had been bad but it lightened the general atmosphere and everyone relaxed a little.

'Does your investigation have anything to do with Greg Matthews?' asked Ash.

'It didn't at first,' explained David, 'but that's all changed, it seems that while much of his family tree is a mystery…'

'It is my belief,' interrupted George, 'that Greg is a variety of Dryad. His family has always lived near or in forests and woods, technically his surname is Meliai but in the nineteen hundreds, the family changed it to Matthews. By tradition, the Meliai were the Dryads of the Ash trees and I find it slightly ironic that Greg befriended Ash. Dryads live for a very long time and they are vital to the ecosystem of the planet, they are the guardian of the trees. We think the birds wanted him because Dryads are immensely strong and supposedly can make trees walk.' George laughed, 'Greg may have none of those powers and I may have been reading too much mythology for my own good.'

'But he is still missing,' said David, 'and we want to find him,' taking a deep breath David continued, 'alive!'

'Do you believe he is still alive?' asked Ash, 'He and I were good friends and I miss him, but I can't help feeling that something really bad has happened to him.'

'To be honest,' said David reluctantly, 'we have no idea, but until we find him we are going to work on the premise that he is alive.'

'Did you find any clues in the cellars?' responded Ash. 'There were so many files there, we, I hoped it would lead you to him.'

'I'm sorry we found nothing,' replied David, 'all the filing cabinets you and George mentioned are gone and the place was swept clean. We even found the entrance to the corridor of rooms you examined through the spy holes; each was set up for human or animal experimentation but was clinically wiped clean. The crime scene investigators found nothing, no fingerprints, epithelial cells, hair or DNA. I have never seen such a professional clean up, it must have cost a fortune to have been done so quickly, I wouldn't like to be one blamed for that!'

'That's really disappointing,' understated Fin, 'we all saw the files but didn't have time to read them,' aware that this was only a partial truth he looked at the others. Jenny nodded her head in slight agreement and Fin realised that the group wanted to trust David and George but did not feel able to yet.

'Do you remember anything at all?' asked a frustrated David.

'I flicked through Greg's file,' admitted Eiry trying to be helpful, 'it mentioned that he was being moved to a place called the farm, but it did not say anything about what or where that farm is.'

'Thank you,' replied a grateful David, 'that may be little to you but it does gives us somewhere to start.'

'It all happened in a rush,' said Eiry waving her arms around, 'George was there too, and we had no time to give anything other than a quick glance.'

'If I'd know they were going to clean it all out,' snarled Ash, 'I would have stolen the bloody lot!'

Looking up at the clock on the wall David double-checked the time against his watch, 'Elizabeth is due in any minute, what do we do?' Noticing the confused look on the young people's faces he continued, 'We think we should try to see if we can get Elizabeth to work with us, but we don't know if we can trust her, what do you all think?'

'I think you can trust her,' said Ash.

'I'm not sure,' said Jenny, 'she is very kind and I love her to bits but I don't know, so I am going to be safe and say, no.'

'She has always been good to us,' indicated Eiry, 'so I say yes.'

Nodding her head Sed agreed, 'Definitely a yes.'

'I'm not sure either,' said Fin, 'but it doesn't matter what I think as I am already outnumbered. But I trust Ash and the rest's judgement so I would have said, yes too.'

'So be it,' said George, 'but please let us do the talking, we certainly do not want to implicate any of you in anything or put you at risk.'

While everyone waited for Elizabeth to arrive David went to the hotel fridge and extracted sodas for everybody. The conversation moved away from Ravenswood and turned to football and a gentle argument began about which football team was the greatest. When Elizabeth entered, she relaxed immediately both by seeing George whom she knew and everyone laughing. George walked across the room and gave Elizabeth a big hug while David passed her a coffee and invited her to sit down.

The jovial atmosphere continued as George introduced David formally to Elizabeth. 'We've met,' she said, 'but only in passing but it is a pleasure to be introduced. I was expecting to sit in on an interview between Special Branch and these young people, is that still going to happen or do you have another agenda?'

'Yes and no,' replied David, 'Yes they will be interviewed by Special Branch, but in this case that means me, and no as George is not a member of Special Branch.'

'Why is George here?' asked Elizabeth.

'May I?' requested George looking at David, when David nodded his head he continued, 'In many respects this meeting was about seeing you and not just our young friends here.' Noticing the puzzled look cross Elizabeth's face, 'Something unusual, you might even say ominous, is occurring at Ravenswood House, it has caught Special Branches' attention hence the reason they have facilitated this meeting.'

'I'm not sure I understand what you mean.'

'How long have you been involved with Ravenswood?' queried David.

'I have been on the staff for just over four years, but have been involved with it and its predecessor all my life, my mother's brother is Mr Byrd,' a slightly embarrassed look crossed her face, 'to be honest that's how I got the job in the first place.'

'You're Birdie's niece,' exclaimed Fin, 'you look nothing like him!'

A smile crossed Elizabeth's face, 'He looks like my grandfather and his nickname was Birdie too.' Dropping the smile she turned towards David and George, 'Let's stop beating around the bush, what do you want?'

'In brief, we believe that Ravenswood is being used as a facility to discover, train and groom its students to serve a terrorist faction called The Flock,' explained David.

'Go on,' said a slightly shocked Elizabeth.

'The Flock is part of underground movement that

infiltrates society to the highest level, once there it uses corruption, blackmail, intimidation and violence to get what it wants.'

'And how does this affect me,' asked Elizabeth, 'or more importantly these young people?'

'We have known for a number of years that there are supernatural, no that's wrong word, extranatural people living among us. These extraordinary beings are broken down roughly into three factions, The Birds, Mythical Creatures and a controlling group that everyone is too scared or afraid to mention.'

'And you think I am part of it?' asked Elizabeth.

'Yes and no,' said David, 'Yes we do believe that you, Elizabeth Gosling, are one of The Birds, but no we do not believe that you are a member of The Flock, although you seem to be intimidated or scared of them.'

Outside the window the sky darkened and it began to rain heavily, pigeons huddled up on the window ledge in an attempt to seek shelter, thunder crashed but failed to make an audible impact through the double glazing. Glancing up Fin subconsciously noticed the flash of lightening but was lost deep in thought considering all that he was hearing.

'We particularly believe that a militant section of The Birds, known as The Flock, uses Ravenswood to identify specially gifted young people out of its broken, troubled and abused students,' said a disturbed David, 'and groom or eliminate students like…'

'Greg Matthews,' interrupted Elizabeth, 'I have never been satisfied with the explanations that Mr Chough has given me about his disappearance,' Staring at David she continued, 'but who could I tell, my concerns are grounded in mystery and the truth sounds too unbelievable?'

'We believe you,' said George, 'and we are trying to do something about it.'

Sitting silently, Elizabeth nodded her head and a look

of relief crossed her face.

'Have you heard of the Farm?' asked George taking advantage Of Elizabeth's honesty.

'Yes I have,' replied Elizabeth, 'but only in passing. I once overheard Mr Chough trying to reason with my uncle,' she paused, 'Mr Chough hates my uncle and would like to get rid of him if he could, but I believe that one of the Governors served with him in the army and my uncle saved his life on more than one occasion, so his position is protected.'

'Do you know which governor?' asked David.

'No, my uncle said it had something to do with the Special Forces they both served in; when I showed interest and asked questions he said he couldn't tell me anything because it was tied up in the Official Secrets Act.'

Pausing for a moment David considered what Elizabeth had just said, 'Special Forces, do you know which branch?'

'My uncle keeps a sandy coloured beret which he gets out on Remembrance Day,' she thought for a moment, 'the badge has a sword between a pair of wings, or it could be flames and there's some writing too.'

'Who Dares Wins,' said George.

'Yes that's right,' agreed Elizabeth.

'The emblem of the SAS,' said David, 'if Mr Chough was a member of the SAS then I might be able to discover more about him,' he paused, 'or not, Hereford are not always as helpful as they could be. Sorry we digress, you were talking about the Farm?'

'My uncle was confronting Mr Chough about sending students to the Farm on placement. It is not safe, he said, but Mr Chough told him to mind his own business and stick to teaching. He even threatened my uncle with the sack but they both knew that was never going to happen.'

'Did they give any clues as to where the Farm might be?' David asked.

'They never gave any indication of where it was but I

got the impression from the way they were talking about it that it was near Ravenswood.'

'Do you know why your uncle did not like student placements at the farm?' asked George jumping in to the conversation.

'Sorry, I thought I said that already,' said Elizabeth, 'my uncle was so concerned because none of the students that went to the Farm ever returned to Ravenswood!'

'None,' said David, 'that's very unusual.'

'That's what my uncle said but Mr Chough accused him of being jealous of their success and assured him that all the students went on to greater and better things.' Elizabeth took a breath, 'I think they heard me coming so they changed the topic of conversation, but I could tell that neither of them was happy about me overhearing their conversation. So I pretended that I had been lost in thought and acted surprised to see them.'

'Elizabeth,' asked David, 'I want you to think carefully, is there anything more you want to tell us about what is going on at Ravenswood?'

'Not really,' she replied, 'I obviously don't trust Mr Chough but other than that and the apparent disappearance of Greg Matthews, no.'

'Are you one of The Birds?' asked George.

Elizabeth took a deep breath, 'Yes, but I am not part of The Flock.'

'Are there others like you at Ravenswood among the staff?'

'Birds, yes,' said Elizabeth, 'we tend to keep together for mutual support, but all we want to do is coexist in peace, we love working with the young people. Which leads to me to ask why these young people are here?'

'We believe that Greg Matthews was a Dryad,' said David, 'and we consider that Ravenswood has more than its fair share of extranatural students,' pausing he looked around the room, 'let's face it even one or more of these young people may have special talents.'

An uncomfortable silence settled on the room as David, George and Elizabeth looked at the young people.

'Okay, I'm going to come out,' stretching out a hand Ash said, 'I am the son of the Phoenix.' From nowhere, flames erupted out of his hand, turning his palm up a bright ball of flame just floated there.

'Ash,' said Eiry, 'what are you doing?'

'Oh come on Eiry,' began Ash.

'You will set the fire alarm off!' she shouted!

'Sorry,' apologised Ash and the flames went out. Turning to face everyone he reasoned, 'I am sure Elizabeth has known about my talent for a while and David and George needed to see this, to know that their nightmares are true.'

'Amazing,' exclaimed George.

Looking around at the adults Ash continued, 'But you need to know I will never serve The Flock,' and then he gave a warning, 'and I will use all my powers to see my friend Greg again.'

'Do any of the rest of you have,' Elizabeth looked at David and then the rest, 'extranatural powers?'

Out of the adults line of sight Ash gently shook his head, Fin instantly understood what Ash wanted them to say. 'No Elizabeth,' he said, 'not that we know of,' then he laughed, 'but it would be fun!'

'I wish we did,' said Jenny, 'I would love to have a gift that compensated for being blind.'

Noticing Elizabeth's eyes fill with water, Fin walked around and sat next to Jenny, 'That's why you have friends,' he said giving Jenny a big hug.

'I'm just an ordinary girl,' complained Sed.

'So am I,' said Eiry, 'but having Ash around makes us feel special.'

As all the adults eyes were on the girls, Fin looked at Ash in time to see him grimace and they shared a smile. When it came to telling a story and gaining sympathy, the three girls were in a league of their own.

of you are ordinary,' said Elizabeth, 'you are all ...ary to me.'

behind Elizabeth's back Ash pretended to be sick and Eiry slapped him, 'That's kind of you, we love you too,' she said glaring at Ash.

George and David watched them all get excited but managed to stay out of the inevitable group hug. Looking at his watch George spoke to David and he nodded in agreement.

'I am sorry to break up the fun, but George has to go to another meeting while he is here in town,' interrupted David, 'I have to ask, Elizabeth will you help us?'

'In any way I can,' replied Elizabeth, 'I assume you want me to let you know what's going on at Ravenswood and let you know if anything unusual happens.'

'Perfect,' said David, 'and if you hear any news of Greg...'

'Of course,' she said, 'that goes without saying.'

'Elizabeth, I would prefer it if nobody knew I was a Phoenix,' explained Ash, 'what with the royal visit and Greg vanishing, I don't want to be next!'

The conversation now over, George left for his other meeting; everyone else met in the dinning room of the hotel suite and had an extravagant meal. Once everyone had eaten, they retired to the meeting lounge. Fin instigated a loud and violent game of cards, while Elizabeth read the newspaper.

Slipping out David disappeared for an hour or two until he returned accompanied by George, 'Have any of you been watching the news?'

Sitting up Fin realised that the hotel had television screens and he had not thought of watching anything, 'Why,' he asked, 'has something happened?'

Picking up a television remote, David turned on the twenty-four hour news station and they all sat down to watch. Cycling round and around again was the story of the murder of a couple whose bodies had been stabbed, crushed and their eyes pecked out. The scenes too graphic to show sounded horrific, it was only when the photographs of the brother and sister, John and Susan Martin, were shown that they recognised them.

'That's the fire officer who attended the false alarm at Ravenswood the other night,' said Elizabeth, 'I remember her because she spoke to me.'

'We believe this couple used to work for The Flock,' said David, 'but it looks like they displeased someone.'

Watching Elizabeth Fin saw her face loose colour as the realisation settled in, 'I recognise they as they have visited Ravenswood before as guests of Mr Chough but this time their uniforms fooled me. This is not good news as it means The Flock are on the move again. How on earth am I supposed to pass messages on to George if we are being watched?'

'Write me a note and put it into your collection envelope when you visit the church,' said George, 'mark it special collection and I will fish it out.'

'That will work,' said a relieved Elizabeth, 'I do go once or twice a month so no one should notice.'

The news of the Martin's murder disturbed them all and they retired to bed.

After breakfast, the following morning they all met up with David and George again for one last chat before the black range Rovers took them back to Ravenswood.

'David,' began Elizabeth, 'when I was drifting off to sleep last night I remembered something.'

Turing to Elizabeth David gave her his full attention.

'Do you know why His Royal Highness Price Hugo, the Duke of Karmania, is visiting Ravenswood?'

'Only what I have been told,' he replied interested in what Elizabeth was going to say, 'that a distant cousin of the Queen needed to be entertained and that he asked to visit Ravenswood.'

'You don't think that's strange?'

'I do, but I served in Royal Protection for a while and I quickly gave up thinking anything was strange when it had to do with royalty. Why do you ask?'

'You said last night that there are three factions...'

'I did, The Birds, Mythical Creatures and a controlling group that everyone is too scared or afraid to mention.'

'I know the name of the controlling group,' stated Elizabeth, 'and you are not going to like it!'

'I haven't liked any of this so far,' said George, 'I can't imagine how it can get much worse by knowing their name.'

'The Royals,' said Elizabeth simply, 'and you are about to bring one under your protection to Ravenswood.'

CHAPTER 11 – THE HOOK NOSED PRINCE

Mr Chough seemed a little disappointed that his announcement of the imminent visit of His Royal Highness Prince Hugo, to Ravenswood received little more than a murmur. However Fin, was not at all surprised, the fuss of the last few weeks had destroyed any anticipation he and the others had been feeling. Fin was also struggling to digest Elizabeth's news that Prince Hugo was not just a relative of the Queen but also a member of the Royal faction. Lost in a dream world he chewed over the implications and only stirred when Mr Chough announced that he had cancelled the rest of the day's lessons.

Rushing back to the lodge, everywhere he looked ancillary staff, teachers and press-ganged students cleaned and polished, even the gardeners seemed to have woken from their summer stupor.

On arriving back Fin discovered the others waiting, 'Things are getting out of hand,' said Jenny, 'I think I trust David and George and I want to trust Elizabeth but for the moment I don't think we can.'

'I agree,' said Ash, 'with a Royal coming here we can't trust anyone or anything until we know where we stand.'

'That means going through the photographs,' suggested Jenny.

'On top of that,' said Ash, 'we need to put the photographs somewhere so safe that they can't find them.'

'Agreed,' added Eiry, 'but somehow we will need to make working copies of them.'

'How?' groaned Sed, 'it's not as if we can photocopy them and if we tried to copy the information by hand it would take days.'

'Why can't we photocopy them?' asked Eiry.

'There's no way we can get to the village and do it,' said Fin, 'they would recognise us in a second, that's if we managed to get out of the well and get past the farm they are rebuilding.'

'Why don't we just use the library photocopier?' suggested Eiry smirking.

'Because this bloody place doesn't have one,' shouted Ash, 'we're lucky to be allowed a ballpoint pen and pencil!'

'Yes it does,' said Eiry, 'remember when we found the secret panel in the library and Dr Swan helped us find the books we needed for our project, when I signed the books out, he left the door open to his back office and there was an old photocopier there.'

'So do we read them first or do we risk trying to copy them?' asked Fin.

'I vote for reading them,' said Ash, 'if we are caught copying them and we will lose them and still be in the dark!'

'It's a no-brainer,' exclaimed Sed, 'we went to a lot of trouble to find and get them; it would be foolish to risk everything without reading them first.'

Sitting around the lounge, they waited for the light to fade following the sunset. Birds sang evening songs in the trees and the fading light turned everything a shade of pink.

'What time is it?' asked Ash.

'Five minutes after you last asked,' replied Eiry, 'and if you ask again I will plant you headfirst into the garden and the staff can polish your feet in the morning.'

'A rough translation,' said Fin, 'and I'm paraphrasing here would be, Ash shut up you are starting to annoy me!'

Outside the light faded irritatingly slowly, but they all knew that they had to wait for everyone to go to bed; they could not risk anyone visiting.

Finally, the light faded and they asked Jenny to get the photographs.

'I can see Elizabeth heading this way,' whispered Sed.

They all ducked and picked up books and Fin began to read to Jenny. There was a knock on the door and Elizabeth popped her head in.

'I just wanted to check that you are all okay before we endure tomorrow's royal visit.'

'We're fine Elizabeth,' yawned Jenny, 'but we plan on hiding, the last thing we want to do is to attract the attention of a Royal!'

'That's what I was thinking too,' Elizabeth agreed, 'sadly I think Mr Chough might have other ideas. Anyway I'm off to bed, see you tomorrow.'

Elizabeth closed the door quietly behind her as she left, Ash ran to the window and watched her disappear, 'No it's okay; she's gone around the side to her rooms,' he said while clicking the snip on the door and closing the blinds, 'But better safe than sorry.'

Running upstairs Jenny collected the photographs; Eiry went to the kitchen and returned with a carton of apple juice and five glasses while Ash double-checked that all the blinds were closed. After turning off any unnecessary lights, Sed sat down as Jenny returned with the photographs.

'I have an idea,' said Ash, and ran up to his room returning with a magnifying glass.

'I've got one too,' said Eiry, 'and so have you Sed; I will get them both.'

'Can't we just look at the photographs?' complained Sed and then watching Fin stand up and then sit down again she groaned, 'you've got one too, well go and get it, don't just sit there, move!'

A sheepish Fin eventually returned with his magnifying glass, 'It was at the bottom of my stuff,' pulling a face he exclaimed, 'well I've never needed it before.'

'Finally,' said Sed picking up one of the photographs and looking at it, pausing for a moment she smiled at Eiry and picked up the magnifying glass.

Silence descended on the room and Fin smiled to himself as he watched them all examine the pictures. Sed was concentrating so hard her tongue was out, Eiry lay back on the sofa staring up at a picture, Ash lay on the floor resting his chin in his hands and Jenny sat in the darkest part of the room letting her hair fall over the image.

The clock ticked to itself as the evening drifted into morning as each person examined a photograph and then swapped it for another on the pile. Eventually, they had read them all and with bleary eyes looked at each other.

'Even with a magnifying glass it's hard to read,' said Fin rubbing his eyes.

'Greg's file has been redacted and it's full of blacked out lines,' said Ash, 'I was hoping for so much more.'

'It's not all been struck off,' said Fin, 'it does include a section on his friendship with you.'

'I know,' responded Ash, 'but it's all a bit vague, it appears that David and George were right in thinking the Flock had discovered that Greg was a Dryad, but after that all I can make out is that he was transferred to the Farm.'

'I struggled to make out anything after that,' said Eiry, 'it looks like there was an address written there but it has been obliterated by a marker pen.'

'Is it my peculiar vision,' asked Jenny, 'but I thought I could make out the bottom half of a postcode.'

Excitement reverberated around the room as Ash

grabbed the photograph and held it up to the light, 'Jenny's right,' holding up the magnifying glass he peered at the picture, 'but you can only see the bottom of it, it looks remarkably like the postcode for here, so it's near by.'

Taking the photograph out of Ash's hands Fin looked at it, 'Ash may be right but it could be anywhere.'

'If we had the originals we probably could make it out,' remarked Sed, 'but it's too late for that now they are well and truly gone.'

A disappointed group sat around the photographs until Fin spoke up, 'Maybe we are going about this the wrong way,' he said, 'the postcode is a clue, but without the original it's not enough for us to risk passing a message on to David and George.'

'What are you suggesting?' asked a curious Sed.

'That we concentrate on ourselves, on what they have on us, we might be able to find a pattern,' continued Fin, 'they are obviously looking for something in particular.'

'We know what they are bloody looking for,' snapped Ash, 'they are looking for extranatural powers in us.'

'Of course they are,' growled Fin in reply, 'but they want our powers for a reason, they want to use us in some way, otherwise they would simply just kill us off!'

'Of course they would,' remarked Ash, 'we know all this!'

An exasperated Fin turned to Ash, 'Then tell me this Einstein, what war do they want us to fight in?' then slightly too loud for the conversation, 'What justifies the amount of time, effort and money they have put into taking over Ravenswood and subverting it to their ends?'

'Never mind the jeopardy,' joined in Eiry, 'for a militant secret society all of this is a bit obvious, why risk the attention of Special Branch?'

'I don't know,' replied a subdued Ash, 'why are we so important to them?'

'Exactly,' responded Fin, 'what is so special about us?'

The room went quiet as they all re-examined the photographs, outside dawn changed the colour of the sky and the bird's morning chorus began.

'It's interesting,' explained a tired and slightly disappointed Eiry, 'that among all that detail my file is pretty much blank.'

'I noticed that too,' said Jenny, 'I'm only here because of my friendship with Fin and they are starting to suspect that I might have no powers at all.'

'They obviously haven't a clue,' laughed Fin, 'I don't think any of us have clue of your full potential.'

'Yeah,' said Ash, 'you really can be quite scary!'

'Yours is quite interesting,' said Eiry changing the subject by talking to Sed, 'they believe that your family has a history of raising up especially gifted people and they are simply watching you to see what happens!'

Noticing that Sed was abnormally quiet, Fin looked at her, 'Are you alright?'

'I didn't notice the first read through, it seems that they think they have met my father,' a tear slid down Sed's face, 'I have no memory of meeting him,' pausing she wiped a tear from the corner of her eye, 'and they traced him to Chester.'

'I must have missed that too,' said a confused Fin, 'do they mention him or you by name?'

'No, they traced him by cross referencing a number of my extended family relations, that's why I missed it.' Sed paused to pick up a photograph, 'they mention my Gran, my great uncle and my great, great grandfather, the rest they refer to are distant cousins.'

'I read that too,' interrupted Jenny, 'sorry I had no idea that was your family, if I remember correctly; they followed a big and powerful man down to the banks of the River Dee and tried to trap him.'

'That's the one,' continued Sed, 'when they tried to get close to trap him out he recognised them for who they were.'

'The Flock,' said Fin.

'The river was in flood and when he realised he was trapped he jumped into the river and was swept away,' explained Sed, 'Their report said that no one could have survived the river in flood but no body was ever found.'

'Are you sure that was your father?' asked Ash.

'Yes I am,' responded Sed, 'there's something that rings true about it.'

Tiredness swept across room but no one wanted to go to bed, everyone's attention moved to consider Fin and Ash's stories.

Reaching forward Ash picked up the photographs of his own files. 'I know it's hard to believe but I was concentrating so hard on Greg I haven't read my own.'

Remaining silent for a moment, they let Ash struggle with what the files had to say about him. Watching him as he examined them Fin tried to remember what he had read. Ash was born, Ashley Mackray, not Bobrov, the change of name designed to distance him from his father who had owned the Mackray Bakers. There was no mention anywhere of his mother or her maiden name. Thank goodness, thought Fin, they have not linked my mother with Ash's father. It did not take Fin long to connect what was in his file with that of Ash's, both he and Ash were born in the Scilly Isles and their births had been registered at St Mary's. The arsonist was systematically destroying any evidence of Fin and Ash's relationship, the Mackray Bakery fire, the Registry Office and the fires at his family homes.

Sitting up Ash had put the story together, 'Someone is destroying the physical evidence of us being brothers. What is troubling me is that it's not the Flock, they obviously haven't fully joined all the dots together. They may suspect there a connection between us because they have deliberately put us together but there's no way they could know we are brothers. It's not the courts or Special Branch because they are still in the dark about what's going on here.

'I agree,' said Eiry, 'that's why David needs our help.'

'Then who?' asked Fin, 'Who gains by the destruction of the evidence and why do they leave a calling card?'

Looking up Eiry asked, 'Calling card?'

'The feathers,' answered Fin, 'after the first fire they were left as a message, but who they were left for and what the message is I have no idea.'

'As I understand it,' reasoned Sed, 'You were both born on the Scilly Isles and something scared your parents so much that they split up to protect you, your mum went by her maiden name of Butler and your father changed his name from Mackray to Bobrov.'

'The first fire was different from the rest,' said Ash, 'and I think I know what happened. My father was the Phoenix, he was near the end of his life, his powers were waning and passing on to us his twin sons. I guess one of us,' stopping he looked seriously at Fin, 'and by that I mean me as I can produce fire at will. As a toddler somehow I had an accident and burnt the family home down.'

'It could even have been your father,' suggested Sed, 'especially if he was struggling to contain his powers.'

'Whichever, we survived but mum died later because of the smoke. As I grew older and my father grew weaker the accidents kept happening and he finally died.'

The sun rose and daylight burst in the window illuminating the room, standing up Eiry walked to Ash and gave him a hug, 'Even if it was you it was not your fault as you were just a child.'

'I know that in my head,' replied Ash, 'but I am filled with guilt.'

'That first fire could have been me,' said a subdued Fin, 'but I'm not sure it was either of us, before mum died I was allowed to visit her in hospital and she started to whisper to me a story, but she fell asleep almost soon as she started.'

Sitting up and stretching Jenny said, 'Can you remember what she told you?'

Shaking his head Fin struggled to remember, 'It's so vague.'

Standing up Jenny went to Fin, placed her hands on his head, and whispered, 'Remember.'

Closing his eyes Fin drifted back into his memories, the familiar form of his mother was lying in the hospital bed her blonde hair splayed across the pillow, the nurse had sat him on the bed and his mother stroked his hand. Fin looked around the room it was hospital clean and smelt of disinfectant, in the corner stood a uniformed police officer talking to a nurse. Standing next to the police officer was Jenny, noticing his look Jenny shook her head and pointed at his mother indicating that he was to pay attention to her. Wanting to ask Jenny how she could be there drifted from his mind and he looked into his mother's face. It was older than he remembered and she was struggling to breath, the nurse came over a slipped a hissing oxygen mask over her mouth. The nurse went to pick up Fin and removed him from the room but his mother got so agitated they let him stay.

He must have fallen asleep, because when Fin woke up his mother was breathing slightly more easily. The older Fin looked through his younger eyes and saw the tears of grief and anguish in his mother's face.

'I'm going to be leaving you soon,' she said, 'and I want you to know I love you, I love you both so much but I can't stay.' Gently she lifted Fin's hand, 'I want you to understand that if I could I would be with you forever.' The effort of speaking caused her to cough and her frail body grew week, 'but as I can't I am going to tell you a story; once upon a time there was a firebird and a dragon who argued over what fire was made of…'

As Fin watched, his mother fell asleep and a nurse came over and gently lifted him up and took him out the room.

As the door to the room closed, his mother said the last words he ever heard her say, 'And the Sons of the Dragon ruled the world.'

The hospital faded and Jenny let go of Fin and sat down.

'How did you do that?' Fin asked Jenny.

'I don't know,' replied Jenny, 'I just felt I could help you remember, I certainly wasn't expecting to be in there with you!'

'Is that it?' asked Ash not sure what he had just witnessed.

'She fell asleep,' whispered Fin, 'and I never spoke to her again.' Then with more confidence, 'but with Jenny's help I have remembered her last words, she was warning me about the Sons of the Dragon, maybe they are the arsonists.'

'I've never heard of them,' said Jenny, 'but it gives us something to investigate.'

'Yeah, but were do we start?' asked Eiry.

'Elizabeth,' declared Ash, 'she knew about the Royals maybe she has heard of the Dragons.'

Silence descended on the room and was disturbed only when Sed started snoring, Jenny jumping up looked at the clock, 'It's five o'clock in the morning and we have to be up at seven,' picking up the photographs she walked to the stairs, 'I need a couple of hours sleep and so do you.'

No one argued and they headed up their different stairs to bed, the girls were asleep instantly, Fin tossed and turned and Ash lay wide-awake until the alarm clock woke Fin up. Bleary eyed they met the girls downstairs and headed over to the main house for a silent breakfast.

After breakfast, Ash and Fin managed to find Elizabeth alone and approach her.

'Excuse me Elizabeth,' asked Ash, 'can we have a quick word?'

Noticing the serious looks on their faces Elizabeth

agreed, 'Sure come to my classroom.'

They walked in silence over to the classroom and sat down around Elizabeth's desk.

'This is difficult,' said Ash, 'but I have remembered something my father said to me and I have no idea if it's important or not.' Noticing that Fin was about to object to the lie Ash continued, 'The other day when we talking you mentioned that you had a heard of the Royals, so I was wondering if you have heard of the Dragons?'

Colour drained from Elizabeth's face, 'Of course I have heard of the mythical Dragons, the type that fought with St George is that what you mean?'

'I don't know, I remember my father being very secretive about it,' pausing Ash took a deep breath and gave Fin a look that meant trust me, 'it was a day he was particularly ill and not making sense, but he started telling me a story.'

Having gained Elizabeth attention Ash wove into his story everything that his mother had said to Fin about a Firebird and a Dragon who argued over what fire is made of. He ended his account by saying, 'And the Sons of the Dragon ruled the world. Do you have an idea what he was talking about?'

Staring down at her desk Elizabeth picked the side of her fingernails, the colour had not returned to her face and she seemed to be breathing too quickly.

'We try not to talk about them, there's an old saying 'talk about a Dragon and it is bound to appear.' Dragons are the bogeymen used to frighten children at night, in reality they are the contract killers of our world. If you want something nasty to happen to someone or something for a price they will do it for you.' Elizabeth's voice shook as she spoke, 'Some think they show loyalty only to money and that they are merely mercenaries, but they are so much more. They are so dangerous and you Ash, as the son of the Phoenix, are a direct threat to them because only the Phoenix can handle their fire.'

'Then why have we never heard of them?' asked Fin.

Standing up Elizabeth walked to the door and checked that no one was listening, 'The Flock is terrified of the Dragons and the Royals only deal with them when they have no choice.'

'Why would the Firebird and the Dragon argue over fire?' asked Fin.

'Fire is the natural element of both species, Dragons revel in it and if left unstopped they would use it to subdue everyone to their will and pleasure then, when bored, throw them away as a burnt out cinder. The Phoenix has always respected fire in the way a sailor considers the sea, to be used but never taken for granted. The Dragons have always considered themselves as equals to the Phoenix, but they are not the Phoenix can control, bend and extinguish as well as ignite fire.'

'So the Dragons can start a fire but can't control it,' said Fin, 'no wonder they hate the Phoenix.'

'The Dragons are powerless against a mature Phoenix,' continued Elizabeth, 'that is why the Flock want you Ash, with you on their side they could take on the Royals.'

'But I'm not a mature Phoenix,' said Ash grasping the meaning of Elizabeth's words, 'I'm too young to fight them on my own! How many Dragons are there?'

'I have no idea,' said Elizabeth, 'but more than I can count!'

The Royal visit dominated the rest of the morning, two black Range Rovers containing Royal Protection Officers arrived and began changing all the arrangements. Passing through the entrance hall Fin overheard the initial part of their discussion with Mr Chough.

'Who are you,' demanded one of the officers, 'and why are you here?'

'I am the principle and Prince Hugo is here as my guest,' said Mr Chough haughtily.

'Mr Chough,' said the puzzled officer flicking through

his list.

'Yes,' croaked an unimpressed Mr Chough.

'Then you can stay,' replied the officer.

'What do you mean I can stay?' spluttered Mr Chough, 'This has all been arranged in advance and the itinerary agreed with Special Branch. I and my staff are welcoming Prince Hugo outside the main entrance and then proceeding to the main hall for light refreshments.'

'No,' said the officer, 'Prince Hugo will come straight inside and greet everyone here.'

'Why?'

'We deem it safer that Prince does not linger outside.'

'But this has all been agreed with Special Branch!'

'Local plods,' sneered the officer, 'with no understanding of the seriousness of the occasion.'

'That's outrageous,' snapped Mr Chough, 'who do you think you are?'

'We,' the officer looked down at his papers, 'Mr Chough, are in charge, we are Royal Protection part of the Special Branch of the Metropolitan Police, and we do not care what arrangements have been made in advance.'

'You do not care?' stated a shock Mr Chough.

'No Sir we do not, the prince's safety is our main concern,' said the officer, 'please go and wait over there out of the way.' The officer pointed towards a chair by the far wall and waited until Mr Chough did as he was told. 'We will come and get you when, and if, we need you.'

'You cannot be serious,' said Mr Chow standing by the chair, 'I am going to my office to speak to your superiors,' turning he headed towards his room, 'and I want to know your name?'

Smiling at Mr Chough's discomfort the officer replied, 'You will find that my name is irrelevant but you can have it anyway, it is Eagle and if you cause me anymore bother I will have you removed from Ravenswood until the visit is over!'

Fin left to the sound of Mr Chough's office door

slamming shut and decided it would be wise to return to the others before he was caught smirking at Mr Chough's embarrassment. Walking across the grounds Fin realised that the officer was also a Royal and he, the others and Mr Chough would have to be a little more careful.

To great excitement Prince Hugo arrived proceeded by six-motorcycle police officers, two blacked out Range Rovers and a police helicopter. On stepping out of the car, the prince was rushed into the entrance hall by his security detail and the formal reception took place. Fin took his place with all the students, applauded the prince's entrance and waved his Union Flag. Once the prince was inside, he rushed off to rejoin the others.

'Okay,' said Jenny, 'the plan is simple, but we will go over it again.'

'I head over to the main hall where the teachers are having an informal reception with the prince,' said Ash, 'when all is a clear I will give the thumbs up signal.'

'Eiry and I will head over to the library,' explained Sed, 'if the coast is clear we will copy the photographs and hide them at the back of the secret compartment.'

'If there is any teacher present,' said Eiry, 'I will engage them in conversation and Sed will attempt to duplicate the pictures and hide them.'

'Should anything go wrong,' added Fin, 'I will set the fire alarm off and get the girls out.'

'While Fin is rescuing the Eiry and Sed,' completed Ash, 'I will set fire to the bin outside the library and disappear.'

'If all is successful I will take the copies back to our rooms,' said Jenny, 'if the fire alarm goes off, as a distraction, I will need rescuing by Fin.'

'So that's clear,' said Fin, 'let's do it!'

Picking up a workbook Ash headed over to the main hall, if challenged he was ready to seek out a teacher to ask for help with an assignment. Outside the building stood two black suited security officers, nodding towards them, he walked past and seeing through the window that the teachers were occupied sat down on a park bench, opened his book to read and gave the thumbs up signal.

Eiry and Sed acknowledged Ash's signal and went into the library. Eiry as agreed pretended to have a problem finding a book and sought assistance but there were no staff present. Opening her book Eiry sat down near the entrance while Sed went to the back office, turning the handle she pushed the door, it was locked. Just about to panic she read the sign on the door, PULL, the door opened outwards and she went in, switched on the photocopier and began to duplicate the pictures.

Outside the room Eiry was concerned with the noise the photocopier was making but the library remained undisturbed. In the distance, she could see Fin sitting on the grass reading a textbook, seeing Eiry's look he shook his head indicating everything was okay.

Ten minutes later Sed came out with copies hidden inside her bag and passed them over to Jenny and she went to sit with Fin on the grass. Eiry and Sed ran back into the library to hide the originals.

Out of the corner of his Fin noticed that Ash had sat up and was trying to attract surreptitiously his attention.

'Jenny,' whispered Fin, 'can you see what Ash is trying to tell us?'

The gentle summer breeze caught Jenny's hair and it moved in the air.

'Crap,' Jenny swore, 'Dr Swan is heading this way.'

Before either of them could move or warn Eiry or Sed, Dr Swan had marched into the library. No sooner, had he entered the library there was an enormous crash, Fin and Jenny ran across to the library and entered into a scene of chaos. Eiry was helping Dr Swan up off the floor from a pile books and checking to see if he was hurt.

'What happened?' asked Fin surveying the bookcases

that had fallen and the piles books everywhere.

'Some idiot,' said a hurt Dr Swan, 'left the library ladders behind the door, I was in an hurry and I pushed the door open to hard, it hit the ladder and it toppled over the bookcase.'

'It was like watching dominoes fall,' said Eiry holding her arm, 'I only got hit by flying books but poor Dr Swan took a blow from a bookcase.'

Looking at Dr Swan Fin noticed that his arm was hanging strangely, 'You look like you have broken your arm.'

Shock crossed Dr Swan's face and he turned white and fainted.

'Did you hide the photographs?' asked Fin.

'Yes,' groaned Sed, 'but this was my entire fault I put the ladders by the door, I didn't expect Dr Swan to come bursting in.'

'We'd better get him some help,' said Eiry looking sympathetically at Dr Swan, 'call Ash over.'

Sed ran off and brought Ash back, Dr Swan was still out cold, Ash placed his hands on his arm grimaced in pain but Dr Swan's arm regained its normal shape.'

'Stop there!' cried Fin.

'What?' replied a startled Ash.

'If he has no injuries people may ask questions why,' explained Fin, 'the last thing we need during a royal visit is to draw attention to ourselves.'

Regaining consciousness Dr Swan looked around at the debris and the concerned faces of the students. 'I think I'm okay,' he said, 'but you had better go and get help. I'm so cross with myself, I never should have burst into the library like that.'

Within minutes, the library was full of teachers and security staff, only after they deemed it safe did the hooked nose prince come over to talk to Dr Swan.

From a chair that had been provided for him, Dr Swan thanked each of the students for being there and introduced them to Prince Hugo.

'It seems that you done a great service to Dr Swan,' said Prince Hugo, 'it is a pleasure to meet you and I wish you every success in your future.'

Moments later the prince was led from the room and the paramedics arrived to take Dr Swan to the hospital.

'The paramedic approached Dr Swan, "How are feeling, are you in much pain?'

As Fin and the rest, were bustled out Fin smiled at his reply.

'Some bits of me are okay,' he said rubbing his arm, 'but some bits of me could do better!'

CHAPTER 12 – THE CAR CRASH

'All rise,' said the Eagle, 'for His Royal Highness Prince Hugo Earnweald.'

Chairs grated against the floor as the dark figures around the table rose. Fin and Jenny, breathless from dodging Royal Protection and rushing through the secret passageways watched, frustrated that once again they could not see any faces. The hook nosed prince entered the room, followed by the stooped figure of the Crow and sat down.

The Eagle stood at the prince's shoulder and watched the room while the prince surveyed his surroundings. 'How quaint,' the prince said sarcastically, sweeping his arm around the room, 'I do so like the decorations, although I believe the French Flock would like the body of Corneille back.' He waved his hand and the body fell from its chains on the walls and landed with a sickening thud. 'Eagle see to it Corneille gets home.'

The Eagle smiled and whispered into his radio and two security officers entered and zipped Corneille into a body bag and left.

Shivering in the corridor Fin began to feel cold

creeping into his bones and Jenny's hair was standing on its end, inside the room the meeting continued.

'As you requested Corbeau passed your message to his Lords and Masters,' the prince smiled, 'and they were not amused and spoke to us. We had our own little chat with Corbeau and he was most forthcoming. Sadly he cannot be with us this afternoon but I am told that his wounds will heal and that he will make a full recovery.'

The prince wiped the table with his finger and looked at the dust, shook his gently and sighed to himself.

'May I ask why your highness is so interested in the humble doings of our Flock,' croaked the Crow, 'you have never shown any interest before?'

Silence descended as the occupants of the room watched the beginnings of a battle of wills, as the Crow spoke to the prince, Fin and Jenny felt a blast of cold hit them.

'You have never attracted our attention before,' growled the prince, 'it is no concern of ours when you squabble amongst yourselves, you provincial flocks are always pecking at each other.' As the prince spoke, his voice grew quieter and filled with menace, 'Neither were we bothered about your immature experiments with humans nor the occasional snatching and corrupting of specially gifted children. However, when your games gained the attention of the Dragons we decided to act. You may have decided to play with fire but understand me when I tell you we do not want to get burnt!'

'My Lord,' said Raven, 'Royal or not, what right does he have to come in here and question us in our own nest?'

'Silence!' whipped the Crow's vicious voice, 'Though admirable to me your loyalty makes you seem a fool.' The Crow smiled and turned to the prince, 'However, your highness, my honourable friend here does have a point, why does a prince think he can come here and challenge me in my own nest?'

The prince stood to his full height and the shadow of

his invisible wings filled the room, 'You stir Dragon fire and expect no response,' he shouted, 'your petty games among the humans are irrelevant to us but when you seek the tools to destroy our throne do you foolishly think we will remain silent?'

'What evidence do you have, your highness for these outrageous claims,' croaked a smiling Crow, 'none! Come back when you have evidence and are ready to challenge us in the Royal Court.'

The prince raised his right hand slightly and lightning flew across the room towards the Crow. The Crow lifted his arm to defend himself and the lightening bounced off harmlessly.

'You exceed your authority,' snarled the Crow.

Smiling the prince waved a finger at the Crow; he raised high into the air, his body spread eagled and the Crow screamed in agony. 'My dear Lord Crow,' he said quietly, 'I was only toying with you, my powers are greater than yours do you really wish to challenge me?'

'No your highness,' screamed the Crow.

Lowering his finger the Crow fell back into his chair, 'You will cease provoking the Dragons or we shall return and pluck you all!' Standing the prince placed his hands underneath the oak table and threw it into the air scattering the Council of Crows.

From his spy hole, Fin watched the hood fall of Mr Chough's face, the prince and Eagle left and he and Jenny decided it was time they left too.

From the safety of their lodge, Fin and Jenny watched the royal party leave, their cavalcade throwing up dust and gravel as they left the grounds. As the dust settled teachers and students reappeared from their hiding places, everyone relieved that Ravenswood could return to normal. Fin was surprised to see a smiling Mr Chough standing outside the main entrance hall talking to Elizabeth; he thought he would be hiding in his office licking his wounds.

On their way over to their evening meal, Elizabeth joined them and they all enjoyed a light-hearted evening as they reminisced over the royal visit. Fin would have laughed more about the visit of the hook nosed prince if he had not seen the power of the prince in action. Unfortunately, Fin and Jenny had not had a private moment to talk to the others about what they had seen in the torture chamber.

Turning to Ash as they left the dinning hall Elizabeth spoke to Ash, 'Mr Chough passed a message to me that the vicar had found a history book I might be interested in. Do you fancy a trip to the vicarage?'

'Yeah I would love to,' said Ash, 'but are you allowed to take me on your own?'

'Mr Chough suggested I take you,' replied Elizabeth, 'so it will be fine.'

Returning to their lodge, Fin and Jenny shared what they had seen in the chamber and then they played cards all evening. As the clock approached eleven, Jenny sat up abruptly and held her head as if in pain.

'What is it?' asked Sed.

'I've no idea,' said Jenny, 'but I feel something is terribly wrong, my hair is sensing great pain.'

'I'm concerned that Ash and Elizabeth have not returned,' said Eiry, 'and I'm sorry I don't feel very well.'

Outside the lodge, the weather changed and a summer storm struck. Rain poured from the sky in sheets and the temperature dropped dramatically. Outside the rain turned into giant balls of hail that struck the windows and threatened to break them.

Inside Fin realised that Eiry was running a temperature and produced a cold damp cloth to place on her head, as his hands touched her head cold ran through his fingers and she cooled down.

'Thank you,' said Eiry, 'that really helps.'

'No problem,' replied Fin, 'I am a master of the cold

flannel.'

Outside the freak storm passed but inside they all grew concerned at the absence of Ash.

Around midnight there was a knock at the door, Fin opened the door cautiously and standing there was Mr Chough. 'May I come in?' he asked.

Fin invited Mr Chough in and they all gathered around the kitchen table.

'I am really sorry,' a sad Mr Chough began, 'but Elizabeth and Ash were involved in car accident tonight on the way over to the vicarage. It seems their car left the road and rolled down an embankment into a ditch; Elizabeth will be staying in hospital overnight and she has some broken ribs and some cuts and lacerations. The doctors say she is in a lot of pain but it looks a lot worse than she actually is.'

'And Ash,' asked a shocked Eiry, 'you haven't mentioned him is he okay?'

'I don't know how to tell you this,' said Mr Chough gently, 'Ash hit his head really badly and may need to be transferred to a specialist head trauma unit.'

'Why?' asked Eiry trying to hold back her tears.

Mr Chough in the gentlest voice anyone had ever heard him use explained, 'Ash is being maintained in a medically-induced coma, I'm afraid he suffered a critical head injury and the doctors want to rest his brain by slowing its activity to reduce inflammation.'

'What are his chances of recovery?' asked Fin.

'We don't know, if he is stable in the morning the signs are good,' pausing he looked at them with sadness in his eyes, 'but we have no idea about the long term impact,' added Mr Chough, 'we will know more in the morning.' He stood up, 'Try to get some sleep, and if you believe in prayer Ash could do with some.'

As the door closed behind Mr Chough they all started to talk at once, after a moment the buzz of voices stopped and Fin spoke first, 'I don't like any of this.'

'There is nothing to like,' said Eiry, 'poor Ash and Elizabeth.'

'The timing of this just doesn't add up,' said Jenny, 'nothing about this makes any sense.'

'What do you mean?' asked Sed.

'Oh come on,' said Fin, 'Jenny and I saw the Crow and Raven cower before the prince. Then as soon as the prince leaves Mr Chough passes a message on to Elizabeth from George.'

'Why would George trust Mr Chough with a message when he believes he's the Raven?' asked Sed catching on.

'Exactly,' continued Fin, 'and why would Mr Chough authorise a break in our 'Protection for All Policy' by allowing Elizabeth to go off alone with Ash? When Jenny and I came to Ravenswood they insisted on two members of staff accompanying us.'

'They believe that Ash is the Phoenix,' stated Jenny, 'the royal visit has scared them and caused them to act immediately so they have taken him.'

'It's a great conspiracy theory,' pondered Sed, 'and it all fits but what about Elizabeth?'

'I was starting to trust Elizabeth,' said Eiry, 'if she really comes back in the morning from the hospital then maybe Mr Chough is telling the truth!'

'Not a chance,' added Fin, 'if Elizabeth comes back injured then maybe, but I doubt it, she has betrayed us and they have taken Ash.'

They talked for another hour but failed to make any progress so they decided to go to retire for the night. Fin took himself off to bed but could not sleep; the room was too quiet without Ash's constant chatter. In the end he got up, put the light on, and went downstairs to make a drink and found the girls sitting around the table, it appeared that none of them could sleep.

The following morning being a Saturday they had no

lessons so they ate breakfast in the lodge, not that anyone could eat but trying to do something normal helped. Sitting near the window Eiry watched a car stop near the lodge and Elizabeth got out.

Gingerly Elizabeth, with the aid of a crutch, limped across to the lodge and knocked on the door. Opening the door Fin invited her in and encouraged her to sit down at the kitchen table. Everyone wanted to ask about Ash but after looking at the deep and nasty cuts across her face and the way she was struggling to breathe they all decided to wait and let her speak first.

'I don't remember anything about the accident,' she began, 'we were heading towards the vicarage and the sky went dark and the next thing I remember is waking up in hospital.'

'How badly are you hurt?' asked Sed.

'I have deep cuts all over my body and this bad one on my face they glued back together,' Elizabeth started to cry, 'I have bruised ribs and a swollen ankle, but the worst thing of all is they would not let me see Ash. I have no idea how he is or how badly he is hurt, they wouldn't tell me!'

Eiry tore a strip of kitchen tissue of the role and passed it to Elizabeth and she wiped her eyes and blew her nose. Pain was etched into her face and she seemed racked with guilt.

'That cut looks really bad,' Eiry, said gently, 'it must really hurt.'

'It does and they have said that I will be scarred for life,' continued Elizabeth, 'it's so deep I am going to need plastic surgery, they said I was lucky not to lose an eye, but the scar will fade with time.'

'No,' said Eiry, 'Oh Elizabeth!'

'They offered me professional counselling but all I could think about was Ash. I am so sorry, he was in my care and now he's in a critical state.'

'What do you actually remember,' asked Fin, 'or has it

all gone?'

'It's so strange,' she replied, 'I really cannot remember anything.' Struggling to stand up Elizabeth added, 'I am so tired and sleepy from the shock and the pain killers I need to go to bed but I couldn't without talking to you first.'

Walking around the table Fin took Elizabeth's arm, 'I will walk you home,' he said, 'May we come and visit you later?'

'Yes, I would like that. I am so sorry, as soon as I hear anything about Ash I will let you know.'

'There is no doubting Elizabeth has been in a car crash,' said Eiry, 'there's no way this was not an accident, it puts our conspiracy theory to shame!'

'Actually,' responded Jenny, 'I disagree.'

'What?' exclaimed Eiry.

'There is no doubt that Elizabeth has been badly hurt,' continued Jenny, 'but those injuries look nothing like those from a car crash. Yes, her face is cut badly and she has broken ribs and stuff but it all looks wrong. When I was younger, one night I heard a couple arguing in a house across the road, the next day they were both battered and bruised and they said they had been in a car crash. No way, they had been fighting, Elizabeth looks like she has been in a fight and I reckon that cut on her face was inflicted with a knife.'

'Then why doesn't she remember?' asked Fin.

'I believe Elizabeth has been telling us the truth,' said Jenny, 'but someone has wiped her mind clean of what happened.'

'Why would they do that?' asked Eiry.

'I can think of one reason immediately,' replied Fin, 'she can't tell us or the police about anything that happened to her. This means that they can get away with removing Ash from Ravenswood without any suspicion being left on the school.'

'So we are stuck,' groaned Sed, 'Mr Chough is not

going to tell us the truth and Elizabeth can't help us!'

Sitting back in his chair Fin was lost in thought, noticing Jenny motioned the others to be quiet.

'What's up Fin?'

'There's a pattern forming and I can't put it together, I am missing something but I can't remember what it is!'

'Do you need me to help you remember what it is?' asked Jenny.

'No, it's just…,' said Fin, 'I am so stupid,' he said jumping up and shouting, 'it's all about remembering. Elizabeth can't remember what happened to her, I can't remember what happened to me. Ash was right I need to go back to the nightmare room to remember and somehow we have to get Elizabeth there too.'

'No,' said Jenny shaking her head, 'that's too crude. The nightmare room plays on all our fears and the teachers use that as means of physiologically controlling us. We take our own fears in with us and being in a secluded place with,' she paused and then got excited, 'the trains rumbling deep in the tunnels beneath Ravenswood, means our sleep is disturbed, causing us to dream.'

'Brilliant,' said Fin sarcastically, 'what do you suggest?'

'I suggest,' continued Jenny, 'that you try to remember and I help you. If it works with you, maybe, if she is willing, it will work with Elizabeth too!'

After lunch, Mr Chough took them aside to tell them that was no news yet on how Ash was doing but he would let them know as soon as he could.

'Git,' swore Sed, 'he's playing with us!'

Returning to the lodge Jenny sat next to Fin on the Sofa while Sed and Eiry sat in the chairs.

'Just relax and try to remember that night,' Jenny said soothingly, 'and will try to join you.'

Leaning back, Fin closed his eyes and tried to remember, the stuff of Fin's nightmares spilled out into his waking mind. He could hear the persistent beeping of the smoke alarm and he could once again smell the smoke. Suddenly a cool hand held his and he and Jenny were in the room together.

'Hi,' said Jenny, 'fancy meeting you here!'

The panic that had been starting to form eased from his mind and he smiled at Jenny.

'Fin I want you to take a step back with me,' said Jenny leading him to the side of the room.

When Fin looked up, he saw himself lying in the bed peacefully fast asleep.

'I have taken you back to the beginning of your memory but it's important to remember that this is just a memory, none of what happens can touch us, so you do not have to be frightened for me or yourself.'

Nodding Fin acknowledged Jenny's words, this time it was different. His past self was asleep but growing restless, smoke had been slowly creeping under the door and his subconscious brain could smell it. The smoke detector activating still made him jump and Jenny squeezed his hand, the beeping was quickly replaced with sound of the fire alarm going off, its siren piercing the air with a deafening whine. Fin watched himself wake up panic and be tangled up in his duvet. Falling to the floor on his head, he laughed as it was almost slapstick. Aware now of the fire Fin snatched his shoes off the floor and ran for the door. Grabbing the handle he turned and pulled it, but the door would not budge. Smoke seeped under the bottom of the door and Fin watched panic overtake him.

Mouthing with his younger self, he watched him scream, 'Let me out of here!' The more he pulled the more frustrated he got. Panic crept up on him again, and he hammered the door with his fists. 'Let me out!' Fin watched as he coughed and slide to the floor.

'This is where I come in,' said Jenny as the door was kicked open from outside, 'I do like to make an entrance!'

The door flew open and hit him in the shoulder and he fell across the room. Standing in the doorway was a younger version of Jenny, her wild hair, as if taking in everything was sticking out in every direction. Fear was in her bright blue eyes as she yelled, 'Fin, Fin, where are you?'

'Is that what my hair looks like at the back?' said Jenny, 'I need to do something about that.'

'Not now Jenny,' laughed Fin, surprised that he could laugh while reliving a memory.

'Sorry,' said an amused Jenny.

Turning back, he watched Fin climb up off the floor, rub his shoulder, and pick up three feathers off the ground. Jenny grabbed his hand and they ran down the corridor.

'Stop!' commanded Jenny, 'I thought I saw someone over there.' Jenny pointed in the direction of another corridor, 'When I was trapped and running for the nearest exit I met a staff member who redirected me this way, I think I just saw him again!'

Doing as he was told Fin stopped and the memory froze, turning he walked towards the space Jenny had seen someone, in his mind he retraced his steps and the memory went into slow reverse and a figure appeared. Holding hands Fin and Jenny walked up to the figure, his face was out of focus and blurred.

'Why can't we see him,' asked Fin.

'Because this is your memory,' replied Jenny and you never saw his face properly,' she paused, 'but I did.' Jenny closed her eyes and tried to remember and the face.

As Fin watched, the face came slowly into focus and he gasped aloud.

Opening her eyes Jenny stared in disbelief at the man who had sent her in the direction of Fin's locked room, 'Dr Swan!' she cried, 'I don't understand, surely I would have remembered?'

'It was all before you knew Dr Swan,' said Fin, 'and it has taken our combined memory to recognise him.' Pausing he looked around, 'Why was he here?'

Fin and Jenny rejoined their earlier selves, the

emergency lights had come on and the green exit signs glowed in the dark. Hanging back Fin and Jenny watched them run for the exit, but before they could get to it, there was an explosion and the ceiling fell down blocking off their escape route. Pausing the memory again, they searched for any clues to the source of the explosion but there were none. Turning they watched a second explosion send a ball of fire down the wall and ceiling towards them.

Knowing it was only a memory Fin watched as Fin threw himself between Jenny and the flames; using his powers as a Phoenix, he created bubble of clean air around them. Feathers in hand he protected Jenny only to see a figure move out of the darkness and strike her in the face.

Both Jennies screamed and as blood poured down her beautiful face. Fin saw the face of her attacker, it was familiar, he had seen it before...

'Clever boy,' a familiar voice chided him, 'you have remembered, but I see you needed some help.'

Once again the memory paused only this time it was not Jenny's doing, 'Hello Jenny such a pleasure to see you again.'

The same six figures stood in the memory, three frozen in time, and three living and active.

'Why did you strike Jenny,' Demanded Fin, 'did you have to blind her?'

'You know this woman,' Jenny blurted out, 'and how can she be in your dream?'

'Oh I am always with him my dear,' the woman said, 'he has never let me go.'

'Jenny,' Fin struggled to speak, 'this is my mother.'

'What,' cried Jenny, 'this psychopath is your mum?'

'I am truly sorry about your eyes Jenny,' she said, 'but you saw my face and I knew you were Fin's friend and it wouldn't take much to identify me, after all I am supposed to be dead.'

'Why?' asked Fin.

'Oh and you my little man, even your father would

have been proud of that little bubble,' she said and stopped seeing the lack of comprehension on Fin's face, 'My Darling I'm so sorry to be a disappointment to you, but you and Ash were such a surprise, twins we didn't expect that.'

Walking around the memory Fin's mother picked up a chair and sat down, 'Normally when the Phoenix is dying he produces a son, but your father and I produced twins, well that messed everything up. There have never been two phoenixes at a time and we didn't know which of you would inherit his powers. We never dreamt that you would end up sharing different attributes of his powers but we knew the Flock, among others were after you so we separated.'

'Mother,' exclaimed Fin.

'My name is Adalinda,' she replied, 'and as I have been a useless mother call me that.'

'Adalinda,' said Fin toying with name, 'why all the fires?'

'Oh you silly boy,' scolded Adalinda, 'have you not worked it out yet? My name, Adalinda, means noble serpent, I am the daughter of Dragons and that makes you part dragon and phoenix.'

'Very clever,' said Jenny, 'that's why there could be twins you have created a new species!'

'That's right Jenny dear,' Adalinda replied, 'and that's why I have been destroying all the records of my children's lives, if the Royals found out they would destroy them.'

'Why did you do it?' asked Jenny.

'Because we Dragons are fed up of the status quo,' answered Adalinda, 'it is time once again for the Dragons to rule the world and you, my son, will be our greatest warrior.'

'In my last nightmare you said if I remembered who you are it would change everything,' Fin said through gritted teeth, 'Well it has changed nothing, I am a phoenix and not a dragon. I do not believe in blinding children as a route to power, so here and now I choose for myself. I am the son of the Phoenix, a guardian and proud of it.' Fin took a deep breath, paused and took Jenny by hand then continued, 'So get out of my head, my dreams and my memories, but most of all get out of my life!'

Reality snapped back into place and Sed and Eiry stared at Fin and Jenny, aware that something significant had happened, but not sure what.

By late afternoon, there being no news on Ash's condition they agreed that Jenny and Fin should go and visit Elizabeth. Before they left, they created a get-well card and Eiry and Sed collected from the gardeners a bunch of flowers to give her. The gardeners were most helpful when they realised who they wanted the flowers for and the girls came back with a beautiful, if enormous, bouquet.

'Please sit,' Elizabeth, said pain etched across her face, 'these flowers are so beautiful.'

'Shall I put them in water for you?' said Fin.

'That would be kind,' said Elizabeth opening her card and smiling, 'you are all wonderful please express my thanks to Sed and Eiry.'

'We will do,' replied Jenny, 'How are you feeling?'

'I hurt a lot but the doctors have told me that is to be expected.'

'Mr Chough came over before to tell us there is no new on Ash,' said Jenny, 'he said no news is good news but we don't believe him.'

Elizabeth groaned in pain as she adjusted how she sat in the chair.

'You look so tired Elizabeth,' said a concerned Fin, 'maybe we should come back tomorrow.'

'No please stay,' said Elizabeth, 'I am growing tired of my own company, when I am tired I will ask you to leave.'

'Okay,' replied Fin, 'Can you remember anything at all?'

'It's strange but I can't,' said a puzzled Elizabeth, 'I was in an accident once before and I can remember everything as if it was in slow motion, the glass flying through the air and the sound, this time is so different. It's driving me mad; it's like having a hole in my memory.'

'Would you like to remember,' Asked Jenny, 'or do you think it's better not to.'

Sitting forward in her seat Jenny held Elizabeth's hand gently, 'If you really want to remember, we can help you.' Looking Elizabeth in the eye Jenny said, 'I would trust you with my life, so I will trust you with my secret, with your permission I can walk you through the closed doors of your memory.'

Looking stunned Elizabeth responded, 'Oh Jenny you have powers too,' a tear slipped down her cheek, 'I have grown to love you all and I know your special powers cannot replace having sight but to have a gift is wonderful.'

'Do you want to remember?'

'Damn right I do!' anger boiled in Elizabeth's pained face, 'I have never forgotten anything in my life and this feels to me like someone has deliberately wiped my memories.'

'Do you think that's possible?' asked Fin.

'Of course I do,' stated Elizabeth, 'this is Ravenswood home of the weird and wonderful. I want to know the truth, I might not like it, but I want to know it!'

Jenny insisted that Fin pull their chairs together and she sat in the middle and held their hands.

Laughing in the front seats of the car sat Elizabeth and Ash, behind them sat Jenny, Elizabeth and Fin. The car was travelling quickly down the narrow lanes that led from Ravenswood to the vicarage. Overhead the summer evening sky was bright and swallows flew in the wind catching flies.

'That is so good,' said Elizabeth, 'I can breath and the pain has gone.'

Smiling Jenny gave Elizabeth's had a squeeze, 'This is a memory we are in so nothing can harm us, so whatever happens, no matter how awful do not panic.'

'I didn't realise that you could bring other people into someone's memories,' said Fin enjoying watching Ash laughing and joking in the front seat,

'Neither did I,' said Jenny, 'but we have shared memories so it felt the natural thing to do.'

It felt very comfortable in the back of the car as it drove along the country roads, however, as the journey continued a sense of dread started to overtake its extra passengers. The sky grew dark as if a storm was coming, the gentle banter ceased as the cloud drew closer.

Looking out the window Ash cried out, 'That's not a cloud but a swarm of crows!'

Large black crows crashed into the car and Elizabeth had to stop because she could no longer see the road, still the birds came until the window was covered in their blood and feathers and dead birds surrounded the car. In the back, the three visitors watched in horror as the front windscreen smashed and silence fell.

Looking out the window they could see that car was surrounded by dark figures their faces hidden by hoods, all that is except Mr Chough whose hood was thrown back and was laughing. In his hands, he held a heavy staff that he had used to smash the windscreen of the car.

'Hello Elizabeth,' said Mr Chough the Raven, 'how good of you to join us.' Pointing his staff at Ash he yelled, 'Take him to the farm.'

Hooded figures dragged Ash from the car only to drop him in pain as Ash burst in to flames.

'You can't take me,' Ash said, 'I will turn you all ash!'

The Crow smiled, 'You know nothing child, bring Elizabeth to me!'

Pulled from the driving seat Elizabeth was thrown on the floor in front of the Raven, lifting up his staff he swung it, hit her hard and she cried out in pain.

Somehow, now standing outside the car Elizabeth and her students watched as the Crow hit Elizabeth repeatedly.

Unable to contain Ash the hooded figures fell back as he threw fire at the Raven, singed but unstopped the Raven struck Elizabeth again.

'I will keep on doing this until you surrender,' cackled the Raven, 'lift her up.'

Three hooded figures ran over, picked Elizabeth up and held her battered body up by her arms. The Raven walked over to Elizabeth and started to cut her face.

'I surrender,' cried Ash defeated, 'leave her alone.'

'Oh you do disappoint me,' smirked the Raven, 'she is so irritating I so wanted to cut her some more.'

The Raven lifted his staff and the car flew through the air and crashed into a ditch, turning to Elizabeth he said, 'I would love to kill you my dear but someone I bow to wants you kept alive.' Pointing his hand at her Elizabeth hovered in the air, 'I was going to torture you to discover if Ash was the Phoenix, but it is your lucky day because he demonstrated his powers trying to defend you.' Flicking his wrist Elizabeth span in the air. When he next spoke the Raven's voice became all silky and hypnotic, 'You have been in a car crash and Ash is badly hurt, now you will forget everything,' then in a commanding voice cried, 'EVERYTHING!' Flicking his hand with a dismissive gesture Elizabeth flew through the air and fell like a broken doll into the ditch next to the car.

Fin's head span and he found himself back with Jenny in Elizabeth's lounge.

'I'm so sorry,' wept Elizabeth.

'It was not your fault,' said Jenny bitterly, 'you did everything you could!'

CHAPTER 12 – A DAY AT THE FARM

Fin made Elizabeth a cup of earl grey tea while she sat back in her chair exhausted.

'I know what Ash would call Mr Chough,' Fin said through gritted teeth, 'you were in no accident!'

'I am so angry,' said the exhausted Elizabeth, 'but I have no energy to deal with this yet. Thank you Jenny I remember it all now, but I think it for all our sakes it would be better if Mr Chough remained ignorant of that fact.'

'Well he's not going to hear it from us,' said Fin, 'Elizabeth we know now for certain that Ash has been taken to the farm but we have no idea where it is, do you have any clues?'

Sipping her tea Elizabeth thought, 'Jenny I have heard the farm mentioned a few times, but only in passing, do you think you could help me remember?'

'I don't know,' she replied, 'I have only done this twice and I have no idea what I can do.' She turned and looked at Fin, 'Get a pen and some paper and I will try to repeat what I hear.'

'Do you want me to join you?' asked Fin.

'Not this time,' apologised Jenny, 'we will be flitting about and I want to concentrate on Elizabeth's thoughts.'

Once again, Jenny held Elizabeth's hand and they both seemed to fall asleep, Elizabeth's breathing relaxed and the pain seemed to vanish from her face. Sitting in silence Fin waited as the minutes passed he felt himself grow sleepy and jerked awake when he heard Jenny suddenly speak.

'The old farm is starting to look tired now and we need more space,' mumbled Jenny, 'It would be better if we weren't so close to the canal.'

Now fully awake Fin jotted down what he was hearing.

'Those Canada Geese are vermin you can't walk anywhere without treading in their…,'

'It took me an hour to get back from the Farm I got stuck waiting for a herd of cows to return to their field.'

'Take him to the Farm!'

Relaxing Jenny let go of Elizabeth's hand, 'There wasn't much and they might not even be speaking of the same farm.'

'I need to sleep now,' said an exhausted Elizabeth, 'let me know how you get on.' She was nearly asleep; she turned and twitched in pain and then was dead to the world.

Back at the lodge, Fin and Jenny shared all they had learnt from Elizabeth's dreams. No one was surprised at the behaviour of Mr Chough and everyone felt sorry for Elizabeth and frustrated about the lack of clues as to where the farm was.

'As far as I can tell,' said Fin, 'we are looking for a secluded, shabby old farm complex that is close to a canal and less than an hour from here.' Opening an ordinance survey map of the area he laid it on to the table. 'I reckon with all the single track roads in this area the fastest average speed you could manage would be forty miles and hour. We also know that the driver was delayed by a dairy herd on route.' Producing a pencil and compass, he drew a circle with the centre being at Ravenswood, 'This circle represents a thirty mile radius from here.'

'There are two canals that are within the circle,' added Eiry, pointing at the map, 'but this one runs parallel with a railway track and it's in an industrial area and not secluded enough, so I reckon that rules it out.'

'I agree,' said Sed leaning over the map, 'the only other canal is the one that tunnels under Ravenswood and travels east. It comes out here and three miles later, it goes into another tunnel that comes out in the outskirts of Sedgesworth, and looking at this map there is nowhere else secluded with a canal it could be.'

'There are five farms marked on the map,' continued Eiry, 'this one here is a dairy farm and this one about a mile from the Sedgesworth Tunnel has a lake as well as a canal.'

'Perfect for Canada Geese to flourish, 'agreed Sed, 'does that farm have a name?'

Leaning close to the map, Fin read aloud, 'Rooks Cottage Farm and Bakery.'

'What do you think,' asked Sed, 'is this the place or are we just guessing wildly?'

'I have no idea,' said Fin, 'but it's the only place that fits the clues we have.'

After a lunch that nobody wanted to eat, but felt they had to have to keep up appearances, they regrouped around the kitchen table.

'The longer we leave it the less chance we have of surprising them,' said Fin, 'at present the Flock think that we are distracted by the thought of Ash being critically ill and Elizabeth unable to correct us. That is not going to last, they know we want more information on Ash and they can only delay the inevitable enquiry that follows.'

'We can't all go,' said Eiry, 'that would really attract their attention.'

'I agree,' said Fin, 'I think you and Sed should stay and cover for Jenny and I, also you can keep an eye on Elizabeth and make sure she is okay.'

'If anyone starts looking for us tell them that Fin is really upset and that I've gone to comfort him,' suggested Jenny, 'They might suspect that Fin has gone off on his own but it will defuse their suspicions if I'm with him.'

'I would rather be going with you;' said Sed, 'but two will attract less suspicion than three or four. I have been checking the bus timetables and the 189 to Sedgesworth goes every hour and there is a bus stop near the well.'

'We are going to need bus fare,' said Jenny, 'I have some cash but not a lot.'

'I have enough,' said Fin, 'well at least to get us there, we might have to wing it to get back.'

'I'm broke,' added Sed.

'So am I,' complained Eiry, 'I've been broke for weeks.'

'We'll manage somehow,' said Fin, 'we can make it up as we go along.'

An hour later Fin and Jenny sat at the foot of the well, climbing up they both reached the top and the iron cover. All was quiet at the farm, the builders were absent and the place seemed deserted. The cover however, was padlocked shut.

'I thought this might happen,' said a frustrated Jenny, 'we will have to go back and risk the exit near the school wall.'

'There's no time,' said Fin, 'I'm going to try something.'

Wedging himself next to the padlock Fin grasped it in both hands and imagined that it was melting. Watching from the other side of the well Jenny observed the lock change colour as it got hotter, Fin continued to concentrate and his whole body began to glow and the lock burst apart in his hands.

'Wow,' exclaimed Jenny, 'how did you do that?'

'No idea,' replied Fin laughing, 'it just came into my head so I did it.'

Lifting the cover, they climbed out, sneaked past the farm, and headed for the main road and the bus stop. The bus came much more quickly than they expected and Fin used all their money to cover the fares to Sedgesworth.

Leading Fin up the stairs Jenny pointed to the front seats, 'Anyone getting on will only see the back of our heads,' she said, 'and we can see where we are going.'

Sitting down together, they stared out of the windows, twenty minutes later, to their horror, the bus ran parallel to the entrance to Ravenswood and they could see into the main house. Averting their eyes, they hid their faces and hoped that no one had seen them.

The bus seemed to make random turns and stops and even went into Huntley and Wart, where at the main bus stop Gerty and Prude climbed aboard.

'Two for Sedgesworth please,' said Gerty.

Upstairs they heard the sound of the driver printing their tickets as Gerty and Prude's voices echoed around the bus. Thankfully, they stayed downstairs but their constant chatter shattered the peace on the bus, relieved that they were unseen; Fin and Jenny watched the fields go by.

'It's got to be soon,' said Jenny, 'there's the dairy farm.'

'Five more minutes,' calculated Fin, 'or when we see the canal.'

'Why is it that time seems to slow down when you are nervous,' asked Jenny, 'and speed up when you are enjoying yourself?'

Shrugging his shoulders in reply Fin gave his attention to the countryside, the fields were full of crops and it was hard to see changes in the landscape. A flash of red and yellow burst briefly through the fields and Fin breathed a sigh of relief, 'I have just see a narrowboat so I think we'd better get off at the next stop.'

Ringing the bell Jenny stood up and led them down the stairs to the exit, as Fin climbed down the stairs he realised that Gerty and Prude were both looking at him. Turning his back to them, he hoped in vain that had not recognised them.

'Can you watch Gerty and Prude with your hair,' whispered Fin into Jenny's ear, 'they have spotted us and it would be good to know how they are reacting?'

'They whispering to each other and Gerty has just mouthed Ravenswood,' responded Jenny, 'I have an idea.'

To Fin's horror, Jenny walked up the aisle to where they were sitting.

'Hello,' Jenny said in her hypnotic voice, 'it's Gerty and Prude isn't it?'

The women nodded surprised that Jenny had approached them.

'It was so lovely to see you in the village and at St Hubert's at Christmas,' said Jenny, 'the vicar spoke so well of you when we met him recently.'

'Oh we didn't realise you knew the vicar,' said a slightly bemused Prude, 'he's such a lovely man.'

'Yes he is,' replied Jenny, 'we met him just before the royal visit to Ravenswood.'

The bus started to slow for the bus stop and Fin moved closer to the door.

'I'm sorry I have to go,' said Jenny, 'but it was lovely to see you again.'

'You too,' said Gerty, 'you're a long way from Ravenswood.'

'Yes,' said Jenny, 'we are but we have been allowed out to visit an old friend of ours, Greg Matthews.'

'Isn't he the missing boy?' asked Prude.

'I believe he was,' said Jenny starting to move to the door and then stopped, 'I was wondering if you could do me a favour, I promised the vicar that we would let him know that Greg was at Rooks Cottage Farm and Bakery. Could I be cheeky and ask you to ring him and let him know when you get to Sedgesworth?'

'Certainly my dear,' said Gerty, 'what a nice girl.'

'Yes she is,' agreed Prude, 'but we don't need to wait to get to Sedgesworth to tell him, I have my mobile phone in my handbag.'

With a hiss of airbrakes, the bus departed and left Fin and Jenny in the middle of nowhere.

'I saw the canal in that direction,' Fin pointed in the direction of a public footpath.

Leaving the road, they followed the footpath through the fields, in the distance Fin could see a set of black and white painted lock gates sticking up out of the grass. Relieved they reached the canal, the narrowboat Fin had seen early was nowhere in sight, so they began to walk along the towpath.

Overhead the sun was shining brightly and the sky was full of birds, stopping to look up at them. Fin smiled, 'Swallows,' he said, 'and not crows.'

Twenty minutes later, they heard the honking of Canada Geese and in the trees the caw of crows. The closer they got to the Canada Geese the louder the cawing of the crows became. The hairs on Fin's arm started to stand on end and he realised that he was beginning to feel nervous. Turning to him, Jenny took his hand and Fin realised that he was not the only one feeling anxious.

The watchful crows grew in number as they progressed along the towpath until a crescendo of caws caused them to believe they had reached their destination.

'Keep going,' whispered Fin, 'we are going to have circle back through the fields into those trees.' A half a mile later, they stopped at a picnic bench and sat down to discuss their options.

'We need to get a closer look at the farm,' said Jenny, 'but without arising suspicion.'

'It's late in the afternoon on a summer's day,' reasoned Fin, 'what's more natural than a boy taking a girl for a romantic walk into the woods. When the crows attacked me, my laughter drove them away, they couldn't see me.' Taking hold of Jenny's hand Fin looked her in the eye, 'The crows see our fear, our nervousness attracts them but we have to be really happy and distracted.'

'How are we going to do that?' began Jenny when Fin

leaned forward and kissed her. Taken a little aback Jenny quickly caught on and returned the kiss.

Twenty minutes later, Jenny with flowers in her hair was laughing as they walked hand in hand through the fields and to the woods. Every now and then Fin would run ahead and pick another daisy and return and only give it to Jenny if she kissed him. The distraction was working; Fin was enjoying himself so much he had nearly forgotten about Ash. Jenny's laughter was infectious and the sentry crows completely ignored them. Entering the woods Fin regretted their game had ended but Jenny reminded him they could play again on another day.

The woods were quiet and absent of crows, moving stealthily they crept towards the far side of the wood and sat down when they could see the farmhouse. The outbuildings housed the derelict bakery with signs declaring it closed for refurbishment.

'For a bakery that's closed there are a lot off people wearing white coats and hairnets,' commented Fin as he watched a hive of activity.

Leaning back against a tree, Jenny snuggled into Fin and they waited and watched. Bored, hungry and thirsty they waited until early evening arrived. The people wearing the white coats left the building entered the farmhouse and the farm went quiet.

Carefully they made their way down to the farm, slipped through a hole in the fence, and approached the rear of the old bakery.

'This is bizarre,' whispered Jenny, 'look all the crows are facing outwards as if their attention is elsewhere.'

'It's too easy,' responded Fin, 'if this is the Farm why does it have so little security?'

'The birds?' suggested Jenny.

'There must be more,' said Fin, 'let's wait a minute.' Sitting back in the evening shadows they waited, moments later two guards with dogs walked passed them and circled the building.

'That was too close,' groaned a relieved Jenny, 'let's see how long it takes them to walk the grounds.'

Before the guards returned, another set lapped them going the opposite direction.

'If we stay here we are going to get caught,' said Jenny starting to panic, 'I really don't like dogs.'

'Next time the guards pass we head for the second door on the right!' whispered Fin intently.

'Why the second door,' questioned Jenny, 'what's wrong with the closer one?'

'No one used it earlier,' replied Fin.

'Is that it?' cried Jenny, quietly, 'We need to get in somewhere unexpected!'

'Fine,' growled Fin, 'pick one but make it quick here they come.'

'Second on the right,' sighed Jenny, 'how are we going to get in?'

'Maybe it won't be locked!' said Fin, hopefully.

The guards passed them again without noticing although one of the dogs started sniffing in their direction.

'Now,' said Fin running across the farmyard to the second door on the right.

Jenny arrived first, the door was locked, 'Crap,' she said as she heard a dog bark nearby.

Grabbing the door handle Fin closed his eyes and concentrated on the door handle and it began to glow. The sound of excited dogs barking indicating the arrival of the approaching guards, trying to remain calm Fin imagined the lock turning and the handle moving, suddenly the door opened and they fell inside. Lying on the floor in each other's arms, they waited for the guards and their noisy dogs to pass.

The room they had entered into was dressed to look like a bakery reception, but unlike the outside, it was in pristine condition.

'Have you noticed what's missing?' asked Fin.

'No computers,' replied Jenny, 'I have never seen a

reception without a computer screen.'

'What was that you just did with the door,' asked Jenny, 'it was like magic?'

'I imagined the tumblers turning and the lock opening and it happened,' said Fin trying to explain, 'I'm not sure how I did it!'

Now inside the building Fin was not certain where to go next, leaving the reception behind them they decided to explore, a few doors down they found an administrative office and began to search draws and files.

'What is it they have against computers?' moaned Fin ruffling through a pile of papers on a desk.

Twenty minutes later Jenny found a filing cabinet marked 'Test Subjects Beta Two', opening it she saw immediately two names she recognised, 'I found them,' she cried.

'Shhh,' whispered Fin, 'we don't know how many people may still be around.'

'Sorry,' said an excited Jenny doing her best to whisper, 'it seems as if they have only two test subjects here at present, Greg Matthews and the Ash Bobrov!'

'Why only the two?' asked Fin trying to read over Jenny's shoulder.

'The master file says something about the Farm relocating to bigger facilities.'

'Does it say when?'

'No, the other facility is not ready yet.'

'Good,' said Fin, 'that means they are still here. Does it tell you which rooms they are in?'

'They are next door to each other, Greg is 101 and Ash is in 102.'

The deserted corridors gave them an artificial sense of confidence as they looked for the rooms, but Fin had a feeling that it would not last, especially if they managed to find Ash and Greg.

Finally, they went down a set of stairs and arrived at numbered cells, 101 and 102 were easy to find. The doors were solid steel with industrial frames; Fin thought they were strong enough to resist a bomb blast.

Fin tapped on Ash's door, 'Ash are you in there?'

'Bloody hell, is that you Fin?' replied and excited Ash.

'Jenny and I are both here,' replied Fin, 'I'm going to try to open the doors.'

Fin approached the door but there were no handles or obvious locks, standing feet and hands well apart, Fin lay his hands on the door. Concentrating hard Fin allowed his heat to fill the door, slowly the door began to vibrate and glow, a deep rumble fill the corridor and the walls began to shake. Suddenly the door burst open and in the distance, they heard an alarm go off.

Falling back from the door Fin allowed Ash to pass him, 'I'm exhausted,' he said falling to his knees.

'Fin you are going to have to do that again,' yelled Jenny, 'Ash if anyone comes down that corridor stop them.'

Helping Fin to his feet Jenny dragged him to Greg's cell door and placed him against the door, 'You can do this,' she encouraged.

'I'm not sure I can,' said Fin leaning against the door.

Down the corridor came the noise of dogs barking, doors slamming, shouts and the sound of running footsteps.

Running to the corner of the corridor, Ash filled his hands with fire and shouted, 'Fin you've got to hurry, they're nearly here!'

Shaking as he stood against the door Fin tried to concentrate but the effort was weakening him even more. Placing her hands on his shoulders Jenny tried to meld with him and encourage him, her hands began to glow too but the pain was too much and she had to let go. However, the boost was enough to tip the balance and Fin screamed and reapplied his hands to the door, it began to vibrate and glow, once again a deep rumble fill the corridor and the walls shook so much that the ceiling panels started to fall in.

The door flung open and Greg burst out into the corridor, 'Ash what the hell is happening?'

At that moment Ash was throwing fire down the corridor, turning round he yelled, 'Meet my brother Fin and his girlfriend, Jenny!'

A smile spread across Jenny's face as she dragged Fin up from the floor, 'We've got to get out of here.'

'Tell me about it,' said Fin, 'but I am knackered, I've got nothing left.'

'Yeah, well I have mate,' growled Greg, 'I have been a prisoner for nearly a year and I have had just about enough of this test tube factory.'

'I can't hold them,' yelled 'Ash there are too many of them!'

'Send the biggest ball of fire you can manage down the corridor and then follow me,' yelled Greg and ran down the corridor.

Tucking in behind Greg, Jenny half-carried Fin, Ash as instructed threw a ball of fire and caught up with them. Leading the way, Greg smashed through an old oak door, led them up a rear set of stairs and burst out into the farmyard.

Once outside they realised what trouble they were in, surrounding the farmyard were twenty black cloaked members of the Flock, overhead the sky was full of circling birds and behind them standing slightly out of breath were the guards and their dogs.

One cloaked figure moved forward and croaked, 'Greg I see you have found some friends, how kind of them to come to visit us. I'm afraid none of you will be allowed to leave.'

'I think you will find Rook that you are mistaken about that,' said Greg, 'my friends and I will be leaving immediately as you will be busy saving the farm.'

'Foolish boy,' said the Rook, 'your powers are puny compared to mine.'

'Maybe but together we may surprise you,' said Ash throwing a ball of fire at the roof of the farm where it instantly burst into flames.

Following Ash's cue, Fin grabbed a ball of fire off Ash and threw it at the farmhouse. Behind them was an almighty crash as the old tree next to car park swung a branch and flattened one of the cars, another tree swiped at the upper floor of the farmhouse half-demolishing it. Inspired by Greg's power over the tress Ash threw a ball of fire into flattened car and it exploded.

'Run,' shouted Fin leading them into the chaos, through the grounds and out into the woods.

Behind them, the chase began but as soon as the guards and their dogs entered the woods, the trees turned nasty and beat them away. The tress prevented any bird from landing and hid the guardians as they escaped.

'We need find some cover,' said Jenny, 'Fin is too exhausted to run much further.'

'Head for the canal,' said Fin, 'maybe we can hide in a boat or in a tunnel, but we can't stop yet.'

To everyone's amazement Greg, lifted Fin up and threw him over his shoulder and followed Jenny; as a result, they travelled much more quickly and soon reached the canal. Thankful that it was dark, they walked through the night until they reached a wooded cutting before the canal tunnel.

'I may be strong,' said Greg, 'but I can't carry Fin any further.' Greg gently laid Fin down on the ground in the shelter of the trees. 'We can sleep here,' he continued, 'I have asked the trees to watch over us. It is fortunate that it is summer and that they are so awake, in winter they sleep more deeply.'

Fin fell to the floor and dropped into a deep sleep. Ash and Jenny sat beside him and chattered quietly and Greg walked around their camp stroking the trees until he was satisfied they were safe. Just before dawn Fin awoke to fox looking at him, he laughed and the fox ran off. Feeling refreshed he looked around the camp, everyone was asleep and the trees swayed in a wind he could not feel. Closing his eyes, Fin sank back into sleep and dreamt of trees that walked and talked.

'What do you mean it's the wrong tunnel?' Greg asked exasperatedly.

'There are two tunnels both close to each other, one leads into the outskirts of Sedgesworth and the other tunnels under Ravenswood,' explained Jenny, 'in the night we have travelled the wrong way.' She pointed west, 'The tunnel we want is three miles away in that direction.'

'How can you be so sure?' asked Greg, refusing to believe Jenny.

'Because the sun rises in the east and sinks in the west,' growled Jenny, starting to get annoyed, 'and we needed to go west.' Seeing Greg was about to argue some more she swung all her hair snaking it in Greg's direction, 'Listen tree boy, if you don't want to be turned to stone pay attention to my lips; I studied the map before we came to rescue you and we have gone the wrong way.' Jenny paused, daring Greg to object again, wisely, he chose to be quiet, 'Somehow we have to get from here to the Ravenswood Tunnel without getting seen or caught.'

'Today is Sunday,' said Fin, 'Eiry and Sed will be able to cover for us over the weekend, but if we are not back by tonight all hell will break loose.'

Sitting down together, they discussed their options, having no money meant getting the bus back was impossible and walking along the roads would only get them caught.

'If the Sedgesworth Tunnel is the same as the Ravenswood one,' said Fin, 'then there is no way we can use or hide in it, there's no towpath.'

'We are going to have to go across country,' said Ash, 'but the fields are all open and we would be seen for miles.'

'That's the problem,' said a frustrated Greg, 'while I

was at the farm someone escaped and they were seen and caught by the birds.' He looked around the tree canopy, 'we are sheltered here but once away from the trees we are exposed.' Standing up Greg stretched, 'Everything that flies is looking for us, all the friendly birds will be hiding, so we need to keep close to the ground and out of sight.'

'I think it makes sense to keep close to the canal,' said Jenny, 'it has more cover than the fields.'

In the absence of argument, they set off keeping close to the trees, at the edge of the cutting they kept low to a hedgerow. Every few minutes they were over-flown by crows flying in square search patterns and they would lie still against the ground. They made slow progress and at some points crawling and stopping was all they could do.

'I need a wee!' whispered Jenny, 'I'm also thirsty but I can't go on much further without bursting.'

'Up ahead is a copse of trees,' said Greg, 'can you wait that long?'

'Well I'm not peeing here in front of you,' said an indignant Jenny.

Fin wanted to laugh but he was getting desperate too, 'Keep moving I think we all need a comfort break,' he said and then to himself, 'why is it in books that characters never need the toilet?'

After a reaching the copse, they spread out and returned feeling greatly relieved, but still thirsty and hungry. They continued to crawl along underneath the bushes, they were filthy and they complained about all the scratches and bites. Still they were sheltered from the birds that patrolled the skies overhead but in the distance they heard a narrowboat approaching.

'We are hidden from the birds,' complained Greg, 'but anyone in a boat is going to spot us instantly and let's face it, we look pretty stupid.'

Realising there was no escape they lay down and tried to hide behind the tall grass at the foot of the hedge. Fin lay there and watched the narrowboat approach, it was dark green with yellow and red coachwork, it was a bit shabby and needed a repaint but he liked it. The man steering boat seemed to be lost in a dream world and the birds overhead, occasionally flew over him but ignored the boat.

The narrowboat slowed down and the man jumped off and pulled the boat to a stop. 'Don't just lie there get in the boat,' he said loudly without looking in their direction, 'the crows are about to come back and I want to be moving by then.'

With no other options, the four of them ran over to the rear of the boat, climbed down into the engine room and into the boat. The man pushed the boat away from the bank and the boat chugged away down the canal. The approaching crows swung down low to fly over the boat but seeing nothing amiss carried on.

'It's okay they've gone,' he yelled over the noise of the engine.

Fin climbed out and stood next to the man as he steered, he looked up and all the birds were flying in patterns over the fields and he breathed a sigh of relief. The boat top had been recently repainted and there was the simply design of a fish painted on the hatch.

'It's an 'Ichthus',' said the man, 'it's an early Christian symbol, and it means Jesus Christ, Son of God, Saviour.' Smiling the man said, 'The early disciples used it as a secret symbol in times of persecution.'

'Why did you stop?' asked Fin.

'George, the vicar of St Hubert's is a friend of mine; he got a message from two of his parishioners, Gerty and Prude, and thought you might be in trouble.' The man laughed, 'He knew I was on holiday around here and asked me to look out for you, I saw the birds hunting so I guessed you would be near by.'

'Can you get us close to Ravenswood,' asked Fin.

'I can do bit better than that,' said the man, 'George told me about the maintenance passage in the Ravenswood

Tunnel, I will drop you all off there.'

CHAPTER FOURTEEN – THE SIEGE OF NARCISSUS LODGE

The crows ignored the Narrowboat and they cruised along at two-miles and hour until the late afternoon when they arrived at the Ravenswood Tunnel. Instructions issued by the canal authority indicated that they could only enter the tunnel within a ten-minute period after the hour.

'It takes about twenty-minutes to pass through the tunnel,' said the man, 'so if we stick to the time slot we shall travel through without the possibility of meeting a boat coming the other way.'

The Narrowboat tied up at the mooring while they waited for the time slot to arrive, overhead a canopy of trees kept them hidden from view.

Jumping out onto the towpath Fin read the name of the boat, 'Marshwiggle, I like the name,' he said, 'Where is it from?'

The man laughed, 'It's from C.S. Lewis' Narnia story, "The Silver Chair," Puddlegum was a…'

'Marshwiggle,' finished Fin, 'I read the series years ago, I'd forgotten about Puddleglum.'

Climbing back onto the boat the man started the

engine and with Fin's help untied from the moorings. Switching on his headlights and navigation lights the man steered the boat into the tunnel.

'It'll take us about ten minutes to reach the maintenance tunnel but I have no idea where it is as I have not been this way before,' said the man, 'so keep looking.'

Standing next to the man at the helm, Fin struggled to see, it was hard to make anything out other than shadows in the spotlights.

'It can get a bit wet,' said the man, as they chugged through a deluge.

'No kidding,' said a soaking wet Fin.

As they progressed, the height of the tunnel varied greatly and at times, they both had to duck to avoid hitting their heads. Behind them the entrance was a spot of light in the distance, everything in front was dark.

'There's a slight bend in the tunnel coming up,' said the man, 'George reckons the entrance to the maintenance passage is around here.'

The boat slowed down and began to move from side to side, 'It's harder to steer the slower you go,' he said, 'but we can't risk going passed it.'

Slowing down to a crawl the boat glided along, the only noise being that of the diesel engine that was magnified by being enclosed.

A dark shadow approached on their right, 'I can see it,' cried Fin pointing to the wall.

The helmsman put the boat into reverse and stopped the boat next to the shadow, the boat bobbed about as he tried to jump off with the centre rope. Moments later the man had pulled the boat into the side and indicated that they should climb out. 'George is waiting for Greg and Ash at the church and a friend of his is arranging a police escort to safety,' he said, 'you two need to get back to the school before you are missed.'

'Thank you,' said Ash shaking the man's hand, 'you never told us your name.'

'No I didn't,' he replied, 'but we all need some mystery in our lives!' Laughing he climbed back on to the boat and moved off, 'Be careful and good luck.'

With Jenny leading the way, they made good progress through the passageways and after a tiring, but uneventful, journey they arrived in the church cellar to find George waiting for them.

'Greg,' he cried, 'it is so good to see you again!'

'You too,' he replied in a drained voice.

'If you and Ash will come with me, I will get you to safety.'

'I'm not coming,' said Ash.

'What?' exclaimed George.

'I have something I need to do first,' he said, 'I need to see Elizabeth.'

'I can pass a message on,' said Fin,

'Not this one it's something I have to say myself.'

'No way,' said George passionately, 'if you go back all of this rescue attempt will have been in vain.'

'I'll go with you mate,' said a tired Greg, 'you'll need my help.'

'Thanks but no thanks,' replied Ash, 'get to safety with George, if you are found alive and well it will change everything. This is something that I have to do myself.' Getting up Ash climbed back into the passageway and headed back to Ravenswood and it took a moment or two for Fin and Jenny to catch him up.

The trip back was made in a companionable silence, Ash was in no mood to speak and the others did not know what to say to him, yet they all drew strength from their friendship.

On arriving at the wood store, it was obvious something was wrong; everywhere was silent. Looking around Fin could see everywhere was deserted, against the side of the wood store a sign had been posted: WARNING: GAS LEAK, PLEASE WILL ALL STUDENTS RETURN AND STAY IN THEIR

LODGES UNTIL TOLD THAT IS SAFE TO LEAVE.

'I don't believe it,' commented Fin, 'it's another scheme to isolate us.'

Joining him Ash looked around, 'Why's it so quiet?' he asked suspiciously, 'Can you see those shadows up there?' Ash pointed at the eaves of Ravenswood House.

'They're crows,' said Jenny, 'I can see them everywhere, hiding, watching, waiting,' she shivered, 'it gives me the creeps.'

Keeping low in the shadows of the buildings, they made their way to Elizabeth's apartment but it was empty. Carefully, they edged around to their lodge and saw that it was guarded too, standing in the dark shadows under the trees were black hooded figures.

'Bugger,' swore Ash, 'the Council of Crows are here too.'

'We need a distraction,' said Fin, hiding quietly he waited for an opportunity to come, 'something, anything…'

An hour later, there came a throbbing sound that vibrated the ground, in the distance two RAF helicopters were engaged in a fight exercise, twisting in and around each other. Come this way thought Fin, noisy and violent as they were they kept their distance, frustrated all Fin could do was watch and wait.

'This has happened a few times since I've been here,' whispered Ash looking at the helicopters, 'only once have they flown across the school.'

Frustration mounted as the helicopters danced their way across the sky to the south of Ravenswood; slowly they moved further away and then vanished from sight.

Shrugging his shoulders to the others Fin said, 'Oh well.'

Suddenly, out of nowhere the helicopters roared overhead barely skimming the tops of the trees.

'Bloody hell,' swore Ash.

'RUN!' yelled Jenny grabbing both boys by the arms

and dragging them across the paths to the lodge.

Distracted by the helicopters' over flight the watchers failed to see them running, the birds scattered horrified by the noise of the engines also saw nothing. Bursting through the door, they terrified the girls and Elizabeth, slamming the door behind them they lay on the floor laughing.

'Ash,' screamed Eiry pulling him off the floor, giving him a big hug, and then kissing him, 'you're safe!'

'I think I'm far from being safe,' replied Ash and then turning to Elizabeth who was limping towards him, 'I am so sorry,' he said, 'they shouldn't have hurt you.'

'It wasn't your fault,' Elizabeth said painfully, 'they wanted you and there was nothing I could do to stop them.'

Reaching up to Elizabeth's face Ash stroked her scar gently, 'Look what they did to you because of me,' a tear ran down his face, 'some guardian I'm turning out to be.'

'It really wasn't your fault,' said Elizabeth wiping the tear from Ash's face, 'you're alive and we have got to get you to safety.' she said wincing with pain, 'Sorry, my ribs hurt.'

'Right now my safety is unimportant, I could have gone to George's with Greg, 'he replied.

'You saved Greg too,' smiling she hugged Ash gently.

Ash accepted the hug and pulled her close into him, Elizabeth screamed in pain, but Ash ignored it. As Fin watched, pain wracked through both their bodies and Ash began to glow; soon only Ash was screaming and he collapsed to the floor. Everyone rushed to him and picked him up, he was barely conscious. Lifting his hand Ash gestured towards Elizabeth, 'It was the least I could do,' he said before he fainted.

Walking over to him Elizabeth picked him up, carried him to the sofa, and laid him down to sleep, opening his eyes Ash whispered, 'I will alright soon, my body needs to refresh itself.'

'How did you manage to carry him,' asked Sed, 'you are too wounded.'

'Not anymore,' said Elizabeth.

Elizabeth was correct, the scars on her face had gone, and she was breathing without pain and walking without a limp.

'The Phoenix has the power to bring healing,' explained Fin, 'the only downside is he had to feel all your pain to remove it. Ash will recover but not for a few days, the greater the trauma the longer the recovery time.' Pausing for a moment Fin looked at Elizabeth, 'This is why he refused to go to safety he wanted you to be whole and free from pain.'

Kneeling down next to Ash, Elizabeth stroked his forehead, 'Thank you, I love you too.' Standing up her voice filled with confidence, 'We are a family and we stand or fall as a family. Thanks to Ash, I am now strong enough to fight with you. The gas leak story is nonsense and when they realise that you have sneaked passed them they will come for you. I'm not sure what I can do to help, but you have my word, they will only get to you over my dead body!' Elizabeth's eyes blazed and Fin did not doubt her for a second.

As evening approached and the light began to fade, Elizabeth insisted that they all eat. Outside crows began to gather around their lodge, soon every branch and ledge held a pair of watching eyes. From the shadows of the trees emerged the hooded watchers, Fin recognised Raven and Rook but could not see the Lord Crow.

A stumbling old man walked across the grass to the lodge ignoring all the gathered watchers and was stopped by the Raven.

'Birdie,' he cackled, 'what are you doing here?'

'I'm not intimidated by you, Raven,' replied Mr Byrd, 'I've known for a while that you have been making a nest here, well I have seen it all before and it is pitiful.'

'Where do you think you are going?' growled Raven.

'Oh for goodness sake,' replied Mr Byrd through clenched teeth, 'I am going to talk to my niece, she has been in a car accident you know,' Mr Byrd considered the Raven and nodded, 'of course you know, you did this to her!'

'Go back to your rooms Birdie before you get plucked!' said the Raven angrily.

'Or what?' asked Birdie, 'Just because you are using a silly voice and have covered your face with a hood does not make you scary Raven, or should I say Mr Chough!'

Watching Raven through the window Fin smiled at Birdie's courage, he may be doddering but steel ran through him.

'Be gone old fool,' said Mr Chough, 'before you get hurt, crawl off to your rooms and make yourself a cup of tea.'

Ignoring them Birdie walked to the front of the lodge and knocked on the door, 'I'm sorry Elizabeth, Mr Chough has gone too far this time and I am sorry that you got hurt. I will see what my friends can do.'

'Enough!' cried Mr Chough and Mr Byrd flew through the air and landed in a heap by the main house.

'You will be sorry you did that Raven,' he said standing up.

'Children,' said the Raven addressing the lodge, 'you will surrender yourselves to the judgement of the Flock or you will die.'

Inside the house, Elizabeth barricaded the door, 'Cover the windows,' she said, 'lock all the doors and keep out of sight.'

Outside the sky darkened as a summer storm approached, the wind got up and the flock's cloaks fluttered in the wind. Suddenly it began to rain heavily yet the figures stood there regardless as if waiting. Finally, a small hooded figure arrived; watching from the window Fin was convinced that his feet were not touching the ground. The air temperature dropped and ice began to form on the windows of the lodge.

Recognising the figure Fin realised why they were waiting the Lord Crow had arrived. Three figures walked forward into the empty space in front of the lodge, Crow, Raven and Rook.

'My Lord,' said Raven, 'We are ready.'

'Good, good, you may proceed,' said the Crow, 'and Raven?'

'Yes lord'

'No mistakes this time,' growled the Crow, then turning to Rook, 'any news on the Matthews' boy?'

'None my Lord,' cringed Rook.

'I will deal with you later,' he replied ominously.

Standing by the window Eiry watched the figures outside; the freak summer storm had turned the rain into hail and snow. Outside the figures began to chant, raised their hands and pointed at the house. The watching crows all cawed at once and attacked the house, bouncing of the doors and windows. Locked inside the sound was terrifying as the birds attacked, the noise of the wind howled until the full force of winter drove the birds for shelter. Snow fell and world became silent, evening turned into night and snow lay thick on the ground. Still the figures stood chanting, Sed pulled Eiry away from the window and sat her down.

Outside the storm settled but the snow remained, 'I have never seen it snow in June before,' Sed exclaimed, 'how can we fight them if they can harness the weather?'

'I have never heard of the Flock being able to control the weather,' said Elizabeth shaking her head, 'they are ignoring it but it's hardly helping them, the crows and ravens have had to seek shelter from it.'

'Why don't they just walk in and get us,' asked Sed.

'Because they know I am here,' said a very tired Ash, 'I feel much better now thanks,' he said noticing their looks of concern, 'the pain has gone I'm just a little tired.'

Outside the hooded figures approached the lodge,

Raven nodded his head and one walked forward and tried to open the door. Realising that it was locked he hit it with palm of his hand and it burst inwards. Stepping over the threshold a ball of fire caught him and he flew out and crashed at the Raven's feet.

Ignoring the struggling figure at his feet Raven nodded and five hooded figures moved forward and walked through the door. A second ball of fire flew towards them but was waved away as if it was nothing.

'Sorry,' said Ash struggling to create another fire ball, 'I'm a bit more tired than I thought.'

'Give that to me,' demanded Fin taking the ball of fire off Ash, immediately the fireball grew in intensity and power and Fin threw it at the figures in the doorway. Exploding on contact it blew the five figures back out into the snow.

'That's not possible,' exclaimed Elizabeth, 'Ash is the Phoenix and there can be one only at a time!'

Slamming the door shut, 'Ash is my twin brother,' replied Fin, 'somehow there are two of us now, but neither of us is a true Phoenix.'

'Can we hold them off,' asked Sed who was holding Eiry, 'Eiry's running a fever; she's so hot I can't cool her down.'

It was then Fin noticed that Sed had been laying a cold cloth on her forehead, not much of an army he thought, Ash too weak to fight and Elizabeth, Sed and Eiry powerless. 'Jenny,' he asked, 'can you do anything?'

'I don't know,' she said, 'but I can try.'

Taking hold of Ash's hand, she willed strength into him and his face became less grey, 'Ash cool Eiry down.'

Going over to Eiry, Ash kissed her on the forehead and she cooled down a little and gave him a smile.

Looking out the window, Jenny thought hard, her amazing hair standing on end and moving gently from side to side.

'Do you all have powers I know nothing about?' asked

Elizabeth.

'We're normal,' said Eiry and Sed at the same time.

'If you call that bloody normal!' laughed Ash.

Feeling better Eiry went into the kitchen and came back with two saucepans, 'I may not be Supergirl but I can smack people over the head if they annoy me.'

'Tell me about it,' said Ash rubbing his head.

Screams of pain echoed from outside, Jenny was gently singing a nursery rhyme and rocking side to side:

'Tick-tack! tick-tack!

White old face with figures black!

So when dismal, stormy days

Keep him from his out-door plays,

Most that he cares for is to sit

Watching, always watching it.

And when the hour strikes he thinks,

A dear, wise head has the little Jinx!

'The clock strikes one,

The mice ran down!'

Outside the hooded figures were flailing side to side in pain as the nursery rhyme embedded itself into their minds.

'What is she singing?' asked Ash.

'Hickory Dickory Dock,' replied Elizabeth, 'remind me not argue with her if she can do that much damage with a nursery rhyme.'

One hooded figure remained unperturbed, smiling the Crow said, 'Very good little girl,' and then cawed at the lodge; a wave of sound struck the windows smashing them all at once.

Blasted by flying glass Jenny fell to the floor her face bleeding from multiple cuts and stopped singing. Angry Ash ran to her and picked her up,

'It's okay,' she said wiping some blood off her face, 'I'm just a bit dazed.'

Bursting through the door a crow grabbed Ash by the shoulders and threw him to the floor, there was a double clunk as Eiry and Sed struck at the same time. The crow fell to the floor unconscious with a massive bruise forming on his forehead. Jumping up Ash sent a fireball out of the door to deter anyone else from trying to enter.

Following their leader's example, the crows began to craw and the noise battered the sides of the lodge. Ash kept producing fire but in his weakened state he was unable to keep it up and the crows began to approach the lodge.

Determined to resist they all stood in a line and encouraged each other. Ash produced fire and Fin propelled it outwards their attackers. Jenny began to sing again and Elizabeth and the girls swung pans. There was a loud cry and the crows attacked, in the end the sauce pans became their best line of defence, as each crow entered they were battered by three angry women.

'We can't keep this up,' said an exhausted Elizabeth, 'we are outnumbered.'

Looking out of the window Fin watched the Crow, Raven and Rook laugh aloud, 'Enough,' shouted the Crow, 'we have enjoyed the sport but apart from being amusing your defence is futile.'

The Crow walked forward slowly and stopped outside the door, 'I do not wish to hurt you, harming you is the last thing I want to do, although, I cannot say the same for Raven.'

'I have already felt what Raven is capable of,' shouted Elizabeth, 'I would rather die then let him touch me again!'

'Yes, I am sorry about that,' the Crow sighed, 'I will be having a word with him later, he will regret his misguided enthusiasm for inflicting pain.' The Crow's voice hardened, 'However, it is time to face reality there is nothing you can do to stop us taking the Phoenix from you, I'm not interested in the rest of you, hand him over and we will leave.'

Out of sight of the Crow, Jenny had her hands on Ash's shoulder, 'I have done all I can,' she said, 'I have nothing left to strengthen you with.'

'It will be sufficient,' said Ash, 'it has to be.'

Hearing nothing from inside the Crow walked away. 'Raven I want the Phoenix and Elizabeth left alive,' the Crow said menacingly, 'the rest I am not interested in.'

'If you do not want to see your friends die,' gloated the Raven, 'then come out and face me.'

'I have no choice,' said Ash, 'I have to face him.'

'No,' said Eiry, 'stay here with us.'

'You heard the Crow he only wants me,' said Ash softly, 'at least this way you will survive to come and find me again.' Holding Eiry's hand for a moment he said, 'Everything will be alright, I promise.'

With sadness, they watched Ash walk out the door and two of the crows take him by the arms and lead him away. Sobbing Eiry wanted to go with him but the others would not let her.

'Kill them all!' cried Raven.

'What about Elizabeth,' asked Rook, 'our Lord said she was not to be harmed?'

'Kill them all!' said Raven dismissively.

'No!' shouted Ash throwing off his captors and prepared a ball of flames, 'You will leave my friends alone,' he yelled as he sent one ball of fire after another at the Raven.

Caught off guard the Raven was engulfed in flames and screamed in agony. Burnt and singed he threw the flames off and pointed a finger at Ash who was propelled high into the air, 'Die you little slug,' he cried and let Ash fall.

There was a sickening thud as Ash hit the concrete pathway and did not move, a pool of blood formed around his body and his sightless eyes stared up into the night. Silence filled the grounds as everyone realised that Ash was dead.

Screaming in agony Fin rose off the floor as wings of fire erupted from his back, his hands burst into flames and his body began to glow white. Flying through the doorway

Fin hovered in front of the Raven, 'You killed my brother,' he yelled in anger, 'up and until now we shared the fire but now there is only one, I am the Phoenix! Fly away little bird before I destroy you and your flock.'

The flock tried to fight the Phoenix but his power and strength were too great for them, and they fled. Landing on the grass Fin noticed he had melted the snow around him in a perfect circle.

Running over to Ash, Fin wrapped his arms around him and tried to revive him, but Ash was lifeless. Falling to his knees, he began to cry, Eiry joined him and together they wept.

Realising that it was too late for Ash, Elizabeth spoke to Jenny and Sed, 'Go to the main house and go into Mr Chough's office and telephone the police and the ambulance.' Producing a card from her pocket, she handed it to Sed, 'If you can, ring David and George too and get them here when you have finished return to your lodge. I will try to raise the rest of the staff from their hiding places.' Taking her Jacket off Elizabeth draped it over Ash's body, 'Fin take Eiry back home and make her a drink and stay with her until the police get here.'

Wanting to stay with Ash, Fin was going to object but now his fire had receded he was dithering with cold, Eiry looked like she was going to be sick, and the look on Elizabeth's face gave him no option.

An hour later, they all sat around the fire, the warmth of the summer evening was melting the snow but they were old cold to the bone.

Sitting in silence shock had overwhelmed them all; even the noise of the air ambulance landing in the grounds did not disturb them.

It was not until David walked in that they stirred, 'What happened?' he asked sitting down next to them, 'Start from the beginning and tell me everything.'

Everyone looked at Fin and he nodded, and told David the whole story. It took a while, because every now and then one of the others would fill in a detail that he had missed. Listening David took notes but mostly he sat and listened.

Around two in the morning George arrived, walking in he looked at David and shook his head, 'There is no sight of them anywhere, wherever they have gone they have vanished.'

'And Mr Chough' asked David, 'I would like to have a word with him?'

'He has disappeared with the rest.'

A Special Branch officer entered, looked at David and indicated that they should step outside.

'It's okay Michael,' David said, 'these children know more about what's going on here than we do!'

'Very good Sir,' he replied, 'we have captured one of the crows, she was trying to escape from Ravenswood House, and Williams caught her jumping out from a upstairs window.'

'Where is she now?' asked David.

'She's handcuffed in the back of one of our cars,' replied Michael.

'Good,' said David appreciatively, 'when you have finished your report escort her in.'

Yes Sir,' acknowledged Michael, 'our team have just reported back from the Farm, there is nothing much left. A fire had damaged a good section of the property but the Flock destroyed the rest as they left. Forensics is examining the place but they told me not to hold my breath as it's been wiped clean.'

Nodding David dismissed the officer and sent him to go and get the prisoner. 'Thank you for telling me everything,' he looked at them, 'Do you mind if I speak to the prisoner while you are here, I would value your thoughts?'

No one objected and moments later Michael walked in escorting one of the crows. She was tall and with her hood thrown back, they could see she had dark black her and her eyes shone with anger.

'Where is the Raven hiding?' demanded David.

The woman ignored his question and stared defiantly back at him, obviously determined not to answer any questions. David persisted but she remained silent.

'Do you mind if I talk to her?' asked Jenny.

'Be my guest,' he replied.

'I am going to ask you to tell us what you know,' said Jenny, 'and you probably think that silence will serve you well, but I am afraid you will be wrong. You see I have the ability of walking through peoples' minds and while it does not hurt me, I can't promise that it won't hurt you. So you will answer David's questions or I will enter your mind and take your memories from you.'

The woman remained silent.

'What is your name?' asked Jenny.

Closing her eyes the woman ignored the question, Jenny reached across and touched her and she sat bolt upright with a look of surprise on her face.

'Oh I see,' said Jenny, 'they took your name away from you and you can't remember it. Well your name is Maria Yvonne Croft and you come from Leeds.'

The woman fell forward and Jenny touched her again, only this time more gently, 'Remember.'

The whole demeanour of Maria changed and the anger left her body and she began to cry, 'I had forgotten my name, they took everything from me and turned me into this.'

'Please Maria, tell us your story,' said Jenny gently, 'what happened to you.'

Maria's story was long, complicated and catalogued a series of abuses of the mind; she had been kidnapped, stripped of her memories and made to serve the Flock.

'Can you tell us what happened to the Raven?' asked Jenny.

'He's dead and hanging from the walls of the underground chamber,' she whispered in a horrified voice.

'What happened?' asked Jenny.

'The Lord Crow, the Raven and I went down to the chamber after the Phoenix drove us away. The Crow was very angry and argued with the Raven.

'So Raven,' began the Crow, 'I give you one instruction and you ignore it.'

'No my Lord,' grovelled the Raven.

'Silence fool!' snarled the Crow and whipped his hand out, Raven flew into the air and crashed into the wall, the chains wrapped themselves around him and began to crush him, 'I told you not to hurt the boy or Elizabeth and you killed the boy and wasted any opportunity we had to convert him.' Then in anger he yelled, 'I told you Elizabeth was under my protection and you ignored that too. So you will die in great pain,' The chains tightened further around the Raven, 'but before you die, I want you to see my face and realise your stupidity.'

The Crow dropped his hood and the Raven screamed out, 'No it can't be!'

'They were his last words,' said Maria.

'Did you see his face?' asked David.

'No,' replied Maria, 'he had his back to me and I never saw it, but whoever it was it devastated the Raven.'

'Thank you Maria,' finished David, 'Michael please take her somewhere safe, she is as much a victim as poor Ash.'

Maria and Michael left, leaving David, 'Well I think that covers everything, you need to go to bed now and get some sleep, if you can, tomorrow's going to be a long and busy day.'

Not expecting to sleep Fin went to his room and climbed into bed, ignoring Ash's empty bed he switched the light off and prepared himself for a long night staring at the ceiling. In seconds, he was asleep.

EPILOGUE – THE POWER OF THE PHOENIX

The memorial service at Ravenswood took place a few days later, little mention was made about the night Ash died, instead Mr Byrd dwelt on Ash's life, the impact he had made on the school and his friends and how much he would be missed. Special Branch tried to hide how Ash had died but everyone there knew that the Flock had infiltrated Ravenswood and that Ash had died trying to save his friends.

Afterwards at the crematorium, Fin felt the loss more keenly, it was so real, so different, and so personal. Dressed in their most respectable clothes, Fin, Jenny, Eiry and Sed sat together. Watching over them and sharing their grief, Elizabeth and David sat together, and representing Ravenswood stood the new acting head, Mr Byrd. Sitting next to Fin, Jenny held his hand trying to offer him some physical support, but Fin was oblivious to everything. Outside the crematorium Special Branch officers guarded the funeral service and kept the press at bay with a DA-Notice.

'We have come here to do three things,' said George

233

dressed in his vicar's robes of a cassock, surplus and black scarf, 'to say a last goodbye to Ash, to remember him for who he was; to pray for you his friends and to come to God who alone can bring comfort to us in times of grief and loss.'

The service drifted by Fin without him noticing anything until the curtain closed around the coffin and everyone started filing out. Lifting his head Fin looked around, so few people, he thought, to remember a life that had burnt so brightly.

The small funeral party returned to the vicarage where George's housekeeper had prepared some finger food and light refreshments for them. Thankfully, Mr Byrd after a cup of tea left and returned to Ravenswood. Afterwards, Fin was not sure who started him laughing, but soon they were all telling stories of Ash's antics and his ability to swear and get away with it.

When finally, the food was finished and the stories told they all got ready to return to Ravenswood.

'I had to wait until Mr Byrd had left,' said David but I wanted to you to see these. In his hand, he held copies of all the national daily papers; the headlines were variations on a theme: Escaped from Hell, Human Guinea Pig Found Alive, Abducted Child Escaped Experiments. Picking one at random David began to read aloud, 'Missing schoolboy, Greg Matthews (14), was found alive and well by Yorkshire Police. Detective Inspector David Llewellyn Jones explained, 'Early this week, the missing schoolboy Greg Matthews escaped from a group of activists that wanted to use him for illegal human experimentation. Greg is very lucky to be alive and is now in a place of safety. I am afraid that all other aspects of this case are covered by a DA-Notice 04-05 and cannot be reported."

'That's fantastic,' said Jenny.

'Greg is going to be placed with a foster family,' explained David, 'we have given him a completely new identity and moved him far from here.'

'Can we speak to him?' asked Eiry.

'Yes you can,' replied David, 'but only from a safe phone, we don't want to put him back in danger again, but you are his friends and it would be terrible to isolate him completely.'

'Thank you,' said Eiry, 'I'm really tired and exhausted do you mind taking us home?'

After a quick thank you to Helen for feeding and looking after them, David took them home in one of the Range Rovers belonging to Special Branch.

During the weeks that followed, life returned to normal at Ravenswood, Mr Byrd continued in his role as acting head while the police forensics teams sifted through the house and grounds. To Fin's relief the only secret passage discovered was that to the underground chamber but after Mr Chough's body had been removed, the entrance vanished and was never found again. Sonar teams sought to find another entrance but all they found was solid rock.

The death of Ash had a profound effect on Fin and his friends and David, with help of George, arranged for bereavement counselling for each of them. They celebrated Jenny's birthday but afterwards no one could remember much about it. At the end of a week of brilliant sunshine, as the end of the summer term approached, Elizabeth asked them all to meet them in her garden.

In her hands, Elizabeth carried a small wooden casket, 'We didn't want to scatter Ash's remains in the crematorium,' she said, 'we thought it would be more fitting for them to be scattered here.'

'May we all do it?' asked Fin.

Elizabeth opened the casket and produced a plastic bag of ashes, passing it over to Fin he spread some among the flowers and passed the bag on to Eiry. Each in turn spread some of Ash's remains onto the garden until Elizabeth, finally, sprinkled the last. No one spoke or cried; instead, they stood each lost in some personal memory.

'With your permission,' said Elizabeth, 'I would like to plant and ash tree in the gardens and put a garden bench next to it, so when we need to we can all sit and down and remember.'

'That would be nice,' said Fin, not sure what he really thought, 'I'm sure Ash would have something apt to say about it!'

That night Fin asked Elizabeth if she would join them in the lodge so after their evening meal they all sat together.

'This last year has been an amazing one,' said Fin, 'Jenny can see in the dark and read memories; I discovered that I had a brother and that my mother was a dragon-child. Ash and I for a while shared the powers of the Phoenix and we found Greg.' Pausing Fin looked around the room, 'Ash had the amazing ability to heal people and it is wonderful to see you truly healed Elizabeth.'

Everyone smiled at Elizabeth and she blushed.

'But there is one thing that has bothered me,' continued Fin, 'Jenny please come here.'

A confused look crossed Jenny's face as she went over and held Fin's hand, 'What?'

'Jenny I know now that it was not my fault that you were struck blind,' Fin said with tears in his eyes, 'it was my mother's and I can't do anything about that and the pain you went through.'

'Fin it's alright,' said Jenny smiling, 'I know that.'

'But I have had a lot of time to think,' said Fin thoughtfully, 'Ash's death taught me something,' Fin lifted Jenny's hand and pulled her into a tight hug, 'I am the Phoenix, the son of the Phoenix, a dragon and I can do this.'

Tears rolled down Fin's face and dripped onto Jenny, wings of fire erupted from his back, he encircled Jenny with fire, and they both burst into flames. In agony Fin screamed, the flames went out and he collapsed unconscious to the floor.

When he awoke an hour later, Jenny stared at him with her bright blue eyes; Fin reached up and stroked the beautifully smooth skin on her face.

Taking Fin's hand Jenny kissed it, 'Thank you,' she said as a smile lit up her face.

COMING SOON

Fin Butler
and the
Ice Queen

PHILIP JANVIER

OMEN OF THE ICE-QUEEN

I heard the moan of the Ice-Queen's lament,
I heard the Mermaid shriek and fall,
I heard the Phoenix weep in the woods beyond,
And I heard the Dragon haggle as it died.
I saw the kiss of the wild-flower girl,
I saw the Crow sitting feathers in hand,
I saw the royal-bride dance and sing,
And I foresaw that the Wyvern will awake.

Ancient Fragment

CHAPTER 1 – THE POWERLESS GUARDIANS

Screaming in agony Fin tossed and turned in his sleep. Wings of fire erupted from his back and encircled the girl with the crazy hair and the bright blue eyes. Delirious Fin reached up and stroked the beautifully smooth skin on her face. Fighting with his duvet Fin fell out of bed and watched smoke seep out under his bedroom door and out into the landing. Outside his room, in the roof space, the smoke alarm began to beep persistently and Fin groaned and waited for the inevitable

'Fin, Wake up, Fin!' shouted Jenny from the foot of the boy's stairs, looking up at Eiry and Sed on the girl's landing she shrugged her shoulders, broke the house rules, ran up the stairs, and hammered on his door. 'Fin Butler, you are smoking again,' then slapping the door with the palm of her hand she yelled, 'If you don't open this door at once I am going to kick it in!'

The bedroom door opened in a cloud of smoke and a

bleary-eyed Fin stood and stared, 'I guess I was dreaming again, 'he said.

'You think!' yelled Jenny, her bright blue eyes shining and her hair standing on end, 'What was it this time?'

Lost for words Fin felt it was impossible to tell Jenny that he was dreaming about her again, but as usual she managed to read his mind without actively doing so.

'Stop dwelling on it,' said Jenny softly, 'you lost your powers giving me my sight back.'

'Yet somehow when I dream they come back and burn my bed,' groaned Fin, 'do you know how embarrassing it is to keep having to get new bed linen?'

Looking into Fin's face all Jenny could do was laugh.

'I think you should go downstairs before Elizabeth responds to the smoke alarm, finds you up here and gives you a detention,' said Fin feeling slightly hurt and bemused.

'Fine,' Jenny cried with a twinkle in her eye, 'next time you can burn to death!'

Returning to the empty room Fin opened the window and allowed the smoke to dissipate. The nightmares had changed but they were just as persistent, now instead of being trapped and burnt alive, he kept dreaming that he was the mythical Phoenix and had wings of fire. Looking down at the scorched bed sheets and the imprint of the wings burnt into them he sighed, what was the use of special powers if they only became apparent when he was asleep.

Sitting down Fin stared at the spare bed in his room and thought about the last year. It had started badly, arrested and charged with being an arsonist called the 'Firebird'.' Being found not guilty and moved with his friend Jenny to Ravenswood, a home for suspected extranatural young people. Jenny a blind girl, turned out to be a gorgon. She could see in the dark with her hair and could read and walk in people's memories. Made close friendships with Eiry and Sed, and discovered that his roommate Ash was his twin brother.

The smoke cleared finally from his room, Fin closed the window and sat down on the edge of his bed. That was the good stuff, he thought; the head teacher, Mr Chough, turned out to be the evil Raven and died at the hands of his own master Crow, ironically, in a torture chamber beneath his own study. His own mother, who he thought was dead, blinded Jenny and was a member of the traitorous Dragon sect. With Ash he shared the powers of the Phoenix until the night the Raven killed Ash and he became the Phoenix, one of the Guardians. Fin laughed aloud, some Guardian, he thought I used up all my powers giving Jenny her eyesight back.

The smoke finally clear and the burnt sheets removed, Fin headed downstairs, smiling at Jenny he realised that if he had the choice again he would choose Jenny every time.

Standing in silence in Elizabeth Gosling's, their houseparent's garden, Fin, Jenny, Sed and Eiry gathered around a newly planted ash tree and a hand crafted garden bench. Quietly they were joined by Elizabeth and their old friends Detective Inspector David Llewellyn Jones and the Reverend George Oak.

'I'm sure Ash would have hated the fuss,' said Elizabeth sadly.

The wind blew gently through the trees and made a mournful sound that filled the silence, Eiry began to cry and Fin put his arm around her.

'I knew my brother for a less than a year,' said Fin with difficulty, 'and I know you all loved him, but I think Eiry loved him more than any of us.'

Tears welled up in Eiry's eyes, she broke down and wept. Fin sat her down on the bench and everyone gathered around her.

George cleared his throat and was about to speak but David shook his head so he said nothing. Together in silence, they said their last goodbyes to Ash.

'I have prepared some food,' said Elizabeth, 'will you all join me?'

'Do you mind if I stay here a while,' asked Eiry, 'I would like to be alone for a moment?'

'Of course,' said Elizabeth and led the rest away.

Wiping the back of her hand across her eyes Eiry paused and then spoke into the silence, 'I will never forget you Ash and I don't know how I'm going to live without you.' Tears ran gently down Eiry's face, 'From the moment we first met you made me smile and I think that in the whole of my life knowing you was the first thing that ever made me feel happy and feel not alone. I hoped one day that we would go and look for my father, but now even that hope is gone.' Taking a deep breath Eiry looked at the sky, 'I'm not sure that I want to live without you.'

Overhead dark clouds began to form and rain began to fall. The daylight faded all except one beam of light that pierced through the darkness and lit Eiry's face. Unexpected hope leapt in her heart and she laughed aloud, 'Okay, okay, I get it,' she said, laughing some more, 'you always hated me feeling miserable and depressed; so I will try not to let myself crash. I know it won't be easy, but for your memory's sake I will try!' The rain began to fall heavily and in the few yards that Eiry ran to Elizabeth's apartment, she was soaked.

Seeing Eiry standing inside the doorway dripping David handed her a towel, smiling she took it and tried to dry her hair.

Inside the apartment, they all watched the wild summer squall batter the windows, 'I've never seen anything like it,' said David, leaving his hand on Elizabeth's shoulder, 'unless it is a symptom of global warming.'

'Climate change,' said Elizabeth correcting him, 'because this is certainly not warming me up!'

Over the next few days the weather worsened, Fin felt as if he was being constantly soaked when he moved between buildings. Thankfully, the beginning of the September term was days away so he could remain indoors and keep out of the rain.

Taking off his waterproof, Fin sat down next to Jenny in the kitchen and looked at the painting she was busy creating, 'That's an amazing,' he said admiringly, 'that peacock looks so alive!'

'All I could think about at night,' said Jenny, 'when I couldn't sleep was that I would never see another peacock.' Jenny paused and picked up the picture, 'Before I lost my eyesight I took sight for granted and then in a moment it was gone.'

'I wish I could have stopped her!'

'You saved my life,' stated Jenny, 'in the scale of things, being alive was more important than being blind. Of course it did help that I could see with my hair,' Jenny reached up and tried to smooth down her wild hair, 'I still can you know. It's strange, now I have my eyesight back it has sort of withdrawn, but in the dark or when something spooks me I can see everything in every direction.'

'I love your hair,' said Fin laughing, and then changing the subject, 'have you noticed something strange has happened here at Ravenswood?'

'Apart from the fact that Ravenswood is the home for extranatural beings gifted with strange powers?'

'Yes,' replied Fin, 'but something less strange than you making out we are characters in an X-Men movie!'

'Okay,' said Jenny, 'give me a clue?'

'We live in Ravenswood.'

'And?'

'And what's missing these days from Ravenswood?'

'Apart from psychopath head teachers who want to farm our special abilities?'

Putting his head in hands Fin pretended to scream, 'Are you trying to be difficult?'

Laughing Jenny put her arms around Fin and hugged him, 'Of course I am and I have noticed something is

243

different or wrong but I can't seem focus on it. It is like when you forget a name; it's there but out of reach and it drives you mad. I'm glad someone else has noticed what is it?'

Sitting up and leaning back in his chair, Fin looked Jenny in the eyes, 'All the Ravens have left Ravenswood, they used to be everywhere but now they have vanished.'

'That's it, it's so quiet now,' replied Jenny as she ruffled her wild hair, 'and that feeling of always being watched has gone too!'

'But is it a good thing,' asked Fin, 'because I'm not so sure?'

Finally, the rain stopped and Elizabeth and David drove Fin, Jenny and Eiry to Huntley and Wart so they could buy presents for Sed's birthday.

'When is it?' asked David from the passenger seat of Elizabeth's Volkswagen Beetle, 'Not that I mind being pressed ganged into being a taxi service.'

'Who is the taxi driver here?' asked Elizabeth failing to dodge a pothole in the road.

'The twenty-seventh of August,' replied Eiry as she bounced in her seat as the car hit another bump in the road.

'Sorry about that,' shouted Elizabeth over the noise of the engine, 'but we are still not allowed any computers at Ravenswood not even in the staff cars.'

'I knew I should have driven,' groaned David as his head hit the roof.

'We agreed it was my turn to drive,' replied Elizabeth indignantly.

'You could have driven my car,' laughed David, 'at least it has suspension.'

'That's not a car,' said Elizabeth, 'it's an armchair on wheels, this car's a classic and anyway it was all I could afford after the Raven destroyed my car.'

'Wasn't it insured?' yelled Fin.

'Yes it was,' replied Elizabeth, 'but there was no other car involved. I could hardly expect them to believe that I was attacked by a maniac and a murder of crows. They are refusing to pay out due to, "deliberate or contributory negligence."'

'That's ridiculous,' said a frustrated David, 'you were attacked by the Raven and the Flock! Would you like me to see if I can sort out some compensation from one of our Special Branch contingency funds?'

'If you could,' said Elizabeth giving David a smile that made him blush, 'it's not as if I can get a crime reference number,' seeing the look on David's face she continued, 'otherwise I am going to insist on driving my classic car!'

'Consider it done,' he groaned as the car hit another pothole, 'I was going to do it anyway but I think if I am ever going to walk upright again I will need to do it quickly.'

Huntley and Wart had changed little from their last visit and the shops were as welcoming as ever. Slamming the doors shut on the car they all headed up the street.

'Excuse me,' said Jenny, 'but do you mind if Fin and I go over and chat to those two old ladies over there?'

'What?' asked Fin lost in a daydream, Jenny poked him and pointed across the road towards the women, 'It's Gerty and Prude!'

'So that's what they look like,' said a bemused David.

'Off you go,' said Elizabeth, 'you do owe them a thank you.'

Crossing the road Jenny linked her arm through Fin's and they joined Gerty and Prude.

'We haven't seen you since we on the bus,' said Jenny, 'thank you for ringing the vicar when we needed help.'

'It was kind of you,' agreed Fin, 'it saved our lives.'

'It was our pleasure,' said Gerty blushing, 'George was so grateful we rang.' Turning to face Prude, Gerty was shocked to see her staring into Jenny's face, 'Don't stare Prude, it's not polite!'

'But look,' stammered Prude, 'she has her eyes back and the scars are gone!'

'Don't be so silly,' snapped Gerty turning to face Jenny 'the poor girl is blind and maimed.' Then seeing the change with her own eyes she muttered, 'Oh my.'

'It's okay,' said Jenny in her most soothing voice, 'a miracle happened after the incident and I was given my sight back,' Jenny ran her hands around her face, 'and I have been restored to full health.'

'Oh my,' repeated Gerty, 'you have such beautiful eyes. A miracle you say, well thank God for miracles, but I reckon such miracles only come at a great price.'

'It did,' said Jenny her eyes filling up with tears, 'a friend died and Fin here gave up everything to make it possible.'

'How,' asked Gerty, 'you were blind?'

'I don't truly understand it myself,' said Jenny, 'but once I was blind but now I can see.'

'I heard the vicar speak on that,' said Prude, 'well I must say what goes around comes around. I am thrilled for you my lovely, it's not often a miracle happens around here, it's usually bad news we hears.'

'Thank you again,' said Fin realising that the conversation was heading into a subject he would rather avoid, 'I think we need to return to the others before the shops shut.'

'Well it's been lovely to see you both again,' said Prude, 'it's grand that you've got you sight back.'

To Gerty and Prude's surprise, Jenny gave them both a quick hug and a kiss on the cheek. More awkwardly Fin shook their hands and they turned to return to the others.

'Well look after yourselves,' shouted a smiling Gerty determined to get the last word in as they crossed the road finally and then more quietly to Prude 'I reckon we'll be seeing more of them as days go by.'

'I reckon you right Gerty,' said Prude, 'but I imagine that girl getting her sight back were more than a normal miracle, if you get my drift, and that there's trouble a coming.'

The morning of Sed's birthday began poorly with the bad tempered return of Smith and Fount grumbling loudly about having to be back at Ravenswood. Stomping across from the main house Fin heard Fount's voice and groaned he really had hoped he had seen the last of them.

'This place has gone to the dogs,' stated Fount loudly, 'it was crap before Mr Chough left, but at least you could have some fun.' Looking around at the rebuilt accommodation and the freshly landscaped gardens he continued, 'How the hell did that bloody gas leak cause so much damage?'

'Oh come Smithy,' replied Fount, 'surely the words, gas and leak, say it all. Anyway, that poor kid was blown up and killed by it, it's no surprise they sent us away until things were rebuilt and restored.'

'That poor kid,' mimicked Smith, 'was called Ash and he was a snotty nosed little sod and the place is better without him!'

Overhearing this conversation, Fin fumed with anger and looking down at his hands Fin expected them to burst into flames, but they remained cold and empty. The lack of fire in his blood ruptured the heat of his anger and Fin found he did not care about anything else Smith and Fount had to say. Still, Fin issued a sigh of relief he watched them disappear around the corner and heard their complaining voices fade in the distance.

Sed's birthday party was a subdued affair, Eiry in her own words was still 'down in the dumps' but tried her best to be happy for Sed. Sed smiled to herself as Jenny and Fin tried a little too hard to be the life and soul of the party but she was still thrilled with their presents. 'Thank you so much.' She cried as she opened her presents and danced around the kitchen wearing her new t-shirt, woolly hat and gloves, over the top of her existing clothes. 'I love this series of books,' she said holding up the C.S. Lewis, Narnia box set up in the air, 'and I haven't read them for years.'

The following morning David and Elizabeth arrived early, woke everyone up and asked them to come down so they could have a discreet chat with them. Sleepy eyed and still in their pyjamas they all met around the kitchen table.

'I need your help,' began David, 'we have found another Guardian but she needs somewhere to live.'

'Why do you need our help,' asked Eiry trying to stifle a yawn, 'isn't that what Ravenswood House is all about?'

'It's not that simple,' continued David, 'we know that she is special but we really want to keep it from the rest of the staff, we still do not know who to fully trust yet. What we were hoping was that she would live with you, you would know her secret but no-one else would.'

'How old is she?' asked Sed.

'She's six months younger than you,' said Elizabeth joining in, 'and while that is a standard academic school year below you here at Ravenswood she will just blend in.'

'But why are you asking us?' repeated Eiry.

'To be honest,' said David, 'we could not keep her secret without your help and we only thought it polite to ask you first.'

'I am assuming that she will be sharing with me then,' said Jenny, 'now I have my sight back I cannot expect to have special treatment anymore.'

Elizabeth nodded her head.

'It's fine by me,' responded Jenny, 'and I guess the rest of us have no problems either.'

'Sounds fun,' said Fin, 'what's her name and what's so special about her?'

Taking a sip of his hot coffee David sat back and smiled, 'I thought you would respond this way.' Putting the cup down on the work surface he continued, 'Mr Byrd, as acting head, has had a request from the courts to take another student and it just so happens that the only suitable space is with Jenny. We are expecting Mr Byrd to bring her over to introduce her to you so the less you know in advance the better.'

'Oh come on,' said Fin getting fed up of David's reasoning, 'just tell us, if we can keep our powers secret I'm sure we can pretend that we know nothing about hers.'

'Fair enough,' agreed David, 'you are to be joined by Chloris Scylla, she's a Nymph.'

'You are kidding,' cried Eiry, 'a Nymph means nothing but trouble!'

'What's the problem?' asked Fin a little bewildered.

'Nymphs,' continued Eiry, 'are often quite beautiful, incredibly selfish, rude and arrogant.'

'Sounds like she will fit in fine,' said Fin laughing.

'Laugh it up fire boy,' said a serious Eiry, 'but their reputation is that they have a dark and nasty side.'

'Come on how bad can she be?' said Fin refusing to back down.

'According to legend,' continued Eiry, 'Nymphs are usually in love with flowers and trees but if angered can turn into a three headed monster.'

'Figuratively or literally?' asked Fin, 'Because I know a few people who turn into three headed monsters when they lose their temper.'

'Look guys,' said Jenny, 'in this house we have always accepted people for who they are and not by the type of their genes. I am happy to share with Chloris, and to be honest, after all we have been through in this last year I would be glad of a roommate.'

'Come in,' called a harried looking Mr Byrd from behind the principle's desk, mounds of papers forming precarious towers on either side of the desk, 'please sit down.'

Quietly the four sat down and considered the chaos around them.

Noticing their looks Mr Byrd waved his arms in the air,

'Since the explosion the paperwork has quadrupled and I am barely keeping up with it. On one side I have the Health and Safety Executive's investigation into the gas explosion that killed Ash and on the other I have government inspectors lining up to take Ravenswood over from the private sponsors. Then there's the police investigation into the alleged terrorist infiltration from a sect called the Flock.' Seeing Jenny for the first time Mr Byrd smiled, 'There is even a paperwork pile on the miraculous healing of Miss Cato here. It's not as if I can say it was Ash's last act of kindness as the Phoenix.' Seeing their surprised faces he continued, 'Oh I was made aware of Ash's special powers by Special Branch and it was a very generous act on his behalf to heal Miss Cato before he died.'

Stunned no one dared speak; if Birdie thought it was Ash that had healed Jenny it made life much safer for Fin.

'Anyway,' said Mr Byrd, 'I am aware that Elizabeth has told you that there may be a new student joining us, this is true. I was approached by the family court and asked could we take in a young orphan, who was in danger of being, err… exploited and urgently needed to be moved to enclosed safe environment. You will understand that I tried to put them off, I explained the situation here at Ravenswood but they felt this would be the safest option.'

Outside the sun came out and the rain stopped, the sunlight was so warm that steam began to appear from the woodwork fencing outside the window.

'Chloris Scylla is now waiting with Miss Gosling, I believe she likes to be called Chloe,' continued Mr Byrd, 'please be kind to her she has had a harrowing time and was only just rescued in time.'

'Yes sir,' said Jenny reacting first, 'we will be delighted to welcome her and help her to make Ravenswood her home.'

'Very good, very good,' said Mr Byrd vaguely, the conversation with him was over and he picked up a file and began perusing it.

'Come on,' said Fin leading the rest out and out into the sunshine.

Making the most of the sunshine Elizabeth was sitting on the bench in her garden, next to her was a girl with long white blonde hair, 'Hi guys, I would like to introduce you to Chloe,' said Elizabeth.

Chloe stood up and offered to shake hands with everyone. Fin thought she looked nervous and withdrawn, her face was pale with dark bags under her eyes and she was covered in bruises.

Ignoring the hand Jenny gently drew her into a hug, Chloe seem startled but Jenny's look projected kindness and Chloe smiled responding to the warmth of Jenny's hug.

'I'm Jenny you roommate,' she said, 'and you are with friends now,' Jenny considered all her bruises,' and if I have anything to do with it nobody will hurt you ever again!'

'That's what the kind boy said,' said Chloe quietly, 'he said that you would always be there for me and that I could trust you.'

'Which boy was that?' asked Elizabeth.

'I've no idea,' said Chloe, 'he just came over and sat next to me, laughed and chattered to me and then went off in that direction.'

'I don't know,' said Jenny, 'first day here and you have an admirer.'

Chloe's face turned white, 'I don't want admirers, I just want to be left alone!'

'I was only joking,' said Jenny guiltily, 'come let me show you our room.'

Excitement filled Chloe's face, 'Please that would be great.'

Taking Chloe's hand Jenny gave her a smile and they ran off to the lodge. For the rest of the day Jenny took it upon herself to be Chloe's guide to Ravenswood House, after a full tour of the facilities they ended up back at the lodge and met up with the others in the kitchen.

'You are all so talented,' said Chloe admiring the artwork around the place, 'and I have never stayed anywhere so beautiful,' she said looking out the window.

Eiry and Sed jumped up and made everyone drinks, Fin who was sitting lazily in the corner was made to get out some chocolate biscuits and soon they were all relaxed around the table.

'Chloe can you tell us a little about yourself?' asked Jenny gently, then seeing a look of horror cross her face continued, 'Only what you feel able to, we don't want to pry or raise up nasty memories.'

'It okay,' said Chloe nervously, 'David said I could trust you and there are things you need to know. What do you know about me already?'

'We know nothing about your background,' replied Fin, 'we know you are a Nymph,' seeing a panicked look cross her face continued, 'don't worry that's our secret, I'm the Phoenix and Jenny here is…'

'I'm a Gorgon,' finished Jenny, 'I can see with my hair and I can read and enter into people's memories and dreams.'

'The Phoenix and a Gorgon,' gasped Chloe, 'in the same room.'

'Chloe,' said Jenny, 'you need to know that Fin has lost all his powers, well all apart from some residue that flares up when he dreams, he lost his powers when he healed me of my blindness.'

'But surely it will come back,' reasoned Chloe, 'I thought that was a characteristic of the Phoenix?'

'We just don't know,' said Fin sadly, 'I will just have to wait and see, but for now your secret is part of ours and we will do everything we can to look after you.'

'Thank you,' Chloe exclaimed, 'I have never mixed with other Guardians before, I thought I was the only one left.'

'Sadly,' said Eiry, 'Sed and I have no special powers even though we suspect that we are descendants of extranatural families.'

'You guys are amazing,' said Chloe, 'I'm so glad I'm here.'

To cover everyone's embarrassment Fin offered around the chocolate biscuits.

'You know I'm a Nymph,' continued Chloe once they had all had another biscuit, 'and I am aware that our reputation goes before us, I can be selfish, rude and I have a quite vial temper.' seeing everyone look slightly worried she added, 'But I have never grown three heads,' she suddenly laughed, 'well not yet anyway!'

'To be honest,' said Fin, 'I know nothing about Nymphs.'

'Nymphs are Guardians of the trees and lovers of wild flowers,' explained Chloe, 'we have a reputation of being loving and fun, carefree you could say, but with nasty tempers. If Jenny can walk in memories and dreams, I can awake gifts that lie dormant in people, well in theory I can.'

'Then why were you kept a prisoner?' asked Sed seeing fear in Chloe's eyes, 'Sorry, I am just guessing here, but you are scared, covered in bruises and I can think of no other reason David would want to hide you here with us.'

Starting to cry Chloe answered Sed's question, 'I was taken as a child from my mother, and she was sold to someone to be the mother of their children. I have been moved around from country to country and from one barred room to another. I was being groomed to...' Breaking down she could not continue.

'The children of Nymphs often become Guardians and immortal,' Jenny said quietly, 'the Flock, the Dragons and the Royals all see them as the perfect breeding stock and when they reach sixteen they are used and afterwards they are disposed off.'

'That's disgusting,' cried Eiry, 'you mean Nymphs are sold off as sex slaves and then abandoned!'

'I have seen things you would not believe,' said Chloe through her tears, 'They used to beat me because I kept trying to escape; they said if I tried to escape again they would kill me and feed my body to the birds.'

'What happened?' asked Sed placing her hand gently on Chloe's shoulder.

'They beat me because I refused to eat,' she continued, 'I just wanted to die so they left me alone in a dark room. There was a fire and one of the other slaves was sent to check up on me; instead, she led me out to rear of the building and told me to run. So I did, I escaped out of an open door and I ran and as I climbed over a wall I heard a terrible scream. I think they killed the slave girl for letting me escape. I was not going to be caught again so I ran into the woods where I was rescued by old man who found me shivering in the dark. He drove me to a hospital, I was terrified, I lost consciousness and when I woke up your friend David was there. At first, I was too terrified to speak to him, but eventually he guessed most things and got me to tell him everything and then he brought me here.'

Frustrated and angry Fin stood up and paced the room, 'I am so fed up of this, we are experimented on, used and abused, just because we are different!' Deep anger welled up from with him, 'and if I ever get my fire back…'

Noticing Fin's words trail off but the fire remain in his eyes, Jenny got up from the table, walked over to Fin and took his hands, 'One day there will be a reckoning, but it's not today, we need to get stronger and learn how to use our abilities first.' Turning to Chloe, though she did not know it, the anger burned as bright in her eyes as it did in Fin's. 'Chloe, you have seen and experienced things that no one should see, you are part of our family now and I feel sorry for anyone who tries to get to you, because they are going to have to get through all of us first!'

ABOUT THE AUTHOR

Philip Janvier was born in Liverpool in 1957 and studied Theology at Trinity College, Bristol. He is an award winning documentary videographer, has written both Christian and secular material including a novella, audio plays and magazine articles. He is addicted to reading, loves children's fantasy novels and Doctor Who. He is married and lives in Liverpool where he is the Team Rector of St Stephen's, Gateacre.

14586448R00148

Printed in Great Britain
by Amazon.co.uk, Ltd.,
Marston Gate.